Hamelin's Child

DJ Bennett

Hamelin's Child
Copyright © 2012 DJ Bennett
All rights reserved.

www.debbiebennett.co.uk

ISBN-13: 978-1470131036
ISBN-10: 147013103X

ACKNOWLEDGEMENTS

Cover design by JT Lindroos
Cover photo by AndYaDontStop

All characters and events in this story are fictitious. Any resemblances to real people, living or dead, are purely coincidental. This book is sold subject to the condition that it shall not, by way of trade or otherwise, be lent, resold, hired out, or otherwise circulated without the author's prior consent in any form of binding or cover other than that in which it is published and without a similar condition being imposed on the subsequent owner. No part of this publication may be reproduced, stored in a retrieval system or transmitted in any form or by any means, electronic, mechanical, photocopying, recording or otherwise, without the prior written permission of the author.

Note that this book contains adult material and is not suitable for minors.

Other books by DJ Bennett

Paying the Piper

ONE

Michael Redford died on his seventeenth birthday – the night Eddie picked him up off the street, shot him full of heroin and assaulted him.

Michael had been drinking steadily all night, matching Jenny's Breezers with export-strength lager, and when he saw Jen wrapped around his mate's brother across the dance floor, he didn't feel at all inclined to slow down. Totally oblivious to observers, they were all hands and lips – a human octopus of limbs on the red chesterfield sofa with Jenny's long dark hair covering both their faces. She'd dropped an E in the toilets; he could tell by the shine in her eyes and the way she moved when they'd been dancing earlier – she always came onto him when she was high, then pulled away when he got interested. Michael kicked the pillar next to him in disgust. He hated nightclubs anyway.

'She came with you, didn't she?'

Michael turned to see a man standing next to him. Blond hair, cream chinos, polo shirt and too much jewellery. He seemed older than the rest of the punters.

The man waved his hand in Jenny's direction. 'The girl,' he added, by way of explanation. 'I was watching the two of you earlier.'

Michael nodded. 'Don't think she'll be leaving with me.'

'Girlfriend?'

'Ex.'

'Evidently.' The man smiled sympathetically. 'Women are bitches, aren't they? He's a dealer, by the way – saw him outside the bogs before. What're you drinking?' He pointed at Michael's empty glass.

Michael shook his head. 'No, thanks.' *Now fuck off, creep.* Something about the stranger made him uneasy.

'Suit yourself.' The man shrugged and went off to the bar, returning a few moments later with a pint and what looked like a whisky chaser. He held the pint out. 'Got you one, anyway. You look like you could use it.' He had an impressive assortment of gold rings on his hand, which suggested serious money, even if the guy was a poser.

Oh, what the hell... 'Cheers.' Michael emptied half of it immediately. He had less than a fiver left from the eighty quid his dad had given him earlier that day and not enough for a taxi home. Still, he couldn't complain – there weren't many parents who'd let their underage son celebrate his birthday in a club, and it was largely due to the intervention of his elder sister Kate that they'd let him go at all. On top of that, she'd even managed to talk them into giving him enough money to enjoy it in style. The money had come with strings of course, but listening to the ten-minute *evils of drink and drugs* lecture had been a small price to pay for his freedom.

Seventeen today. Or was it yesterday now? It was well past midnight. Some of his mates were on the other side of the dance floor; Jenny and her new friend were all but shagging on the sofa and everyone seemed to be one half of a couple apart from him. Glancing sideways, he saw the man had melted into the crowd. Michael wondered whether he should just go home and he was starting to consider the idea seriously when the stranger appeared at his side again.

'Still here?' The man smiled. 'D'you want me to have him warned off?'

'No.' *Who is this prick? Some kind of gangster?* 'He can have her.'

'What's your name?'

'Michael.' His voice sounded weird – in fact, everything sounded weird. The music seemed distorted and hollow and it echoed around his head, the bass making his teeth ache. *Too much booze, Redford, that's your problem. And far too much imagination.* Sure, the guy was a bit strange, but – shit – wasn't everyone in this dump?

'Hi, Michael. I'm Eddie.' He touched Michael's shoulder with an air of concern. 'Are you OK?'

Michael shook his head, trying to clear it. His pulse was pounding in time with the music. 'What *is* this?' He held out what was left of his drink, wondering whether the man had spiked it with anything.

'Holsten. It's what you were drinking earlier.' Eddie sounded hurt. 'It's all right, isn't it? Chuck it, if it's off, and I'll get you another.'

'No ... I don't know.' The lights seemed brighter and sharper, the music burning into white noise. He stared at the pint in his hand. *What the hell is in this drink?* He took a step forward and staggered, but Eddie caught his arm and deftly took the glass out of his grip.

'I think you've had enough, Michael,' he said softly. 'Let's go get some fresh air, shall we?'

Trafalgar Square was bitterly cold and the wind cut through Michael's shirt as he followed Eddie down the steps. The night air cleared his head a little and for the first time he paused to consider what he was doing. Yet Eddie seemed pleasant enough and he had prevented a potentially embarrassing situation, so Michael wasn't entirely ungrateful. And it didn't look like Jenny would have any problems getting an escort home.

The Square was quiet. There were still night buses around, but few people. February wasn't the weather for sitting outside; that would come with the summer, when there would be people in the fountains, even at this hour of the night. He'd paddled himself once, last August, when they'd spent the whole day in town, laughing at the tourists and seeing who could get off with a girl fastest. Michael had been the first to climb a lion and sit on the top, doing an impromptu Hillary impression for a group of French girls. Then he'd jumped in the fountain and had been about to embark on Jacques Cousteau, when he'd been dragged out by a policeman. He'd got off with a warning, but it had impressed the girls to the extent that he'd succeeded in getting his hand up Carine's T-shirt later that evening.

Last summer seemed a long time ago.

'You got enough money to get home? I'll find you a cab.' Eddie sat down on the step, lighting a cigarette behind a cupped hand. 'Wait a sec.' He took a long drag. 'God, I've been wanting a smoke for hours.'

Michael hesitated and shivered. He'd left his coat behind, but he wasn't sure he was sober enough to return to the club and collect it. They probably wouldn't let him back in anyway. The cold air was sharp in his lungs and he retched suddenly at the metallic taste in his mouth.

'Sit down, Mikey.' Eddie reached up and grabbed his arm and Michael let himself be pulled down onto the step. He didn't feel at all well. His brain was fogging again and he was having difficulty seeing straight. Being pissed had never been like this before.

'Put your head between your knees,' Eddie instructed. 'Go on. It will make you feel better, I promise.'

Michael did as he was told and closed his eyes. The ground lurched crazily and he stayed that way for a minute before looking up again. Eddie was watching him, a curious look on his face, and Michael frowned, trying to work out what wasn't quite right. His mind was doing cartwheels, fuelled by a sudden fear and whatever it was he'd drunk. *Who is this guy?*

'Hey, come on, Mikey.' Eddie reached for his arm and Michael pulled away. 'You scared of me? I won't hurt you.'

Scared? Bloody terrified, more like. But he couldn't get his tongue round the words and he simply sat there and stared stupidly at the man. He wasn't as young as he'd first seemed, maybe in his thirties, and his eyes were slightly bloodshot. Maybe the guy was coming on to him? *Oh, sick!* He swallowed and realised he felt very sick himself. Pushing the man away, he threw up, splattering partially-digested spaghetti bolognese down his trousers and across the steps.

Eddie leaned forwards and held his shoulders. 'Go on, Mikey. Chuck it up. You'll feel much better afterwards.'

Michael didn't protest, he was too busy avoiding his feet. In the back of his mind, he knew that last pint had been spiked with something, but he was still far too drunk – and ill – for it to bother him. Light-headed, he sat up and let Eddie's arm slide around his shoulders; he knew he should pull away, but his body didn't seem to want to obey his mind. He wondered where his phone was and remembered he'd left it in his coat pocket. Stupid, but it was an old model and not worth nicking – pay-as-you-go had become borrow-if-you-can and he doubted there was more than a few pence credit left on it.

'Feel better now?'

Michael nodded. It was true. He did feel better, although everything was still fuzzy and unreal. The Square swam in and out of focus, but it didn't seem to matter.

'How old are you, Mikey?'

'Seventeen.' It was difficult to connect his brain to his mouth and he couldn't get his lips to work properly.

'Perhaps you should go home. Should I take you home? I'm not sure you'd manage it by yourself.'

God, no! If his parents saw him like this, they'd go ballistic. Alcohol was one thing, but drugs were a different matter altogether. He could imagine the reaction, the anger followed closely by the sadness, the head-shaking. His mum would cry and somehow the whole incident would become a major catastrophe. Home was not a good idea right now. *Need to sober up – get straightened out. Need to sleep.*

Eddie could have read his mind. 'Tell you what, Mikey. Why don't you crash at my place? I guess you don't want to go home in this state. You can phone your folks from mine if you want – tell them you're at a mate's.'

Michael tried to argue, but Eddie wasn't having any of it and the man pulled him to his feet. Michael stood there, swaying unsteadily. He felt dizzy and sick again, and he wasn't too sure he could stand alone, much less walk anywhere.

Eddie slipped an arm underneath his shoulders and half-carried him across the Square. There were black taxis parked up in a rank, but they walked past them and down a side-street before Eddie finally flagged down one of the many cruising private cabs. He gave the driver some address Michael had never heard of. The cabbie sniffed pointedly, looking at Michael's trousers, but Eddie pulled a wad of notes from his pocket and waved them enticingly.

The driver still wasn't impressed. 'Thirty quid. And another twenty if he pukes again.'

More negotiation and finally the driver nodded. Michael tried to speak, to say something – anything – but Eddie's grip on his arm tightened as he shoved him into the back of the cab. Something wasn't right and when Michael staggered out of the taxi twenty minutes later, he was even more uncertain. Wherever they were, it was nowhere that he recognised and he'd lived in London all his life. Mind you – he giggled, suddenly finding the situation incredibly funny – he wouldn't recognise his own family right now. *Nor would they recognise you*, a small voice said in the back of his mind and in a brief moment of lucidity, he opened his eyes wide and saw the puke stains on his trousers.

Eddie caught his look, hurriedly taking his arm as he led him down a narrow alleyway away from the safety of the main road.

'Where we goin'?' asked Michael. He was aware he was slurring his words, but he couldn't seem to help it. What the hell had he been drinking? Where was he? The streetlight at the other end of the alley was in painfully sharp focus, yet he couldn't see his hand in front of his face without squinting.

Eddie smiled reassuringly. 'Just somewhere you can sleep for the night. Your mother would never forgive me if I abandoned you in this state, now would she?' He unlocked a steel door halfway down the alley.

But – parents don't know you – do they? Michael was confused now. Was this guy a friend or something? Christ, he felt sick. He couldn't get his legs to do as they were told and he felt stupid when Eddie sighed before lifting him over his shoulder and carrying him up several flights of stairs and through more doors. He threw up again down Eddie's back, crying out as the man dumped him on a bed and slapped his face.

'You little shit.' Eddie pulled off his jacket in disgust, rolled it up and tossed it into the corner of the room. He turned to a second man who was standing in the doorway. 'This is Mikey. He's seventeen and quite a looker under the puke. Let me clean him up a bit and you can see.'

Hands stripped him, but Michael was barely aware of what was happening. He could see the dust dancing crazily in the light of the bedside lamp and there were patterns in the shadows on the ceiling. *So pretty!* Somebody slapped his face again, but he didn't feel any pain.

'He's well gone.'

'He'd been drinking heavily when I found him. Girlfriend dumped him.' Eddie sat on the window ledge and calmly took off his shoes. 'What d'you reckon?'

'Family?'

'Parents, I think.' There was a long pause. 'I know, I know – but just look at him, Joss. This kid's got class, not like your other street brats.' He leant over the bed and took Michael's face between his hands. 'Come on, Mikey – let's have a birthday smile for your uncle Eddie.'

Michael obliged and Eddie let him go. 'See? Cute, you've got to admit. Seventeen going on twelve.'

'Where did you pick him up?'

'At a club. All alone and very impressionable. Keep him under for a few weeks – 'til the media lose interest – and he'll be perfect.'

'I can see the attraction. All right.' Joss pursed his lips. 'You've not convinced me yet, but I'll give him a shot and we'll see how he takes it.'

Michael was aware he was naked. Both men were looking at him appraisingly, but he wasn't embarrassed. He wasn't anything at all – just a body and a detached mind floating and watching as a syringe appeared in his field of view.

'This won't take a minute, Mikey. It'll make you feel better.'

This wasn't right. He fought to connect brain to body. *No!* He couldn't string the words together to speak. *What the hell is happening? I want to go home!*

Hands on his wrist and elbow turned his arm, squeezing. He could feel the pulse in his wrist, feel his heartbeat racing away out of control. But he couldn't struggle, couldn't get his muscles to function properly and as the needle entered his skin, it seemed like every nerve in his body was screaming.

And then everything changed. The universe shrunk to a single point of existence, then exploded and he was flying on the wave of the liquid in his veins. Higher and higher he soared, above the building and out into the night city, the stars bursting like fireworks. All his senses had suddenly doubled in strength and he felt more alive than he'd ever felt before. Patterns skittered in the air, patterns of smell and sound and pure sensation – every part of him was alive with sensation – and he could feel the dust in the air, settling on his flesh like soft snow. It was incredible.

Joss tossed the used needle and syringe into the waste basket by the bed. He turned to Eddie. 'I suppose you want a finder's fee? Two hundred?' Michael could hear the voices clearly, yet they seemed to be coming from miles away, distant and booming.

Eddie snorted. 'I ain't no charity, Joss. Five.'

'He's risky. He'll cost me two before we start.'

'He'll make you that in a night. Four-fifty.'

'Three. And that's my highest offer. Take it or get him out of here.'

'I might just do that.' Eddie sneered. 'Set up on my own.'

'You couldn't take the pace, Ed. Now do you want the money or not?'

'I'll take it. As long as I get to take *him* first. He stays.'

'Deal.' Joss crossed to the door. 'I'm out of here.'

The shadows on the ceiling rearranged themselves and Michael smiled warmly. The light was too bright; his eyes hurt and the darkness was so much softer. There were patterns here too – swirly shapes in the shadows and he could see each pore on the man's skin. He smelt faintly of alcohol and his clothes held the residue of cigarette smoke. Michael could hear the sounds of a fox raiding dustbins in the alley below and the distant music from a party somewhere down the street, or maybe it was a car stereo. He was turned over and he could feel the silky touch of pillows against his face and neck. Then there was pain and he heard someone screaming. It went on for a long time.

And as he lay there afterwards, he heard Eddie leaving the room, closing the door behind him. The man was whistling softly.

TWO

There was a comforting solidity in the smell, something Michael could recognise and hang on to.

Bacon frying.

Memories of a thousand Saturday mornings poured through the hole in his mind. He was lying in bed and listening to his mother in the kitchen directly below his bedroom. Soon she'd be knocking on the door and he'd be down at the shop an hour later, counting black dustbin liners into sets of five and wrapping them in an elastic band. His Saturday job was as boring as hell, but it gave him the extra cash he needed.

Saturday job? Michael's mind climbed to the next level, hauling itself up into the conscious world. *Bacon?* He hadn't worked on a Saturday since his spectacular failure in his mock exams, at which point his parents had reluctantly agreed to give him the same amount of money as an allowance, provided that he spent the time studying. And as for bacon – that had stopped the minute Kate had decided to try to turn the family vegetarian. At twenty his sister had developed an alarming social conscience and Michael was forever arguing the issue with her: *What would happen to all the animals if we didn't eat them? Would there be a lamb chop mountain? If God had intended us to only eat veggies, he wouldn't have invented mint sauce* ... But Kate was twenty-two now and getting married soon; Michael was looking forward to the reintroduction of bacon sandwiches to Saturday mornings.

He was awake now, lying uncomfortably on his side, with his cheek against something cool and smooth. For some reason, he didn't move immediately, but lay there, eyes still closed as he tried to remember the previous night. He'd been out on the town, hadn't he? Oh, yes – the birthday date with Jenny – which meant that today was Sunday and he was seventeen and one day old. And minus a girlfriend. Today was lunch with the family followed by tea with the relations. He could think of better ways to spend a Sunday, but it wasn't worth risking the inevitable arguments by trying to get out of the visit. He'd learned long ago that sometimes it was easier just to give in.

Michael rolled over in bed and stretched. It must have been quite a night, as he had no memory of getting home. In fact he couldn't recall anything after the row with Jen, and he hoped he hadn't done anything embarrassing. Still, if mum was cooking breakfast, he couldn't have disgraced himself too badly.

The first time he'd come home drunk, he'd been sixteen and the atmosphere at home had been frosty to say the least; the episode had culminated in his father taking him to one side and having a *man-to-man* talk with him. As he'd had a God-awful hangover at the time, Michael hadn't paid too much attention, until his father started on the *things you should know about sex* lecture – then he had to try hard not to laugh. Dad meant well, but Michael hadn't the heart to tell the man that he'd actually lost his virginity to one of Kate's friends six months earlier.

He grinned at the memory. Then he stretched again, yawning loudly and cut off in mid-yawn as a jolt of pain shot down his lower back. He opened his eyes in surprise. Something *hurt*.

The first thing he saw was the deep-red fringed

lampshade. *Maroon?* Then the matching curtains and pale grey walls. *Dream colours.* A darker grey carpet covered the floor and the whole effect was set off by the expensive-looking maroon satin sheets on the double bed. Everything exactly as it had been in his dreams.

Michael forgot the pain completely as he raised himself up on his elbows and stared around the room. Where the hell *was* he? Last night seemed a lifetime away as he recalled the club and the row with Jenny. *Then what happened?* He remembered talking to a blond man – *He came on to me! Wait until I tell that one to the guys at college* – and he vaguely remembered walking down to Trafalgar Square and watching the night buses. After that his mind was a total blank. And if he'd been that pissed when he'd got to this place, it probably wasn't surprising that he'd dreamed about it so vividly. And dream he had – dark dreams which had seemed to go on forever, full of pain and confusion. Fleeting shadowy figures had floated in and out of the nightmares and he remembered dreaming that he wanted to wake up, scared of sleeping any longer in case this fantasy world turned out to be the real one.

Well, he wasn't at home – that much was obvious and it certainly explained the smell of bacon, though he wondered who was doing the cooking. Michael sat up, about to get out of bed, and another jolt of pain shot through his lower body.

What was I doing *last night?* He couldn't remember any women being involved, but then again, he couldn't rule out the possibility either. Swinging his legs over the edge of the bed, he leaned forward to scratch his foot and stopped mid-reach. On the inside of his arm were numerous pin-pricks and a fading blue bruise.

His mind whirled frantically, spiky fragments of memory returning and cutting through his composure like shards of glass. He had a sudden vision of someone holding him down, while a disembodied pair of hands held his arm and gave him a swift injection. There was more pain and then strong arms around him, holding him while he cried himself hoarse.

But there was nothing more; the images didn't connect up. *Why can't I remember?* His brain felt like syrup, thick and sticky and he was worried now. Had he been ill? Swallowing experimentally, he couldn't decide if he really did have a sore throat or if his mind was playing tricks on him. He certainly felt all right – apart from the pain in his lower back and a slight stiffness in his legs. There was no trace of the hangover he knew he ought to have.

He stood up and crossed the deep-pile carpet to the door, where he found a silk robe hanging from a brass hook. Maroon again. Where were his clothes and his mobile? He needed to phone home and make his apologies; tell them he'd be late back for lunch. Slipping the robe on, he went over to the window, looking out through white-painted bars over a flat roof to dirty buildings and wilting pot-plants on roof-top gardens. As he watched, a train rattled past on overhead rails and the windows creaked in sympathy. It was raining and the vibrations of the window frame made the water trickle down the glass.

Michael had no idea where he was and he was beginning to realise that he had no idea how long he'd been here either. Something told him that last night had been a long time ago and he felt disorientated. Where was he? And more importantly, why? *Are they really memories, or just bad dreams?* He was awake now and they should be gone.

There was a sound behind him and Michael spun quickly, tightening the belt of his robe as the bedroom door opened. A man strolled in with a tray balanced on the palm of one hand, as if he'd once been a waiter. He looked vaguely familiar.

'Hello, Mikey. You must be hungry.'

Mikey? Someone had called him that before. *The man in the club?* Was it the same guy? 'Who are you?'

'You don't remember me?' The man spoke cheerfully as he set the tray down on the bedside table.

'I don't know. You look ... familiar.' Michael frowned. *Why can't I remember?* He glanced at the plate of bacon, eggs and beans and realised he was ravenous.

The man laughed suddenly and waved at the food. 'Eat. We can talk at the same time.'

Michael picked up the tray and sat down on the bed, taking a gulp from the mug of coffee before he started on the meal. He'd eaten half of it before he looked up again, to see the man leaning on the window ledge and watching him thoughtfully.

'Who are you?' he asked again, through a mouthful of beans. 'Where am I? And why am I here? Have I been ill?'

'So many questions.' The man hesitated. 'I'm Eddie, although I think you already know that, don't you?'

Michael nodded. *Eddie. Yes, that's right. But who is Eddie?*

Eddie nodded too. 'I thought you did. Do you remember how we met?'

'In the club. You were wearing a blue shirt.' *And too much jewellery.*

'Good.' He made it sound like a test. 'Anything else?'

Michael shook his head. 'Not really, but ...' He hesitated. 'It wasn't last night, was it?' There were hazy memories drifting across the back of his mind – snatches of conversation, movements and images of people around him.

'No, Mikey, it wasn't last night. It was three weeks ago.'

'Three *weeks?*' Michael dropped the fork with a crash. *Three weeks? Three whole weeks just ... gone! It's not possible – is it?*

Eddie laughed and Michael couldn't quite understand the tone of the laugh. He'd apparently been here for three weeks, yet this guy was behaving as if it was all some huge joke. Suddenly the food lost its appeal and he put the tray down on the bed. Alarm bells were ringing in his mind, and he knew there was something in the air – some secret he shared with Eddie which he should know and didn't. Instinctively he shivered, pulling the robe tighter around his shoulders.

He glanced up at Eddie, who hadn't moved from the window and was watching him with that strange look again, as if waiting for a certain reaction. *But what? What am I missing here?*

'I don't understand,' he said carefully, selecting his words as if they were explosives which might detonate in the wrong combination. 'What happened? Where are my clothes?'

'You really don't remember any of it, do you? All the nights I sat with you, all the times I fed you and cleaned you. You were awake a lot of the time, you know – you even spoke to me. Your memory is really shot to shit.' The man shrugged. 'Still – maybe it's better that way.'

'Maybe what's better?' Michael felt his cheeks burn scarlet. He remembered thinking that Eddie was some kind of pervert when he'd come on to Michael in Trafalgar Square. *He drugged me with something. Spiked my drink.* But had he been right? Or had he really been that sick? Surely if he'd been ill he should have been in hospital, or at least at home with his parents?

'Look at your arms, Mikey.'

Michael turned his left hand over, although he'd already seen the needle marks earlier. 'Injections?' he asked, knowing the question was naïve even as he asked it.

Eddie nodded. 'Heroin.'

Michael's eyes widened. He'd never done drugs – never even been tempted to try them, not after seeing a girl almost die in the park once. He'd been twelve at the time and there were a crowd of them – Goths, mostly – who spent the long summer evenings hanging out by the bridge. Michael was fascinated by them. He talked to them eventually – even got to know a few of them – and drove his parents frantic for a few months when he tried spiking his hair with Kate's hair spray.

Then one of the girls got sick and although they'd taken to Michael, they shut him out, suddenly fiercely protective of their own. He wanted to help, but they wouldn't let him and so he watched Maria as she alternated from a near-catatonic stupor to screaming fits of agony. It terrified him – both what was happening to the girl and the group's attitude to it. 'Bad cut, Mike,' they said to him. 'Don't ever touch smack – it fucks up your life.'

And they moved on. Michael never saw them again and he never knew what had happened to Maria. He remembered the expression on her face, and that had been enough to deter him from furtive joint-rolling at parties. Or the ecstasy tablets his mates and Jenny were so fond of buying in club toilets. They told him to grow up, but he'd seen that version of grown-up and it wasn't for him.

'Heroin.' Michael repeated the word slowly, wondering if he was being incredibly dim today, or if events really were moving too fast for him to keep up. 'Heroin. *Why?*'

Eddie rolled his eyes. 'Mikey, don't be naïve. I'm not going to spell it out for you.' He turned and looked out of the window.

Michael considered the situation. *Jesus Christ – heroin!* It was hard to think straight. Round and round his head the words were echoing: *Don't ever touch smack – it fucks up your life. Don't ever touch smack – it fucks up your life.* He stared at Eddie's back, trying to put all the pieces together.

Heroin cost money. Lots of money. He had no idea how much or where it came from, but he knew it was expensive stuff and not the kind of thing dealers made a habit of giving away for free. So presumably Eddie wanted a return on his money. But what? What had happened in those lost three weeks? And what was going to happen now? He frowned, concentrating, and dredged up another murky image. He was pissing into a plastic bottle and then someone – *Eddie? No, a different, older man* – was holding him steady. Pressure on his arm while another needle went in.

He remembered Maria and felt a twinge of panic. *I don't want to die!* But he didn't feel like he was dying. In fact apart from the pain in the small of his back and the stiffness in his thighs, he'd never felt better. *Pain?* Michael wriggled experimentally. There were bruises on his upper arms too. Bruises where someone had held him down. And it wasn't just his back that hurt.

No more dreams. It was beginning to fall into place.

Dust dancing in the lamplight. Shadows playing across the ceiling.

Skin on skin.

Pain. Screaming.

Silence.

Michael's eyes widened as drugged memories crystallised and realisation slammed into him with all the force of a ten-ton truck. *Oh, God. Please God. I'm wrong – I have to be wrong.*

This isn't happening!

He jumped up instinctively, a wild animal seeing the cage bars for the first time and as Eddie swung round, Michael could read the confirmation written on his face. Limbs frozen, Michael was sure his heart had stopped beating.

Eddie came towards him as if to offer comfort. The movement broke the spell and Michael shook his head, incredulous, as the truth filtered through. As Eddie came into range, Michael leaped forwards and managed to land a couple of good punches to the jaw before the man overpowered him, twisting his wrist sharply and throwing him back onto the bed.

'You finished?' Eddie's face was expressionless, as if he'd seen this reaction a thousand times before. Michael glared at him, wishing he could kill the man by looks alone. Jesus Christ, this had to be all a bad nightmare.

'No.' His voice was still uncertain. There was still a chance he was wrong. 'It's not real.' *Tell me I'm dreaming. Please!*

'It's real.'

Michael threw up over the bed. It wasn't intentional; he didn't even know he was going to do it until he felt his whole stomach flip over and explode. Then he sat there, staring at the mess and unable to move. Arms rigid, he *couldn't* move — couldn't connect his brain to his body — didn't want his brain to be a *part* of his body.

He retched again, but there was nothing left and it hurt his throat, bringing tears to his eyes, but he couldn't cry. Not yet. The horror was too close to the surface and if he cried now, he knew he wouldn't be able to stop.

'You can clean that up when you're done looking at it,' said Eddie from the window.

Michael raised his head. It was an effort, but he forced himself to look at the man. The heroin had faded into insignificance at this latest outrage. 'You fucked me, you stinking queer,' he whispered, wiping his mouth with the back of his hand. 'You drugged me, brought me back here and then you *fucked* me!'

Even now, the rational part of his mind — what little there was left of it — half-expected Eddie to smile and deny it. Call him stupid — call him *anything* — but deny the allegation. Then they could laugh about it and Michael could go home. *Oh God — home. I want to go home. Somebody take me home.*

But Eddie didn't deny the accusation. Instead he came across to the bed and picked up the half-empty mug of coffee from the bedside table. He held it out to Michael. 'Calm down, Mikey. Have a drink.'

Michael flinched as Eddie got close to him, but then he reached out for the mug, took it and flung it at the man's face. Eddie jumped backwards, but the mug caught his shoulder and the contents poured down his arm and chest. It wasn't more than lukewarm now, but Eddie simply stepped up to the bed, grabbed Michael's chin with one hand and slapped him hard across the cheek with the other.

'Fucking perv!' Michael was on his feet before he had time to think. Scrabbling over the bed, he was oblivious to the vomit and his only intention was to get as far away as possible. Heading for the door, he didn't stop to look behind him, but reached for the handle, blood pounding in his temples as he yanked the door open and half-fell out into the corridor.

He swung left and bolted up the hallway, ignoring the shout from behind him. Colliding with what had to be the front door of the flat, he fumbled for the handle desperately.

The door was locked. It wasn't unexpected, given the circumstances, but that didn't stop Michael from pulling at the handle several times as if he could wrench it off by force alone. When he realised it wasn't going to open, he threw himself at the door, then tried to prise it open with his fingernails.

'That's enough, Mikey.'

He froze at the voice, the calm tone cutting through the hysteria. Then he turned around, his back up against the door and his hand on the handle. Eddie was standing at the other end of the hall, his shirt wet from spilt coffee. The man strolled up the corridor, waving a hand at the face which had appeared around a doorway and was watching the proceedings curiously. He shook his head in warning and the face disappeared into the room. Eddie shut the door and carried on towards where Michael was standing.

'Keep away from me!' Michael was surprised he could actually speak coherently – his mind was at screaming pitch and he was breathing so fast, he was shaking. God, this man had touched him while he'd been unconscious. *Fucked* him. The shadowy nightmares were all true.

'All right.' Eddie stopped and held his hands out placatingly. 'Have it your way. But there's no way out, Mikey, and the sooner you realise that, the better.'

No way out. The words were made of lead, puncturing

his mind like bullets. Three little words to reshape his life. *No way out.* But Eddie couldn't keep him here forever. Could he? *What's the point of all this?*

Michael let go of the door handle. For the first time, he realised that he was near-naked in the silk robe and he clutched it round his body, barely noticing the mess down the front. He watched Eddie warily, but the man didn't make a move towards him and finally Michael relaxed enough to back into the corner of the hallway.

'Come on, Mikey. Let's get you cleaned up and I'll do you another breakfast.'

Michael didn't reply. He might not have any means of escape, but he was damned if he was going to *co-operate* with the man. There was no way Eddie was getting within ten feet of him, let alone touching him again.

There were no other doors to try, not without getting past the man first and Michael just couldn't make himself do that. As far into the corner as he could get, he sank slowly to the floor, bare toes squeaking on the wood-laminate floor. Bringing his knees up to his chest, he hugged them tightly.

No way out.

The owner of the face he'd seen earlier came out of the room and looked at him. It was a boy of indeterminate age with long brown hair scraped back into a pony tail. He exchanged a few low words with Eddie before disappearing into what was presumably the kitchen, as he reappeared a few moments later with a can of coke and a packet of chocolate digestives.

No way out.

Eddie stared at him for a moment, then shook his head and returned to the bedroom. He came out with his arms full of maroon satin and went into the kitchen. There were sounds of a washing machine starting up.

No way out.

Michael put his chin on his knees and began to cry.

THREE

Kate Redford made a fresh pot of tea and arranged it on a black lacquer tray together with four cups and saucers and a matching sugar bowl. She looked at the overall effect and added a plate of digestive biscuits. Then she carried the tray through to the lounge, where mum and dad were sitting together with the two police officers.

'Thank you, Kate, dear. What would we do without you?' Her mother didn't even look at her and Kate seethed in silence as she sat down on the end of the settee.

It wasn't anything new. Ever since she and Colin had announced their intention to get married, there had been little inferences, odd comments. All implying that she should be staying at home to look after her parents and not contemplating a move up north with Colin's job. It was only Carlisle, for Christ's sake – not bloody California – yet they were acting as if she was leaving them forever. Not so much losing a daughter as losing a housemaid, she surmised, instantly regretting the thought. It wasn't their fault that they found it hard to let go. They were both retired and she was still young and fit. They'd devoted their lives to bringing up three kids, so why should she begrudge them a little of her time? Besides, her problems weren't important anyway. Not since Michael had disappeared.

It had been Kate who had first phoned Jenny on Sunday and discovered that nobody had seen him since he'd left the club. She knew most of Michael's friends, had always made it her business to keep in touch with his age group. After all he was only five years younger than her and although five years might seem like a lifetime to a teenager, it was nothing compared to the great yawning chasm between Kate and her elder sister Marsha, or Kate and her parents for that matter.

Where are you, Mike? Why don't you phone us? It wasn't like Michael not to keep in touch. He'd fought long and hard for the right to stay out with his friends late at night, something mum and dad couldn't understand, and it had been Kate's intercession that had finally won him his freedom. With strings attached of course, but Michael didn't seem to mind them. He didn't even seem to notice them.

'Kate, lovey?'

'Sorry?' She looked up and saw one of the officers glancing at her, an enquiring look on his face. Detective Inspector Darwin. *Derek, isn't it?* He was late thirties maybe, tall and striking with the first scattering of grey in overly-long hair – in fact too much a typical tv detective for Kate to take him seriously. 'I'm sorry, did you say something? I was miles away.' *Are you miles away too, Mike?*

He smiled slightly. 'You mother was just telling me you've heard nothing from Michael since we last spoke.'

Kate nodded. 'Not a thing. It's been nearly three weeks now.' This wasn't fair. Michael was her brother, but she resented having to take all the responsibility for his disappearance. *Well, wasn't it my fault he was at that damned club in the first place? It was me who persuaded the folks it was a good idea.* They still thought their only son was about twelve and generally treated him accordingly. And they'd gone to pieces since he hadn't come home that night. It was Kate who'd consoled them, Kate who'd eventually contacted the police. There'd been numerous visits already from police officers and family liaison, asking endless pointless questions – *Is Michael doing well at school? Does he take drugs? Is he sexually active? Has he ever run away before?* – but so far nobody seemed to be taking the situation seriously.

'Well, I'm sorry to say that we've spoken to most of his friends and none of them have any idea where he might have gone.' DI Darwin paused. 'Are there any other places he might have gone? Any relatives, perhaps?'

'No.' Kate shook her head. 'And he hasn't run away, either.' *Mike isn't like Marsha,* she wanted to scream at them. Teenage rebel Marsha had run away more times than anyone could remember and Kate had heard all the stories. Marsha liked adventure and was now living on some experimental commune in the Australian Outback, a fact which never ceased to embarrass their parents for what seemed to them like a monumental failure in raising their daughter correctly. So they went to the other extreme and Marsha had become the family heroine, off exploring the world while the rest of them stayed at home. Marsha was better out of it, Kate had decided years ago; she'd never really got to know her sister properly and resented the fact that the burden of holding the family together had now fallen onto her. *Roll on Carlisle.*

'What makes you say that, Miss Redford?'

'Kate, please,' she corrected. 'Michael's not the type to run away. He's too well-balanced – too *normal.*' She sighed. 'It's difficult to explain. But he'd have phoned us, wherever he'd gone. He's like that.'

'Like what?'

'Thoughtful. Considerate.' Despite the worry, she had to hide a smile as a memory jumped into her mind. *He's thoughtful, all right. He even sent Emma a bunch of flowers after she screwed him!* When one of her friends had kindly agreed to assist Michael in his coming of age, he'd been gentlemanly about the whole affair, such as it was. But that was Michael all over; that was what came from having parents to whom good manners and etiquette were everything. *Manners maketh man.* Except that in their eyes, he was still a child. A child who, as the only son, would one day go out into the world, have a high-flying career and carry on the family name.

Kate's mother began to cry. Her father leaned over and patted her arm, handing her a cup of tea. Tea solved everything in the Redford household; from Kate's first failed engagement to her father's recent heart attack, everything could be put right with a cup of tea. The day began with tea, was punctuated by tea at various intervals and ended with tea last thing at night. Kate preferred coffee.

The DI coughed delicately, obviously used to situations like this. His sidekick, who apparently accompanied him everywhere – leastways every time Kate had seen him, they'd been together – was sipping his tea and studiously avoiding anyone's eyes. He never said much and Kate wondered if he was a trainee.

She took the initiative. 'So go on, Mr Darwin. What do you think has happened to Michael?' *Put the man on the spot!*

The man sighed. 'Kate, you know what I'm going to say. We've circulated his photograph and we've spoken to everyone we can think of, including the proprietor of the club and the staff who were working there that night. It was a busy Saturday night. None of the cabbies remember him. Nobody's seen him. In the absence of anything else to go on, there's very little we can do apart from keep our eyes open.' He hesitated. 'We'll put a trace on his mobile and check out his internet accounts. I'll even get the relevant departments to monitor facebook and msn. But you'll probably find he'll come home of his own accord when he's ready. It's not uncommon for teenagers to run away.'

'Michael has *not* run away! Why won't you believe me?' This was like watching a police program on television – all platitudes and patronisation, with nothing ever happening.

'Have you spoken to Jenny?'

'The girlfriend? Yes, of course. She claims that they had a row and he went off in a temper. Never saw him again.'

She would. 'They didn't try to make up?'

'Apparently not. Though you may have better luck with her.' He replaced the empty cup on the tray and stood up, unfolding himself out of the chair. DI Darwin was a big man and yet he had a quiet intricate manner about him, as if he was always aware of every inch of his body and what it was doing. *I bet nobody's ever caught you with your flies down*, Kate thought as he turned to face her.

'Look, Kate. Why don't you try speaking to Jenny again? She seems to have been the last one to have seen or spoken to Michael. Have a woman-to-woman chat with her and see if you can find out what they rowed about – what he was thinking when he left. Come and see me at the station tomorrow and let me know what happened.'

'All right.' Kate stood up. 'I'll see you out.'

He nodded at her parents. 'Mr and Mrs Redford. I'll be in touch, just as soon as there's any news.'

Kate followed the two men from the room. Her father hadn't spoken a word, the entire time they'd been there. She wanted to hate him for it, but couldn't. Gone were the times when she'd screamed at him: *Why can't you be strong, dad?* He wasn't, not any more. Maybe he had been once – she'd seen the air force photographs from the Gulf War and she remembered the stories he'd told her about desert life on the front line. He must have been strong then, just to have survived. Now, he was like a deflated balloon, all the air had leaked out gradually over the years and he was little more than a skin, a shell of memories.

She didn't really resent her parents. Kate just felt stifled sometimes, bogged down in yesterdays when she had a bright tomorrow in front of her. Colin was her passport to a new life and Carlisle was beginning to seem like an Eden.

DI Darwin was at the front door. 'I'll see you tomorrow?'

Kate nodded. 'I'll call round and see Jenny tonight.' Though what good it would do, she didn't know. She could cheerfully strangle the girl, just for being the last person to have seen Michael. *The last person to have seen him alive?* She shook her head quickly – thoughts like that were dangerous. She had to be strong, for Michael's sake, if not for her parents.

'Right.' DI Darwin gave his partner the car keys. 'Go and open up, Steve.' Then he turned back to Kate and touched her arm briefly. 'Don't worry, Kate. We'll find him. Or he'll come home. It's just the waiting that's hard.'

Kate closed the door behind them and went back to the lounge. Her mother was still crying and Kate told her father to make some more tea. Then she sat down on the arm of her mother's chair and put a hand on her shoulder. 'Come on, mum. They'll find him.'

'Why did he do it, Kate?' Her mother looked up. 'Why did he run away?'

Kate gritted her teeth. 'He hasn't run away, mum. Why should he?'

'I don't know. Did we do something? He'd tell you, wouldn't he?'

This isn't fair! 'No, mum. You didn't do anything. I'll go and see Jenny later and see if I can find out any more.' If his own parents thought he'd run away, then how was she ever going to get anyone else to believe her? And if nobody believed her, then who would find Michael?

FOUR

Michael. My name is Michael Redford and this is a dream.

'Mikey?'

No, Michael. This is not real!

'Mikey?'

There was another presence now – a boy his own age, or maybe younger.

'Come on, Mikey. I'm not one of them.'

A different voice from the dreams. Michael opened his eyes, unsure whether he'd been asleep or not. He lifted his head and winced as stiff muscles complained. How long had he been here?

Nothing had changed. He was still sitting in the corner of the hallway in Eddie's flat. He'd half-expected to wake up at home and find this was all some nightmare, hallucinations of a hell he'd never have to live through, but it wasn't and in a way it was a comfort. At least it proved he hadn't imagined it all and he wasn't going mad. Not yet, anyway.

There was a figure crouched in front of him on the hall floor. Michael focused his eyes blearily and tried to press himself even further into the corner.

'Don't be scared, Mikey.'

He peered at the voice's owner. It was the kid he'd seen

earlier, the one with the long dark hair, and he was watching Michael with a look of real concern. 'Michael,' he said hoarsely. 'My name's Michael.'

'Whatever.' He smiled. 'I'm Lee. Here.' He handed Michael a mug. 'Don't throw it at me – it's just tea.'

Michael looked at him, eventually stretching out his hand for the mug. He took a few sips. It was hot and comforting and made him aware how cold he was. The sick on his robe had dried to white smears, but he could still smell it. He wondered if he looked as bad as he felt.

The scream in his mind had muted into exhaustion, leaving behind a great yawning chasm of raw red pain. Michael knew he'd have to tread very carefully to avoid falling over the edge. He needed his wits if he was to survive in this place – wherever he was.

'What time is it?'

Lee glanced at his watch. 'Just gone three.' He wriggled round on the floor and sat down properly, crossing his legs. Michael didn't move, but remained in the corner, both hands cradling the mug balanced on his knees.

'How long have I been here?'

'You mean in the flat? Or here in the hall?' Lee smiled again, though not unkindly. 'Eddie brought you back about three weeks ago, I think. You've been out here since about eleven this mornin'.' He grinned suddenly. 'Shit, was Eddie pissed off when you puked all over the sheets.'

Michael took another mouthful of tea as he tried to order his thoughts. 'Is it all true? What he said?'

'What did he say?'

'About …' Michael felt his cheeks burn. 'About what he did to me.'

There was a silence for a moment, before Lee spoke. 'Look at me.' He paused. 'Fuckin' *look* at me, Mikey.' He held Michael's eyes for a moment and then nodded. 'Yes, it's true. I was there.'

Michael didn't reply. Sitting on the floor in a strange flat, he'd never felt quite so alone before and he wondered what his parents must be thinking. *Do you think I'm dead, mum? Is anyone looking for me still, or have you all given up?* Three weeks could be a lifetime.

His curiosity got the better of him. 'Do they think I'm dead?'

'Your folks?' Lee shrugged.

Poor mum and dad. And Kate. 'I have to speak to them. Let them know I'm all right.'

'You can't.'

'I *have* to.' Michael put the mug down and scrambled to his feet, looking round for a telephone. His legs were cramped and stiff, barely taking his weight as he stumbled back against the front door. He felt the panic leap up again in his mind, but he was too tired to answer it. 'There must be a phone somewhere!'

'Mikey, you *can't!*' Lee jumped up and tried to take his arm, but Michael shook him off. 'There *are* no phones. No landlines, anyway. Eddie has a mobile, but he never lets it out of his sight. And in any fuckin' case,' he added in softer tones, 'do you really think they'd want to know where you are now?'

No. Michael knew the answer straight away. How could he speak to his mother and tell her what had happened to him? How could he tell anybody? His parents had enough trouble coping with the idea that people actually had sex before marriage – the word *buggery* would send his father straight back into hospital with another heart attack. Even if he got out of here, he could never tell them what happened. He leaned against the door and hugged himself miserably. In three short weeks, his life had changed forever.

Lee pursed his lips. 'Why don't you have a shower and get dressed?' he suggested. 'You'll feel a lot better when you're clean and you've eaten.' Michael got the impression that Lee was walking a tightrope, trying to get him to accept the situation without pushing him over the edge. He wondered whether Eddie had put him up to it –

perhaps believing that Michael would respond better to someone of his own age – or whether Lee was genuinely concerned for him. Not that it mattered either way. There were no friends in this place.

Michael nodded after a moment. He was cold and stiff from the floor and the smell of puke was making him feel nauseous again. And if he intended to get out of here, he had to look as though he was co-operating. For the time being, anyway.

Lee showed him to the bathroom, carefully ignoring the other rooms along the way. Michael stumbled along behind. It seemed a strange set-up, this flat. Obviously in a rough part of town, judging by the view he'd had from the bedroom window, the flat was immaculate inside; large and roomy, the decor was quietly understated and yet expensive at the same time. Lee presumably lived here, but who else did? *Eddie?* Michael couldn't shake off the thought that he'd been sleeping in Eddie's bed for the last three weeks. The very idea revolted him and he shut it out, knowing it was the start of the slippery slope down into the terror that was still lurking at the back of his mind.

The bathroom matched the rest of the flat for subtle elegance. Done out in pale peach, the suite was creamy white and spotless, with an extravagantly large oval bath across one corner. Lee rummaged in a cupboard and brought out a huge fluffy orange towel.

'Water's usually hot.' He handed Michael the towel. 'Use what you like. I'll be in the lounge, when you're done and then we'll grab a sarnie.' He wandered out, leaving Michael standing in the middle of the room and still not quite keeping up with events.

Michael shook his head and shut the door. There wasn't a bolt. *Maybe nobody ever shuts the door in this place. Maybe they like to watch!*

He went over to the window. The frosted glass was draped with ivory net and standing on the toilet seat, he put a hand to either side and yanked up the bottom sash as hard as he could. The window resisted for a moment, then creaked and moved up several inches. He tried again, but it stubbornly refused to go any further.

Come on! Michael put all his strength into it, and succeeded only in catching one of his fingernails on the wood. His hands hurt from when he'd tried to claw his way out of the front door that morning, and there was already blood under his nails. Eventually he gave up and crouched down, putting his eyes level with the gap. There were white bars here too and he wondered if every window was similarly decorated. Was it just that the flat was in a rough area, or was there more to it? *Bars keep people in as well as out.* He took a deep breath of the fresh air outside. It tasted of rain and wet tarmac – so normal it brought tears to his eyes and he stood up quickly.

Looking up, he saw the reason for the window's refusal to co-operate. On either side of the frame was a large nail, preventing the sash from being raised more than the few inches it was open. Sufficient for ventilation, but not enough to get his head through and scream.

Michael climbed down and sat on the toilet seat. The nails were too long to prise out without proper tools and in any case, he'd never get past the bars. He flushed the loo to account for the silence and turned his attention to the shower.

The water was hot and hard, needle-sharp jets massaging his shoulders as he stood there. For a full five minutes, he turned his face up to the shower-head and cried again with the water, feeling like it was washing away a part of his youth that was gone forever. No matter what happened to him now, things would never be the same again. But the water took away some of the pain as well and left him curiously empty and calm. Lee was right – he had to face the situation.

He examined his body. It felt like it belonged to someone else as he prodded the pock-marks on the inside of his elbows – on both arms, he was dismayed to see. He wondered how many injections he'd had and whether they would affect him in the future. *What future?* He shied away from answering himself and moved on quickly.

The rest of his body was a different matter altogether. Michael couldn't bring himself to look at his cock and touching himself made him feel dirty. And although the stiffness in his neck and shoulders was easing with the warmth, there was a painful reminder of events in the ache in his thighs. The water stung in places it shouldn't, which was embarrassing even though he was alone in the room, and he could feel his face flush with shame.

Grabbing the soap, Michael began to wash himself vigorously. He scrubbed himself several times over, wincing at the sting of soap in his eyes and trying to ignore the revulsion which was threatening to push him over the edge again. He *had* to get clean although he was beginning to think he'd never feel truly clean again. More memories were returning now – fighting through the drug-induced barrier in his mind. Or maybe it was his mind that was trying to protect him from the knowledge that there had been others besides Eddie. Hazy faces distorted by pain and heroin. Michael wondered what kind of people actually got off on fucking someone who was stoned out of their mind and how much they'd paid for the privilege.

By the time he turned off the shower fifteen minutes later, his skin was burning in places, his eyes felt hot and sore, but at least he was as clean as he was going to get. He climbed out of the bath and wrapped himself in the orange towel.

Now what? Lee had suggested he get dressed, but Michael didn't know what he was supposed to wear. He didn't know where his clothes were and he didn't fancy putting on the robe again, so he dried himself off before opening the bathroom door cautiously. Neatly folded on the carpet outside was a pile of clothes.

This is crazy! Things like this just didn't *happen* in real life. Michael picked up the pile and retreated back into the relative safety of the bathroom where he examined the acquisition.

The clothing consisted of some nondescript underwear – pants and socks – a navy blue sweatshirt and a pair of grey joggers. Supermarket clothes, all apparently brand new and still with the labels on. Which was worrying, really. Why had they gone to so much trouble for him? *What does it all mean?*

He dressed quickly, ran a comb through his hair and turned to look in the mirror. He looked thinner than he last remembered and his dark blond hair seemed longer, but the biggest change was in the bloodshot eyes. He could see it for himself. *Seventeen going on forty.*

Michael left the towel on the floor and wandered out into the hall. Lee had said he'd be in the lounge, but where was that? And for that matter, where was Eddie? At the moment, he was in control, but he didn't trust himself not to snap again if Eddie came anywhere near him. Right now, he felt entirely capable of murder, although he knew that if the situation came to a head, the reverse would be true. *Yeah, Mike. Fucking brilliant. First sign of trouble and you go to pieces.* Except that it had been a bit more than mere trouble, hadn't it? Nothing in his life had prepared him for this and he didn't know how to handle the situation. Jesus Christ, he'd been *raped!* How the hell was he supposed to deal with *that?*

It's your choice, his father would have told him. Dad's philosophy on life said that you made your own luck and events happened according to your own reactions. That was how you survived, he explained, by making your own choices from the selection life offered and if you picked something you didn't like – well – you had nobody to blame but yourself. That was what men were supposed to do. Real men, like the ones who had fought for their country and won. Real men would never have let themselves get into *this* situation.

No! Even as he started thinking about it, he could feel

the scream rising with the bile in his throat. He stood in the hallway for a moment, holding the door frame with one hand while he fought down the panic and tried to compose himself. Events were becoming clearer now and images of the past three weeks kept jumping into his mind. Fuzzy flashbacks, most of them, but he knew he'd woken several times, mostly to piss or eat some of the tasteless mush that he'd been spoon-fed. And then there was the sex, though he couldn't recollect more than the pain and the faces. He wasn't entirely sure whether it had occurred immediately after a jab or if it was just that his subconscious was sparing him the intimate details. The more he thought about it, the less he wanted to know, so he ran a hand through his wet hair and started to take note of his surroundings instead.

Immediately to his left was the bedroom. *Eddie's room?* Michael wandered in and quickly examined the window. He wasn't surprised to find a similar pair of nails preventing more than two inches ventilation. He thought about smashing the glass anyway, but he had a fair idea what would happen if he did and he didn't particularly want to spend any more of his life unconscious. No, that action was better saved until it stood a greater chance of success.

'There isn't any point, Mikey.'

He swung round, startled, to see Lee standing in the doorway.

'There's no-one out there,' he added gently. 'Shit, don't you think I tried the same thing once?' Lee came into the room and Michael backed away slowly, still not sure whose side the boy was on. If there were any sides.

'How long have you been here, Lee?' His voice was hoarse and he had to cough sharply.

'Me?' Lee shrugged and sat down on the edge of the bed. The sheets had been replaced with charcoal grey satin. 'A year or so, I guess. Why?' He pulled the elastic band from his hair and began combing it with his fingers.

'But what do you *do* all day?'

'Do?' Lee nearly spat out the piece of gum he was chewing, choking with sudden laughter. 'I sleep mostly. In the day, anyway.'

'What are you – a vampire?' As soon as he'd said it, Michael understood what Lee was implying and he turned away, wondering how he could possibly have been so stupid. *He's gay, dickhead! He and Eddie are ... lovers.* He frowned. *So what does that make me?* Besides, there'd been someone else. An older man. Michael could picture him from the nightmares and he had the feel of authority about him.

Lee laughed again. 'A vampire? I like that.' He paused. 'You haven't sussed it out? Mikey, I'm a rent boy. Did you really not know?'

'You're *what?*'

'You know – people pay for the pleasure of my body.' He did a graceful twirl on the carpet for effect and flopped back down on the bed. 'Fuck me, you really are an innocent, aren't you?'

Michael could feel the stark terror still lurking in his mind. It was growing, a black cloudy shape which was in serious danger of crowding out reason. *If you're a rent boy, then Eddie is – what? A pimp? And I'm ...*

He blinked and sat back onto the window ledge heavily. The black fog was threatening to swamp him and he could feel the blood draining from his face.

'Mikey?'

'Fuck off,' he said through gritted teeth, desperately trying to stay on his feet. *I won't do it – they can't make me! I'll kill myself before he touches me again! Him or anybody else!*

Lee stood up and Michael flinched. Lee sighed. 'Get a grip, Mikey. It's not the end of the fuckin' world. Hell, I even get to go out occasionally – this place isn't a prison and Eddie and Joss ain't screws.'

'Joss?' He'd heard that name before.

Lee dismissed it with a wave of his hand. 'You'll meet

him tonight. Now come on – let's sort out munchies. You must be friggin' starvin'.'

I don't think I could ever eat again. But his body betrayed him and his stomach rumbled at the thought of food. Still shaking, Michael forced himself to stand up, fighting back the rising tide of terror. Panic wouldn't help him – not now or ever – he needed a clear head if he was going to find a way out of this nightmare. But oh God, he had to find a way *soon*.

FIVE

The television was on, but Michael wasn't paying much attention. Out of the corner of his eye, he could see Lee sitting cross-legged on the sofa and rolling a joint. Eddie was reading the *Evening Standard*, a mug of tea balanced on the arm of the chair and the top of a mobile phone peeking out tantalisingly from his shirt pocket. Everything seemed relaxed and yet there was an undercurrent of tension in the air.

Michael was still strung out on what he'd discovered and the implications for his immediate future. Much to Lee's amusement, he'd gone round every room in the flat – not that there were many of them – checking the windows for escape routes. There weren't any. *Surprise, surprise, Mike. What did you expect? A fucking exit sign?*

He'd concluded after much deliberation that they were somewhere in the East End. It wasn't an area he knew well, not beyond the vicinity of the Docklands Light Railway. Michael was a Westerner; born in Hammersmith, he'd grown up around Chiswick and although he knew Central London and the West End reasonably well, East London was largely unexplored territory.

The flat itself seemed to be several floors up over some kind of shop or factory. He could see a tattered awning below the lounge window, but it was old and broken and didn't look like it was still in use. In fact the entire area seemed much the same – dirty and unused. Forgotten, almost. *Perfect for Eddie's little enterprise. Who the hell is going to come around here unless they know what they're looking for?* He'd spent a good few hours watching the alley below, but hadn't seen a single person in all that time.

He sneezed suddenly and the other two looked up.

Eddie nodded. 'Joss will be here soon,' he said, although Michael couldn't see the connection. *Joss. The final piece in the puzzle?*

Lee flipped television channels with the remote control. 'He's late today,' he observed, carefully licking the cigarette paper. Michael noticed that his hands were shaking and it took him three attempts to light up. Lee inhaled and sat back, sighing as he breathed out. He took another drag, then he held the joint out. 'Anyone else?'

'No.' Eddie flicked him a cursory glance. 'And you go easy. You're working tonight.'

'Shit, Eddie. Five nights in a row?'

'You got a problem with that?'

'Guess not.' Lee held the joint out to Michael. 'You want a drag, Mikey?'

'My name,' said Michael, with as much dignity as he could muster, 'is Michael. Not Mikey. Michael.' *So fuck you!*

'Your name is whatever I say it is,' Eddie corrected, without even looking up from the paper. 'And you don't want to smoke that crap.'

Michael didn't answer and wouldn't look at Lee. Instead he stared fixedly at the television screen. Lee sighed again and shrugged. 'Suit yourself.'

Michael chewed a fingernail. *Something's about to happen.* But what? Both Lee and Eddie were on edge and it was obviously something to do with Joss' imminent arrival. He sneezed again and wondered if he was getting a cold. Come to think of it, he wasn't feeling too good. Gone was that *alive* sensation he'd had when he'd woken that morning and he was tired and listless. Not that it was surprising, given the way the day had progressed, but Michael couldn't help feeling there was more to come.

'Who is it, then?' Lee changed channels again.

'What?' Eddie looked up irritably.

'Tonight. Who is it? A regular?'

'Ask Joss. He makes the arrangements.'

'I'm askin' you.'

'No idea.'

'Sorry I fuckin' spoke.'

Eddie put down the paper. 'Shut up, Lee.' He reached over for the remote control and changed the television back to the original channel. Lee blew a smoke ring and smirked.

Michael got up and walked out of the room. The bickering was getting on his nerves. *What nerves? They've already been shot to hell.* After what he'd learned today, he doubted whether he had the capacity to be shocked by anything ever again.

He went into the bathroom, had a piss and was about to return to the lounge when he froze in the hall. There was the sound of a key in the front door.

A chance to get out of here? Michael readied himself for a bolt for freedom, but as the door opened, he found he couldn't move. He knew the man who was standing in the doorway and seeing him brought back more memories. Middle-aged and carrying a black leather holdall, he was dressed in faded jeans and a black silk shirt. An expensive leather jacket hung casually across his shoulders and he held a cigarette in one hand. Michael frowned. It had been Joss who'd been doing the injections while Eddie held him. But had that been all Joss was involved in?

'Mikey?' His voice was educated, with no trace of an accent, cockney or otherwise.

Christ! He's acting like he's my father coming home from work! Michael hesitated. *Come on, Redford. You've got to get past him.*

'Hello, Mikey. Nice to see you awake at last. How are

you feeling?' The man stubbed out the cigarette in the ash tray on the hall table. 'I'm Joss, though I expect you've already worked that out for yourself.' He closed the front door and Michael backed away as the man walked down the hall. Even if Joss hadn't been involved in the sex side of things, he was infinitely more chilling than Eddie. There was something about him – the casual air, maybe – which said he was confident and in charge.

Joss smiled, tucking the holdall under one arm. 'You look confused. Hasn't Eddie explained things to you?'

'Eddie's *explained* a lot of things.'

'That's good.' Joss came closer and Michael felt the closed bathroom door behind his heels. He reached for the handle, but he wasn't fast enough and Joss stretched out his hand, running it through Michael's hair. 'We'll have to do something about this, I think.'

Eyes wide, Michael couldn't move. He wanted to knock Joss' hand away, but he couldn't bring himself to do it. Underneath the man's cool exterior, Michael could sense an iron determination and there was nothing friendly in his touch.

Michael held himself still while Joss looked at him and waited until the man stepped back a pace, turning to go back to the lounge. Then he seized his moment, ducked his head and sprinted for the front door. It wasn't as straightforward as he'd envisioned – for one thing, his legs didn't seem to want to obey his mind and he stumbled twice, pushing himself off the wall with one hand. And then there was Joss' lightning reaction as he tossed the bag to one side and came after him.

He almost did it. The door handle was within his grasp, his fingers brushed it momentarily and he reached forward, trying to make those few extra precious inches. If he could just get the door open, he might have a chance.

But he was out of breath by the time his fingers almost caught the door handle. Coughing, he pulled out of Joss' grip and fell against the wall. *Move, Redford!* He forced himself to his feet and reached for the door again. This time he succeeded and he grasped the handle firmly, pulling the door towards him. It opened easily and he could smell the freedom of the staircase beyond. *Come on! Just a bit further.* He stepped forwards—

—And saw stars as Joss smacked him round the head with all of his weight behind the blow.

Michael crashed to the floor, closing the door as he fell against it. He saw the gap between the door and the frame and watched it decrease almost in slow motion as his mind screamed at him to get up. Unfortunately his body didn't like the idea and he stayed where he was on the hall floor, muscles shaking.

What's the matter with me? Why can't I get up?

Joss stepped over him and dead-locked the door, pocketing the key with an overly deliberate motion. Then he bent and hauled him up, arms under his shoulders. Michael got his legs underneath him and persuaded them to take his weight while Joss moved his grip from Michael's armpits to his shoulders.

'Everybody gets one chance to make a mistake, Mikey. That was yours. Do yourself a favour and learn from it.' He turned away and picked up the holdall. Michael shivered, too scared to move. *This man gets what he wants.*

'Come inside,' Joss told him and Michael obeyed. His legs were still shaking and he was short of breath as he crossed to the far corner of the lounge, not wanting to be near any of them. Joss put the holdall down on the end of the sofa. Lee and Eddie were in the middle of the room and by the looks on their faces, they'd both witnessed the abortive escape attempt.

'You're late.' Lee looked more relieved than anything else and Michael wondered what the object of the visit was.

'Am I?' Joss didn't seem perturbed. 'Getting nervous, were you?' He smiled. 'I have a job for you tonight, Lee.'

'So Eddie tells me.'

'Good. Then let's get down to business, shall we? Then you can shower and get ready. Mikey – you come too. I want you to see this.'

'Fuck you.'

Joss raised his eyebrows. 'That's really not very polite, Mikey. This is for your benefit as well.'

'Says who?' Michael was tired of being co-operative. He was feeling dizzy and sweating now, yet shivering too, despite the heat from the gas fire.

But Lee didn't look well either and Michael recalled seeing his hands shaking earlier. 'Mikey, don't,' he said, crossing the lounge towards him. 'It doesn't help.'

Joss laughed suddenly. 'You really do know how to pick them, don't you, Ed? He may be a looker, but I thought you said he'd be easy? I'm going to pour a drink,' he added. 'Why don't you sort yourselves out and come and get me when you're ready.'

Lee looked up, alarmed. 'Joss, please!'

'You need a shot, Lee? Then you'd better be persuasive.' Joss shook his head. 'Either Mikey does as he's told, or we all wait.' He picked up the holdall and strolled from the room; Michael could hear the sound of glasses chinking in the kitchen.

You need a shot, Lee? He was beginning to understand what this was all about and he didn't like it. He sat down heavily on the arm of the sofa. *Lee is an addict.* Lee was also exhibiting many of the same symptoms as Michael was experiencing – he seemed anxious and jumpy and there was a thin sheen of sweat on his forehead.

The heroin had slipped into the background, dwarfed by the enormity of rape, which had seemed infinitely worse to Michael. Finding out that Lee was not only gay, but a rent boy hadn't improved matters either. But both buggery and prostitution - horrific as they were – could be survived. *Addiction can't!*

Wait a minute! Things were moving too fast. It didn't necessarily follow that he was addicted to the drug.

Addicts were different from normal people, mindless creatures living only for their next fix. *Aren't they?* And he was fine. A bit tired, maybe. Strung out, over-emotional – but fucking hell, that was only to be expected after what had happened. He'd been out of it for three weeks – he was bound to have picked up a bug from somewhere in that time, when his body's natural defences were low. He could find rational explanations for all of the symptoms he was showing.

'Mikey?' Lee touched his shoulder. 'Mikey, please. You've got to stop fightin'.'

He pulled away. 'Why? So you can both get a fix?' Presumably Eddie was included in all this – he certainly seemed as agitated now as Lee clearly was. 'I don't have to do *anything* for you. You might be able to keep me here, but I'm damn well not going to make it any easier for you!'

'You don't understand.' Lee tried again. 'It's no friggin' different for you.' He glanced at Eddie and nodded. Eddie shrugged his shoulders and left the lounge, leaving Lee and Michael alone.

'Something you don't want him to hear?' asked Michael with more than a touch of sarcasm.

Lee nodded. 'Mikey, it's not my fault you're here. Shit, all this happened to me a year ago.'

'My heart bleeds for you. But since you *can* leave, why don't you?'

'Because I need the gear.' Lee wiped his forehead with the sleeve of his sweatshirt. 'Joss supplies good clean smack – none of the street crap that's around – and in return, I do his clients. It's no big deal. I don't have a choice, Mikey. I need the stuff. So do you.' He hesitated. 'An' pissin' Eddie off is only going to make your life fuckin' hell.'

Michael didn't say a word. From being a prisoner, Lee could now leave if he wanted to, but he didn't. He stayed by choice, needing the drugs that only Joss could give him. Well, maybe not only Joss, but certainly servicing Joss' clients was going to be a safer bet than touting for business around King's Cross station, mugging old ladies or jacking cars – and they were the only other ways he was going to get money in sufficient quantities to satisfy his needs. At least this way nobody got hurt.

'Mikey, don't put me through this! Don't put *yourself* through it. You need it as much as I do.' There was a note of panic in Lee's voice now, but still Michael hesitated. True, he felt awful, but he wasn't convinced that heroin was what his body needed. *Physical addiction without the psychological craving? Is that how it starts?* But this wasn't a biology exam – this was real and he had to deal with it now.

Lee thumped the arm of the chair. 'For fuck's sake, Mikey, don't be so friggin' selfish!' He jumped up and ran from the room and Michael could hear him arguing with Joss in the kitchen. A few moments later, he came back into the lounge, left sleeve rolled up and his eyes wide and bright. He threw himself full-length onto the sofa and lay there, staring at the ceiling and humming softly to himself.

Christ, is that what it's like? 'Lee?'

Lee stopped humming. He tipped his head back over the edge of the sofa and looked at Michael upside down. 'Screw you,' he said pleasantly.

Mind over matter. *I am not an addict*, Michael told himself firmly. He had more willpower than that, surely? It was only a matter of discipline. But seeing Lee lying on the sofa, relaxed and obviously much happier than he'd been a few moments ago was hard to resist. Was there any point in him trying to sit it out? He'd seen programmes on television about drug addicts, seen screaming maniacs with bloodshot eyes clawing at the doctors for a fix. He'd watched Maria that day in the park. It scared him stupid.

Joss came into the room. He pushed Lee's feet to one side and sat down on the end of the sofa. 'Lee, go and take a shower.'

'In a minute.' Lee was watching the ceiling intently and

Michael wondered what he could see there. *Heroin doesn't cause hallucinations, does it?*

'Now, Lee,' said Joss firmly, giving him a shove.

Lee swung his legs over and stood up. 'All right, I'm goin'.' He glared at Michael. 'An' I don't know why you're looking so fuckin' smug. Wait 'til you start working – then you'll really—'

'Lee – out!'

'I'm going, I'm going.' He wandered out of the room, muttering. Joss got up and closed the door behind him.

'He'll calm down in half an hour or so. It always hits him like that. He doesn't mean to upset you.'

Michael shivered. Being alone with Joss was not something he relished. Eddie might be physically threatening, but Joss' calm composure covered a sharp tongue and the man reminded Michael of a new teacher he'd once had at school. No matter what the provocation, he'd never let himself be flustered and he'd sit at the front of the class until somehow his sheer presence made them all shut up. And then he'd give them all a detention and none of them would dare to argue. After two or three lessons, he got a reputation for having the quietest classes in the school and all the parents loved him. Michael's parents were no exception; in fact they'd admired him so much they'd taken his advice and dragged their son out of school at sixteen, enrolling him in sixth-form technical college and telling him it would be better for his career.

He drew his legs up onto the chair and watched the man, who was still carrying a crystal tumbler of what looked like scotch. He cradled it carefully.

'OK, Mikey,' Joss said after a few moments. 'I think it's about time we had a little chat. You're not feeling too good, right now, are you?' He smiled slightly at Michael's reluctance to answer. 'Have you ever seen anyone in heroin withdrawal, Mikey? No, I don't suppose you have, have you? But it's not very pretty. It will get worse than you feel now, much worse – in fact by tomorrow you'll be begging me to help you. You'll be vomiting, every muscle in your body will be shrieking and you'll want to die – you'll feel like you *are* dying.'

Michael couldn't look at him. He wanted to cry, but he was damned if he was going to give the man the satisfaction. His whole body was shaking now and he didn't doubt that what Joss said was true – it was going to get worse.

Joss drained the tumbler, stood up and placed it on the mantelpiece. 'Ah, I'm not being fair to you, am I, Mikey?' He paused. 'Tonight, you're going to get a shot whether you like it or not – just so you believe what I'm telling you. Tomorrow, you'll do as you're told, or we'll sit here all night until you beg me for it. And you will, Mikey, believe me. So do yourself a favour and calm down.' He crouched down in front of Michael's chair. 'I really don't want to hurt you, Mikey. I've spent far too much time and money on you already.'

His voice was chilling and for the first time Michael thought beyond the immediate future. *He doesn't intend to ever let me go!* This was no quick fuck by some pervert; this wasn't going to result in him being dumped stark naked in a motorway service station. This was commitment. Joss was investing in Michael and Michael wondered what exactly the man expected of him. It didn't bear thinking about and Michael knew he'd crack up before that ever happened to him. *Yeah, or be stoned out of my mind.*

Joss called for Eddie who came into the lounge holding a small syringe. Michael instinctively tried to stand up but Joss shoved him back again. 'Push up your sleeve, Mikey.'

He couldn't move. *This isn't real.* The syringe in Eddie's hand seemed to have grown out of all proportions; it loomed into Michael's field of view and reminded him of all the times he'd been to the dentist.

'Mikey, push up your sleeve. I won't ask you again.' Joss' voice was calm and business-like as he took the syringe from Eddie. He looked up at the man. 'Got me a fresh needle?'

Michael watched in horrified fascination as Eddie produced a tiny plastic cylinder with an orange cap. He snapped the cap between his thumb and first finger and extracted an orange plastic tip with a needle attached to the end of it. Joss took it from him and – careful not to touch the needle itself – exchanged it with the one on the end of the syringe. He turned back to Michael. 'You still not going to co-operate? Roll up his sleeve, Ed.'

Eddie took his wrist and Michael pulled away sharply. At the same time, he kicked out with both feet, but Joss wasn't stupid – he'd obviously expected this reaction as he was out of the way in a fraction of a second, as Eddie moved round to stand behind the chair. Michael tried to get up but even as he moved, Eddie's hand was on his throat. He coughed, but the pressure didn't ease up.

Joss pushed up the sleeve of his sweatshirt and turned his wrist over, clamping it palm up on the chair arm and holding it with one hand. Leaning forward with his free hand, Eddie squeezed Michael's upper arm hard. Michael cried out and tried to push Joss away, but he couldn't move – the pressure on his neck was choking him. He clawed at the hand on his throat, but Eddie was too strong and the more he struggled, the harder it became to breathe.

Working quickly, Joss located a vein and carefully inserted the needle with an almost delicate precision. 'Hold it there.'

Michael sat very still now. He watched the plunger move slowly down the syringe – none of this stabbing that he'd seen in films. The cloudy liquid entered his bloodstream and he fancied he could feel it in his arm, making its way up to his heart.

He *could* feel it. Every tiny blood cell in his body was circulating with the drug, passing it on, moving it round like a baton in a relay race. But it wasn't blood, it was air and he was flying again, dancing with the sparkles of dust in the room. The sound of running water from the bathroom became a thundering waterfall, cascading down the mountainside and he wanted to fly over it, dive over it and swim it to the bottom. The feeling was fantastic, out of this world and he *could* be out of this world – he was on another planet, listening to the silence of space and watching the earth rotate from a million light years away.

Michael wondered why he'd ever resisted. There was nothing on earth like this. He was a fool. A crazy immature fool not to want to experience this feeling. He laughed suddenly and the others laughed with him.

'Stay with him, Ed. Don't leave him alone 'til he comes down a bit.' Joss looked at his watch. 'I'll see you the same time tomorrow.'

Eddie nodded. 'What d'you want doing with him?' He waved at Michael. 'You got him lined up for anyone tonight?'

'No.' Joss shook his head. 'Not for a week or so. I only got the photos uploaded last night. And he's had enough shocks for one day. Try and get him with Lee later if you can – get him used to sharing – but don't push it. He's worth taking time with.'

Michael wondered what all the fuss was about.

SIX

Kate reversed the Fiat into the last of the visitor's spaces outside the police station. There was a car coming in just behind her; the driver glared at her as if the space was his personal property and Kate was tempted to give him a V sign, but resisted. *Arrogant bastard!* She slammed the car door and smiled at him as he circled the car park like a bird of prey.

She was in a bad mood. She'd been working late, volunteering to cover the Well Woman clinic that the doctor's surgery ran every week. It looked good on her receptionist's record, put her even more in the running for the post of practice manager, and it made up for the fact that she'd decided to take a week's leave at short notice to be with her parents. Colin wouldn't like it, of course – it was a week less to be used for the honeymoon and the move up north, but she reasoned that if she was going to move all those miles away from the parents, it wouldn't kill her to smooth the path a little with some judicious daughterly care and attention. And to be fair, they needed it – Michael's disappearance had hit hard and they were blaming themselves for failing to warn him about whatever it was that had happened to him. Kate wasn't entirely taken in – she knew damn well that this was partly another anti-Carlisle protest, but she didn't have the heart to argue the matter with them. If they wanted her to think that they thought it was their fault, then let them.

Emotional blackmail had always been her mother's trump card, to be pulled out whenever the game looked shaky. What she failed to take into account though, was Kate's ability to recall all the previous cards which had been played in each hand. It was a skill she'd learned at an early age – to watch, listen and remember – and it had served her well so far. *Remember how much you cheered your dad up when he was in hospital?* was the latest ploy and Kate resented being manipulated in this way. Sometimes she wished Michael had been a girl and then perhaps the family duties would have fallen to him; but Michael was a man and thus expected to go out into the world and carve his own niche. *And Marsha can't even manage a phone call.* Yet Marsha was the family's golden girl – Marsha had travelled, spread her wings, made something of her life, while Kate was still living at home and trying to save enough money for the wedding.

It didn't help that Colin was being less than sympathetic about the whole affair; he was concerned, certainly, but he had both feet firmly in the running-away camp and wasn't going to let himself be persuaded otherwise. But then he and Michael had never got on and Kate got the distinct impression that Colin was everything that Michael didn't want to be – predictable and boring. Good old reliable Colin – handling the house purchase in Carlisle with such calm efficiency that Kate wondered if she'd ever have to make a decision again.

Kate locked the car and jogged up the steps. It was a converted Victorian building and the glass double doors looked out of place in the surrounding architecture.

'I'm here to see Detective Inspector Darwin.'

'And your name is?' The woman on the other side of the counter smiled.

'Kate. Kate Redford. He's expecting me.'

'Just a moment.' She dialled an extension and – hand over the mouthpiece – told Kate to take a seat. A few minutes later, the interconnecting door opened to a soft buzz and DI Darwin appeared.

'Kate. Come this way, won't you?'

She followed him at a fast pace up five flights of stairs. He had a nice bum, tightly clad in black jeans with a grey polo shirt tucked in. DI Darwin obviously kept himself fit and Kate couldn't help but admire the way he took the stairs two at a time without even breathing quickly.

'Coffee?' He looked at her and grinned suddenly. 'Sorry – I should have offered you the lift, shouldn't I? Pardon my manners.'

'I need the exercise. Coffee would be great, thanks.'

He led her through an open-plan office where there were a dozen or so cluttered desks, an assortment of computers and trays piled high with paperwork. Empty plastic cups littered every available surface. Across the back wall was a huge map of the area covered with clear plastic and next to it, precariously balanced on an old fridge, was an odd contraption with red and green lights on it, which contained a number of radio handsets. There were only three people apart from Kate and the DI, and there was no sign of the sidekick she'd met last time.

One man looked up as Kate crossed the room to a small office partitioned off with glass walls. 'Like Daniel entering the lion's den,' he commented wryly. 'Pretty girls should be warned. Enter Derek's domain at your peril.'

'Girlfriend left you again, has she?' The DI held the door open for Kate, followed her and turned back, sticking his head round the door. 'Since you've nothing better to do, we'll have two coffees, please.' He closed the door and indicated a chair. 'Sorry about that – they think they're funny.' He shrugged. 'Sometimes you need a sense of humour in this job. Sit down, won't you?'

Derek's office was no different to the main room, with an overall air of organised chaos. He cleared a space on his desk by shoving everything to one side and dropping an empty sandwich wrapper in the bin.

Kate put her handbag down and sat. 'Inspector Darwin—'

'Derek will do, thanks. I'm not that old yet. Though God knows I feel it sometimes.'

'Derek.' She paused as there was a knock at the door and the man who'd spoken earlier brought in two plastic cups of coffee, three sugar sachets and an old plastic teaspoon that had clearly seen several weeks of active service. 'I went round to see Jenny again last night.'

'Michael's girlfriend.' Derek sat down behind the desk. The flippancy had gone now and his tone was serious. 'Did you get any more out of her than I did?'

Kate frowned. 'I don't know. She was crying so hard, it was difficult to get anything coherent.'

'But you got something?' He sat forward, picking up a pen.

'Maybe.' She took a sip of coffee. 'She says Michael was watching them for a while from the other side of the bar.'

'Watching who?'

'Her and another guy. The bitch dumped him on his birthday.' Kate made a face. 'I never did like her. Michael was watching them for about half an hour.'

'While she – no doubt – made sure he had something to see.' He shook his head in disbelief. 'I'll never understand the way women's minds work. Go on.'

'Then she saw him talking to another man. Older. She thought he seemed a bit creepy.'

'Description?'

'Late twenties, early thirties maybe. Blond hair, lots of jewellery.'

Derek was making notes. 'Any more? Did they go anywhere? Talk to anyone else?'

'Jenny thinks they left together, but she couldn't be certain.'

He tapped the pen on the table. 'D'you think she'd

recognise him again?'

'I don't know. She wasn't very sure about it.'

'How about an artist's impression? Or an E-fit? I can get her to come in.'

'You could try, I guess.' Kate sighed. 'She's only sixteen. The whole business has upset her.'

'And you?' He raised his eyebrows and chewed the end of the pen thoughtfully. 'Has it upset you?'

'What do you think?' she snapped. 'Of course it's upset me. He's my brother, for God's sake!'

'I know. I'm sorry.' He reached across and touched her hand quickly, not meeting her eyes. 'You just seem so calm. I'm sorry,' he repeated. 'Here am I presuming to make judgments about a woman I've barely met. Forgive me, I don't mean to make personal comments.'

'It's OK.' She smiled. 'You've seen my parents. Somebody has to do the coping and it seems to have fallen to me.'

There was a silence. Kate finished her coffee and the DI doodled on the edge of the paper. 'Would you come in with her if I can arrange something?' he asked eventually. 'She might say more with you there, and I'll need an adult present. If her parents are OK with it,' he added.

'Jenny? Yes, of course. Anything that helps.'

There was another pause. 'You realise that the longer this goes on, the less chance there is of finding him alive? I'm not being negative – I just want you to understand that the situation is changing.'

Kate nodded. 'You don't think he has run away, do you? Not anymore.'

'I don't know what to think.' He pursed his lips. 'For the first week or so, it's usually the case. Teenagers like Michael often feel the need for independence and just want to get away for a while – they generally come back when they run out of money. But it's been too long for that now.' He paused. 'We've been monitoring his internet account – even sent him an email – but there's been no response. And his mobile isn't even switched on.'

'You think he's dead?' She bit her lip. Somehow if he said it, it would be true. It was as if he could shape the future – *Michael's future* – just by uttering the words. *He can't be dead. I'd know if he was.* She was angry now. *Jesus, Mike, don't do this to us – it's not fair!*

But Derek wouldn't comment. 'Kate, I don't know what's happened. All I can do is try to trace his last known movements. Now if we can get a reasonable picture of this mystery man, we can go back to the club and see if anyone else saw him and Michael together. Ask the doormen – see if someone saw them get into a cab or something. Cabbies are always better with pictures than words. I've already had people go through all the CCTV tapes from Trafalgar Square, but it's a bit of a hit-and-miss process, unfortunately – though I guess we can try again with a new face.'

'What about the papers?'

'Why not? We can involve the media too – get the local press, even the *Standard* to run a story for us. Might as well make the paparazzi sing for their supper.' He looked at his watch and Kate took the hint. It was nearly eight o'clock.

'I'm sorry – I'm interrupting your schedule.' She stood up.

'Not at all. It's not often I get visitors. Despite what that lot out there say.' He stood up and came round to Kate's side of the desk. 'But I do have another appointment, I'm afraid, even at this time of night. Can I see you to your car?'

She nodded and let him escort her out through the main office, ignoring the glances from the other officers. They took the lift this time and he came out to the car park with her.

'Kate?' He took both her hands and she jumped, surprised at the contact. He let go immediately, obviously embarrassed. 'Kate,' he repeated. 'I *will* find him for you if it's at all possible. I know it doesn't seem like much, but we're doing all we can. I'll call Jenny's parents and arrange for her to come in as soon as she's able – maybe tomorrow. The press too. Will you be free then?'

She nodded and he left her, hurrying back into the building. She wondered if he lived the rest of his life at double speed. She could imagine him rushing round at home, coffee in one hand and toothbrush in the other, perpetually on the move. Not like Colin, who had time for everything – he was Kate's antithesis in that department. Colin was never late and always organised. Sometimes, she was amazed how much more time she seemed to have in her life since she'd met him. He was good for her; he'd given her the confidence to step beyond the family boundaries and make her own life. She needed him. She needed the independence he gave her.

But right now, Kate decided, she needed a drink. Driving round to her best friend's flat, she persuaded Rachel to abandon her Open University studying and come out to the pub. Rachel was the practice nurse. At twenty-eight, she was several years older than Kate, but the two girls had a lot in common. Rachel had her own flat, both her parents lived up north in Liverpool and Kate envied her freedom.

Rachel thought she was mad to want to get married. 'When I was twenty-two, I had three different boyfriends,' she said, sucking on a piece of lemon from her glass. 'Couldn't decide which one I liked best.'

'So what did you do?' Kate grinned. 'You didn't keep seeing all of them?'

Rachel raised her eyebrows. 'Which would you choose? Lots of money, a brilliant sense of humour, or good sex?'

'Probably the sense of humour at the moment. I think mine's gone missing.'

'Shit, I'm sorry.' Rachel grimaced. 'Here am I talking about men and Michael's still not back.'

'Oh please, Rach, cheer me up! I can't take any more gloom – it's bad enough at home. Why d'you think I can't wait to get away?' She hesitated. 'You want to see the police guy who's dealing with it, though.'

'But Kate, you're engaged,' said Rachel, throwing up her hands in mock horror. 'You're not allowed to fancy men anymore.'

'Who says I fancy him? Maybe I could just do with a little uncomplicated sex. He's certainly got the body for it.'

'I'd better come with you next time, then. Keep you out of trouble.'

'Hands off. I saw him first. It's just a shame that all we talk about is my little brother. If he's run away, I'll kill him when I find him, the inconsiderate bastard.'

'Kate, he's seventeen. He's not a child.'

She sighed. 'I know. He just seems younger. It's always been him and me against mum and dad. And I'm worried about him, Rach. I don't think he would run away.' She explained what Jenny had said about events in the club, about the man Michael had been seen talking with. Rachel didn't comment and Kate wondered what she made of it all.

Something was wrong. If Michael hadn't come home, it was because he couldn't, she was sure of that. He was out there somewhere, perhaps thinking of his family and she wished she could reach out and touch him with her mind.

Who was the blond guy? *Is he a friend of yours, Michael? Do I know him?* She wondered what kind of a picture Jenny would produce the next day. Was it a clue or just a false trail?

Where are you, Mike?

SEVEN

Michael was dreaming again. He was five years old, playing in the sandpit at the bottom of the garden and driving toy cars over sand precipices into plant-pot lakes. It was August, the sand was hot and itchy and he took off his swimming trunks, trickling sand over his stomach and watching it collect in his navel with a child's fascination.

Suddenly he looked up, aware that he wasn't alone and he saw a man standing in the lane which led to the garages at the back of the houses. He was looking at Michael with an intensity that Michael didn't understand.

His mother had told him about talking to strangers. He got up and ran to the house to tell her that he'd found one. But the man was gone when he came back outside and Michael wondered if he'd ever really been there at all.

'Mikey.'

What? He struggled up through the murky waters of sleep and opened his eyes. This time the view was different. In the pale watery sunlight, he could see that this bedroom was different from the one he'd slept in last night. This was the second bedroom – the one he'd visited only briefly in his examination of all possible escape routes – and it was decorated chiefly in black and white. Stark colours with cold edges and an overall effect which was less than soothing.

He sat up, rubbing his eyes. He'd half-thought he might wake up at home and find that it had all been a dream, but realism had cut that idea dead. His arm was aching from last night's fix, but the rest of him felt all right, though he couldn't remember much beyond the initial rush after Joss had injected him.

'You OK?'

Lee? Michael twisted around, to see Lee lying on his side next to him, one eye open sleepily and his hair haloed across the pillow. Instinctively, he pulled the duvet over to cover himself. Somebody had undressed him the previous night.

'Fuck off, Mikey.' Lee yanked the duvet back. 'It's cold.'

Michael was disorientated. What the hell was he doing in bed with Lee?

'You were talkin' in your sleep,' said Lee, yawning and rolling onto his back. 'Don't know what you were dreaming about, but it sounded well weird.'

A memory he'd forgotten. It had lain there in the back of his mind for years. At the time, he'd not understood what the man had wanted, but now he knew only too well. 'What am I doing here?' he asked Lee, more for something to say than needing an answer.

'Don't know about you, but I'm sleeping. It's too fuckin' early for anything else.'

'No – I mean how did I get here?'

Lee yawned again. 'You were well out of it.' He smirked. 'I'd forgotten how hard it hits when you're not used to the stuff. Eddie put you to bed and I came in later.' He wriggled and scowled. 'Fuck me, I hope Joss doesn't invite that one back again. How anyone can get off on that kind of thing is beyond me.'

Michael shivered, wanting to ask more, but he didn't dare. How could Lee take it all so calmly? 'Is this where I'm supposed to sleep, then?'

'Guess so. Eddie has the other room, so unless you want the sofa, you get to share with me. But for fuck's sake, I hope you don't wake up at this time every morning. It's unhealthy.'

'Where does Joss live?'

'Fuck knows.' Lee rolled over. 'Who gives a shit?'

Michael slipped out of bed and went over to the door where there were a couple of robes hanging up – black and white this time. *Shit, this whole place is colour co-ordinated.* He turned to see Lee leaning on his elbows and watching him appraisingly.

Michael turned away, knotting the robe securely. He found his clothes at the end of the bed and went to the bathroom to dress in privacy. Lee seemed pleasant enough, but Michael found his company unnerving.

There was a clock in the bathroom and it read nine-fifteen. Quarter past nine in the morning and Michael wondered what everyone would be doing at home. He didn't even know what day it was and as soon as he'd dressed, he went in search of a newspaper in the lounge. The *Evening Standard* said Monday, so it was a fair assumption that today was Tuesday, a little over three weeks since his birthday. Tuesday. Michael wondered if his family would still be asleep or whether they'd be up, trying to find him. *Do they think I'm dead?*

And what about Kate? Good old Kate, who'd never been the sort of big sister his mates had complained about. Kate was always there, holding the family together and drinking most of his crowd under the table on the rare occasions she came out with them. Kate stood up for him, persuaded the parents that he was old enough – and sensible enough – to go out late at night. *Well, you fucked up there, Kate, didn't you? Look at me – off with the first pervert I could find!*

Michael realised that the horror in his mind was healing over with a skin of numb acceptance. Still stunned by what had happened, the survival instinct was kicking in now and he knew that if he wanted to get out of this place, he had to keep his head. But the heroin scared him. He could cope with the assault – just. It was something that had happened, he couldn't change the fact that it had happened and he could come to terms with it in his own time when he got out of here. What was important was to escape before it happened again.

No, what was terrifying was the heroin. Joss had forced it on him last night and Joss had been right. It was what his body had been aching for. No sooner had the buzz hit him than all the physical symptoms had gone floating out of the window with his mind. Right now, he felt fine – alert and fit. His vision was crisp and sharp and he was ravenously hungry. But by all accounts it wouldn't last; by this evening the cycle would be repeating itself and Michael wasn't sure he would have the willpower to resist. Besides which, there were yawning gaps in his consciousness – gaps in which anything could happen to him and he wouldn't know about it, never mind object to it.

Michael wandered into the kitchen and opened all of the drawers and cupboards in succession. He wasn't looking for anything in particular – just searching to see if anything useful to him sprang to mind. A knife, maybe? *Cut Eddie's balls off if he comes near me again?* Somehow, he doubted it would work. Even supposing he got the man into that position, he didn't think he could do it – not even in self-preservation. And while Lee seemed happy enough to be friendly, he wasn't going to risk his own drug supply by messing with the system.

Michael rummaged around in the cutlery drawer and came up with a screwdriver. He looked at it thoughtfully and wondered whether he could get the plate off the lock on the front door. But what would he do with it then? Could you pick a lock that way? Michael was uncertain – he'd tried it once before, when he'd been locked in his bedroom many years ago. It didn't happen often. He couldn't remember more than three or four occasions when his father had locked the door and told him it was for his own good, that he had to learn to do as he was told or he'd never get on in the world. Michael had never quite made the connection between the two ideas, but at least it had taught him that he was responsible for his own actions – which in turn made an escape bid seem quite reasonable under the circumstances. On this particular occasion, he succeeded only in scraping the paintwork and snapping a coat hanger inside the lock, at which point he gave up and tried the dormer window instead. Sliding down the wet tiles was easy, and it wasn't until his foot caught in the guttering that he realised it was further than it looked and he couldn't get back up to the window. So he jumped, landed in the rockery and broke his arm on the edge of the patio. His parents had been more upset than angry and in retrospect, he realised that the accident could have been a lot worse.

So where was the key to the front door kept? Joss obviously had his own key, but unless the rest of them were expected to stay in all the time, there had to be another. Lee had said he went outside occasionally, so Eddie must have a key. And a mobile phone too – he'd seen it. He just had to find them.

Michael selected a small but sharp kitchen knife and tucked it inside his sock, pulling his tracksuit leg down over the top. If he didn't make any sudden moves, it should stay put. Then he noisily made himself a cup of coffee and sat down at the kitchen table.

As expected, he heard sounds of life from the other bedroom a few moments later. Eddie appeared in the kitchen doorway, semi-naked in a silk robe and with his shaggy blond hair standing on end in places.

'You wait 'til you start workin',' he growled. 'You won't be up so early then, you'll see.' He paused. 'I'm going for a shower. Stick some coffee on, would you? The real stuff – not that instant shit.'

Michael didn't answer. *Wait 'til you start working.* Lee had said the same thing the previous night. It was fairly obvious what it meant – he would be expected to earn his bed and board, not to mention his nightly fix. Which only made it all the more important that he got out of this place as soon as he could.

He listened while Eddie cleaned his teeth. The sound of the shower started up and the toilet flushed. After a few moments, Michael got to his feet and tiptoed across the hall, opening Eddie's bedroom door with a delicate touch. He'd had years of practice at this. His parents went to bed so early these days, that even if he came back on time, he had to be quiet. Once he'd learned the secret of prowling the house in near-silence, he'd started coming back later, confident they'd never wake up and catch him. It meant he couldn't invite people round of course, but he could live with that – he'd managed to smuggle Jenny in once and they'd made love on the lounge sofa by the light of the imitation coal on the fire. *Jenny.* He wondered if she was still seeing the guy she'd been with in the club, whether she'd slept with him yet.

Michael shook his head. More than ever he felt a sense of urgency. He had to get out of here, while he was still capable. He didn't want to turn into another Lee, trapped into this life by his own body's needs.

Where would Eddie keep keys? Somewhere easy to find – they'd need to be able to escape quickly in case of a fire or something. Probably in the pockets of whatever he was wearing at the time. So the first place to look would be in the jeans he had on yesterday. And the mobile had been in his shirt pocket.

Michael scanned the room quickly, locating a pair of jeans tossed across the chair in the corner. *Fucking maroon chair! I will never, ever have anything of this colour again!* He ran his hands through the pockets, but found only a wallet and some loose change. Glancing behind him, he strained his ears for the sounds of the shower and opened the wallet.

There wasn't much in it other than a couple of tenners and a UK driving licence in the name of Edward Felsen. *Scandinavian, maybe?* He had the colouring for it. Michael checked the other pockets of the wallet, replaced it in the back pocket of the jeans and arranged them in more-or-less the same position on the chair.

He turned to search somewhere else and saw Eddie standing in the doorway, watching him. He wasn't even wet.

'Lost something?'

Shit. Michael backed away towards the window. What excuse could he possibly come up with for being in here?

'Or maybe you were looking for something,' said Eddie smoothly, coming into the room and closing the door behind him. 'These, perhaps?' He held out a set of keys and jangled them enticingly in one hand, while waving the mobile in the other. 'Or this? Do you think I'm stupid, Mikey?' Taking a step forward, he tossed the phone onto the bed. 'Go on – use it.'

Michael didn't need telling twice. He grabbed the phone, but the display was blank. *Switched off – where's the ON button?* He got it right second try and the display lit up reassuringly. He looked up at Eddie who was leaning against the wardrobe, his hand in the pockets of the bathrobe. The phone beeped and asked him for a pin. He tried a few number sequences at random, locked the SIM card and threw the phone back on the bed in disgust. Eddie grinned at him.

Michael backed away until he felt the wall behind his heels. He was going to have to get past Eddie somehow, or defuse the situation. *Or use the knife.* Eddie was almost on him and if he wanted the space to bend and retrieve it, he'd have to do it now. Eyes not leaving the man, he reached down and freed the kitchen knife from its hiding place.

Eddie laughed.

That threw him completely. Michael had expected

aggression, maybe even fear, but not ridicule. He wavered slightly but held the knife out in front of him. He'd cut a boy at school once – when he'd been twelve – and nearly got himself expelled for it. The other kid had been saying something about Kate, and Michael had gone for him with the nearest weapon to hand, which happened to be a clay modelling knife. Not the deadliest of weapons, but he'd succeeded in causing two stitches' worth of damage to the boy's hand. It had cost him a week's suspension, a written apology and a month's pocket money, which he'd been forced to hand over to the boy in person, but he'd been lucky not to be expelled.

Eddie pursed his lips, still smirking. 'I'm going to count to three,' he said. 'You either put the knife down or I'll take it off you. Your choice.'

Michael said nothing.

'One.' Eddie tossed the keys onto the bed.

Michael risked a quick glance at them. Too far away.

'Two. Don't be stupid, Mikey. You're far too pretty to damage.'

Pretty? Michael curled his lip contemptuously, fired up by adrenaline.

'Three. OK, if that's the way you want it.' Eddie tightened the belt on his robe and stepped up to him. Right up – not just out of reach of the knife, but well into Michael's range.

Michael slashed, but Eddie reached beyond the knife and knocked his wrist away. With his other hand, he punched Michael in the stomach and the knife fell to the carpet. Eddie picked it up instantly and before Michael had time to catch his breath, there was an arm across his throat, a face inches away from his own.

Michael felt the blade at his groin.

'You don't want to use them, so maybe I should just cut them off. Huh, Mikey? Would you prefer that?'

Michael couldn't avoid looking at the man. He had a crazy slant to his eyes. *He wouldn't – would he?*

'You don't think I'd do it?' Michael felt the blade cut through the material. 'You want to keep them? Maybe you're right.' Eddie threw the knife to one side and stuffed his hand down Michael's trousers in one quick movement.

Michael gasped. He didn't know which was worse – the knife or Eddie's hand. Struggling only made the grip tighten and he wondered what was going to happen now. He tried to cough, to relieve the pressure on his throat, but Eddie just leered at him.

And then the bedroom door swung open and a saviour appeared in the form of Lee in the doorway. Stark naked, he scratched himself sleepily. 'Leave him alone, Eddie. Give him a chance.'

'Piss off.' Eddie twisted round without loosening his grip.

'You want me to tell Joss?' asked Lee conversationally. 'If you want to fuck so bad, you can have me later.'

'What? Without consulting our lord and master?' His voice was scathing.

Lee yawned. 'Joss doesn't own me.'

'Matter of opinion.' Eddie smiled slightly. 'But even Joss has his secrets.'

'Really?' Lee eyed him sardonically. 'Tell me about it sometime. But leave Mikey out of it.'

Eddie sighed, gave Michael's balls a parting squeeze and released him.

'Come on, Mikey.'

Michael didn't need further invitation. Ducking Eddie's arm, he shot past and out into the hallway. Behind him, he heard Eddie laugh as he picked up keys and phone, and went back to the bathroom.

EIGHT

Joss came early that evening. Michael heard the key in the lock at about five o'clock and glanced at his watch.

He was fidgety and irritable, more so because he knew the reason for it. All day, he'd been arguing with himself about whether he was going to take another hit that night and he didn't like the answer he'd finally come up with. Yes. Of course he was – there was really very little to say in favour of not having a shot, even supposing that Joss gave him any choice in the matter. What good would it do to sweat it out? Joss had proved to him that his body needed the drug, that he was addicted to the stuff and Michael didn't need any more convincing of that. If he refused to co-operate, they'd simply sit it out until either Michael gave in, or he was too far gone to care – at which point Joss would inject him anyway and they'd be back to square one. No, he needed to stay alert and look for a means to escape this prison, and he wasn't going to achieve that by being a shaking mass of nerves. If heroin was the only way he'd keep his mind and body intact, then he'd have to go through with it, like it or not. It was the lesser of the evils. And the more he got used to the drug, the less it would freak him out. Hopefully he'd be able to cope with the rush in a few days.

Joss stuck his head round the lounge door. 'Hi, guys.' He looked at Lee. 'How d'you get on last night?'

Lee shrugged. 'OK. Bit rough, but I'll survive.'

'He'll be back next week. He's good money, that one.'

Lee scowled. 'I hope he is. I'd hate to think my efforts were wasted.'

'You're so droll. You ready to hit?'

'Sure.' Lee jumped up.

'Mikey?' Joss looked at him expectantly, and Michael sighed and got to his feet. He'd made the decision — there was little point in dragging the issue out.

He followed Joss and Lee into the kitchen, where Eddie was leaning against the work-top, a tumbler of scotch in one hand. He and Michael had been avoiding each other most of the day and Michael could sense a pent-up frustration simmering under the surface. He couldn't work out if it was anger or sexual tension and he didn't want to find out. Michael was well aware he couldn't count on Lee to come to the rescue every time, especially as Eddie had declined Lee's earlier offer.

Joss carefully unpacked the black leather holdall onto the kitchen table and Michael's mouth dropped open in surprise. *What's he done — robbed a fucking hospital?* There was an assortment of plastic-wrapped syringes and small tubes containing needles. In another smaller bag were several ampoules of a clear liquid. But by far the oddest item was a transparent thick-polythene package, taped securely with brown parcel tape along all the seams. It was about the size of a bag of sugar.

Joss picked it up and passed it to him. 'That's heroin,' he told him. 'Chinese heroin, to be precise. If you ever see the brown stuff — that's generally Pakistani or Indian. Chinese is better quality.'

Michael turned the package over in his hand and wondered how much it was worth. He put it back on the table in silence as Joss unpacked the final item from the holdall — a small flat wooden case. Opening it carefully, he extracted a tiny set of scales, with equally tiny weights.

'OK, Mikey. Take a seat.' Joss pulled out a chair and Michael sat down. 'Lesson one,' said Joss as he peeled back a piece of the brown tape on the bag, 'is that you never ever take gear from anyone except me.'

'Why not?'

'Because you don't know where it's been,' Joss explained patiently. 'And don't look so sceptical, Mikey. I'm about to tell you why.' With a teaspoon, he collected a little of the powder from the hole he'd revealed under the tape – it was grey-white in colour with a floury consistency.

'This is about ninety percent pure,' he continued, placing the powder on one of the dishes on the scales. 'The crap you buy on the streets can get as low as fifteen or twenty percent or less.' He selected a weight and balanced the scales, scraping a little off the top of the powder and replacing it in the bag. 'The rest of the mix can be anything from caffeine to talcum powder – neither of which will do you any good at all.'

He produced an even tinier spoon from the box with the scales. Picking up one of the ampoules of liquid, he snapped the neck between his thumb and forefinger and carefully spooned the powder into the top. 'If you take gear which contains something your body can't deal with, it might kill you,' he said, shaking the ampoule gently. 'And believe me, Mikey, nobody wants you dead.'

No? Michael risked a glance at Eddie, but he wasn't watching.

Joss held the ampoule up to his eye and examined the contents. 'Lesson two, is that you always use a clean syringe and needle.' He glanced up briefly. 'I'm sure I don't have to explain the reasoning behind that, do I?' He smiled and Michael wondered what the hell he was getting into. The longer he sat here, the less he wanted any of this stuff inside him. But just looking at it, he could feel his body reacting in anticipation, an almost sexual thrill making the hairs on his arms stand up.

Michael was amazed at the lengths Joss was going to. He'd thought drug addiction was all shared needles and AIDS. He wondered where the heroin came from in the first place, but decided he was better off not knowing. He'd seen *Midnight Express* on dvd once and it was not a pretty film.

Joss handed him the ampoule and he sat there stupidly, not knowing what to do with it. The man ripped open one of the sealed plastic bags and pulled out a syringe. With the same careless flick of the wrist, he snapped open the top of a tube and placed the orange-capped needle over the end of the hypodermic. Then he took the ampoule out of Michael's fingers and laughed.

'Say something, Mikey.'

'Such as?' He couldn't keep the sarcasm from his voice.

'I don't know. This is your shot, so how about *please?*'

Michael was confused. His mind was screaming *no!* at him and yet his body was saying the exact opposite. He needed a fix. And as he'd already decided, there was no point in arguing. His hands were shaking already.

'Say it, Mikey.' Joss drew the cloudy fluid up into the syringe. 'Come on – you know you want it. Listen to what your body is telling you.'

'No.' He stood up, kicking the chair out behind him, but Eddie was blocking the doorway. There was nowhere to run – but he didn't want to run, did he? He held out his hand in front of him and tried to control it.

'Mikey?' Joss' voice was sterner now, like a teacher reprimanding a naughty child. Or his father telling him off. God, he could imagine the lecture he'd get if he went home stoned. *Dad? What do I do, dad?* Use your head, his father would say – you got yourself into this situation, so face up to it and make the best of it. Be a man.

'No.' He couldn't do it. It was giving in, wasn't it? After all, he'd not actually experienced withdrawal yet – not really. Maybe it wouldn't be so bad. He'd only been taking the stuff for a few weeks and it couldn't have too much of a hold on him yet, could it?

'Your decision.' Joss shrugged. 'But I'm not staying here all night.' He laid the syringe on the table and supervised Lee, who was carefully mixing his own shot. Michael watched from the doorway, but he didn't leave, not even when Eddie stepped around him for his own fix. Instead he stared with macabre fascination as Joss finished his business and began to tidy away the equipment.

The syringe lay on the table. After a while it seemed to take up the whole of his field of view. His hands were trembling and he had a sudden vision of himself, lying on the ground, his whole body shaking and his stomach contorting in pain. How would he ever escape if he ended up like that? At least he could function properly at the moment – he could see and think. Taking a shot wasn't going to make him an addict – not if he knew what he was doing. Not if he was careful.

Without realising it, his hand reached for the syringe and Joss smacked it away. But his body had already made the decision for him. This time.

Michael dropped his hand. 'Please, Joss,' he said in a small voice.

Joss coughed delicately. 'Pardon?'

Michael shot him a murderous look. 'Please, Joss,' he said more firmly. *It's my decision. I am making this choice freely.*

'Then sit down and push up your sleeve.'

Michael did as he was told, but Joss stopped him and shook his head, motioning to the other arm. Michael sighed and pushed up the sweatshirt sleeve, exposing the inside of his elbow across the corner of the kitchen table.

'Clench your fist,' Joss instructed. 'Makes the veins stand out more.' He leaned over the table and carefully inserted the syringe.

Michael closed his eyes, resisting the temptation to pull his arm away. He could feel it again, feel the rush gathering momentum like a tidal wave threatening to sweep him off his feet, sweep him away completely and drown him in sensation. He felt the needle withdraw this time and he opened his eyes, flexing his arm gently.

The detail was magnificent. He could see the air itself sparkling under the strip light. He could smell the heroin, over and above the scent of coffee and scotch and there was a taste to it too, sharp and acrid. The thunder was still building behind his eyes, rolling in his mind and the focus was getting sharper and brighter to the point at which it was painful to look at the light.

Joss shook his head, smiling. 'Lee, go and sit him in the lounge. He'll be out of it for a while.'

Michael could hear him, but there was no point in replying. Nobody would notice because he wasn't really there at all – he was on a different plane, out of the physical world entirely. He fancied he could see the thoughts in his mind, whizzing around the neurones and sparking off each synapse. Each thought was an individual firework, burning itself out after a few seconds to be replaced by another.

Lee took him through to the other room and Michael was aware of his touch, like a thousand tiny insects on his skin. He was also aware – somewhere in the depths of his mind – that he had to stay in control, he couldn't afford to let the drug take him over. It was only a matter of tolerance – Lee could do it, so he could as well. But Lee's hand on his bare arm sent waves of vibrations through his body, setting up hair-trigger reactions. His nerves were on fire and it shocked him enough to fight the buzz. He didn't want this, he was scared to give in to the euphoria, not knowing what might happen while he was out of it. He needed to build up his tolerance to keep his body happy, but his mind alert.

He woke up an hour later, still sitting in the armchair. The rush had passed and he felt alive but in full possession of his senses. *Shit.* What had happened? Why couldn't he stay in control of himself? *This isn't fair!*

Joss was still there. He was sitting on the sofa, drinking again and watching Michael with an amused look in his eyes. 'Welcome back,' he said dryly, toying with the glass in his hand. 'You fought that every inch of the way, didn't you?'

Michael scowled. He'd co-operated, for Christ's sake – were they going to take the piss out of him as well?

Joss smiled and Michael cringed inwardly. There wasn't a trace of malice in his face and that made it even more chilling; the man seemed genuinely concerned for Michael's well-being and it was confusing, somehow. He uncrossed his legs and stood up, stretching and looking at his watch. 'OK, Mikey. We're going to do something about your appearance. Can't have anyone recognising you, can we?'

What? Did that mean he was going to get out of this damned flat? Or merely that he would be receiving visitors soon? Michael couldn't see that it made a lot of difference in the latter case. Nobody who came to this place was going to be in the least concerned for his welfare and they were hardly likely to call in at the police station on the way home. *Hello, officer. I was fucking this boy earlier and I think he might be the one you're looking for.* No, it didn't seem very plausible, really.

Michael frowned. He was getting altogether too cynical for his own liking, or maybe he was still on a high. And yet, there was no point in letting the grim realism of his situation get to him – he wasn't going to escape if he spent the time in a state of hysteria. He needed a clear head to evaluate and exploit every opportunity which came his way. Perhaps if he was expected to entertain visitors, he might be able to come to some sort of an arrangement with them.

Joss interrupted his thoughts by pulling him to his feet. 'Bathroom, I think.' Michael didn't argue as he followed the man out of the room. Joss collected a chair from the kitchen and placed in front of the bathroom sink. 'Sit down, Mikey. How would you like to be blond?'

'Not really.' *Do I have a choice?*

'That's a shame, because you will be. In about half an hour or so.' Joss threw an old towel around Michael's shoulders and ran a brush through his hair. Then he mixed some powder together in a small plastic bowl with some evil-smelling liquid from a plastic bottle under the sink, and pulling on a pair of plastic gloves, he proceeded to coat small sections of hair in the mixture, wrapping each section with cling-film as he went.

'Lee told me what happened this morning,' he mentioned casually, tearing off another piece of cling-film.

'I'll fucking kill him next time.' The dye, or whatever it was, was cold and Michael shivered. The smell of peroxide was strong and his senses were still heightened enough for him to taste the chemicals in the back of his throat.

'Will you now?' Joss laughed. 'I'd be careful if I were you. Ed's done time for violence.' He paused. 'He won't hurt you – he'd have me to answer to if he did. But he *can* make your life a misery, if you give him the chance. And Mikey?' He stripped off the gloves and pulled the towel up over Michael's head. 'Pull another stunt like last night and you'll lose your freedom indoors. I've found that handcuffs work very well in restoring trust.' He washed and dried his hands. 'There – that should do it. We'll leave that on for a bit. You want some coffee? There might even be some lager left in the fridge, if Lee hasn't drunk it all.'

Michael couldn't make the man out. What was he – a hairdresser as well as a doctor? He did everything with such calm efficiency that Michael couldn't understand why he wasn't earning a decent living out there in the real world. Legally. What was it that made him choose this lifestyle? It couldn't just be the money, could it? Or did he get some perverse kick out of playing with the law?

Joss washed the dye from his hair after about twenty minutes and Michael wondered what on earth he was going to look like. When he finally got to see the results he was surprised. Joss had coloured his hair with generous streaks of ash-blond and while the effect wasn't altogether displeasing, it confused Michael considerably.

Joss nodded approvingly. 'It suits you. Not too extreme, but different enough from the delightful school picture they printed in the *Standard*. And I can finally get some decent front shots for the next set of web photos.' Standing behind him facing the bathroom mirror, he ran a hand through Michael's hair. 'You like it?'

I'm on a website? 'What do *you* think?' There'd been a photo of him in the paper too. When? How long ago?

'I think it's about time you realised that you're here to stay, so you may as well make the best of it. It's for your own good.'

For my own good? That was the story of his whole fucking *life*. Everything was always for his own good. Leaving all his mates and going to sixth form college; not staying out late; giving up his Saturday job; all the stupid little concessions he'd made throughout his life. All supposedly for his own good. And much fucking good had it done him. *I never wanted to go to college, dad. Why couldn't you have let me live my own life?*

Michael was tired of playing by everybody else's rules. Nothing changed. He was seventeen and it was time he made his own decisions. Maybe he wouldn't go home at all when he got out of here – maybe he'd get his own place and do what *he* wanted to do for a change.

Joss washed his hands, collected the black holdall which seemed to go everywhere with him and left the flat shortly afterwards. Michael couldn't face sitting in the lounge with Eddie, who was making obscene gestures with his hands and obviously hadn't forgotten the incident with the knife, so he went to bed. Still floating from the shot he'd had earlier, it wasn't difficult to sleep, but his mind kept returning to the dream he'd had the previous night. He could feel the sand on his skin, the warmth of the sun and he remembered the look in the stranger's eyes as he stood and watched the young Michael play. The boy lay on his back and he could see the horse chestnut tree above and behind him, branches waving in the breeze. There was the scent of new-mown grass and a faint whirr of a lawn-mower in the distance.

Michael opened his eyes and saw the stranger watching him. Only it wasn't a stranger this time. It was Eddie. He tried to sit up, but he wasn't in the sandpit any longer. He was in bed, it was dark and he wasn't dreaming.

A hand pushed him back down onto the mattress and Michael felt the duvet being ripped off briskly. 'Turn over.'

'Eddie, no!' He didn't move. 'Please, I—'

'Mikey, I said turn over.' The voice was sharper now. 'You may as well get used to this – you can't be stoned out of your mind every time you have a punter.'

No! Please God, no! He felt Eddie's hands on his body and his skin crawled. It was hard not to scream. *And he hasn't even done anything yet!*

'On your knees, Mikey. Come on.'

'No. Don't, Eddie. Please!' He could taste bile in his mouth and clenched his teeth. If he was sick now, it wouldn't change anything. All that would happen was that he'd end up getting fucked face-down in his own puke. *Fucked! Sweet Jesus, he really is going to do it!*

'NO!' Something snapped in Michael's mind, releasing a dark burning fury. He'd been semi-conscious on previous occasions, but this time, he was going to fight back. No more being pushed around by this dickhead. No more being pushed around by *anyone*. This was his life and he wanted it back.

As he felt Eddie's weight on the mattress, he kicked out with both legs, glad to be unencumbered by duvet. Feet connected with flesh and he heard a groan followed by swearing. It made him all the more determined not to give in and he brought his knees up again for another go.

'Fuck *off!*' He kicked air and the momentum brought the upper half of his body off the bed. Surprised, he twisted in the gloom and saw that the man had moved round to the side of the bed; his fist caught Michael's side and this time he brought his knees up to his chest in pain, doubling up and coughing as he rolled over.

Instinctively, he'd rolled away from the man, protecting his face and chest, and it wasn't until he felt hands on his body that he realised it was the worst mistake he could have made. Eddie's weight forced him over on to his knees and before he could react, the man was on top of him, pushing him into the mattress. He stank of cigarettes.

'Eddie, no!' There was a note of desperation now as Michael reached behind his head, trying to find something to grab hold of. But without his elbows to support the weight of both their bodies, he was forced closer to the sheets. He could smell the shower gel they had in the bathroom, feel something cold against his arse and—

Shit, that's not shower gel—

He cried out again, trying to throw him off, but Eddie was too heavy and he couldn't move. The puke in his mouth was choking him.

He really is going to do this. He's going to fuck me and I can't stop him!

Michael curled his fists and tried to shut it all out. But it was impossible and as he felt Eddie's body moving on top of him, he had to bite the pillow to stop himself screaming. He'd been so out of it on previous occasions, he'd never been aware of much more than the sharp pain of penetration, but this time he was wide awake, every nerve end shrieking and his mind burning with humiliation.

There was a moment of stillness, a final second where he was teetering on the brink of sanity and then everything exploded in a chaos of white hot fire and pain. There was a soft grunt and Eddie was inside him and *oh God, it hurts! Please! Stop this!* His body convulsed and he couldn't stop himself fighting, trying to twist away from the body which was pinning him to the bed.

NO! Get off me! Leave me alone! Oh God, HELP ME!

The tears were pouring down his face now – tears of anger and shame as much as physical pain. Michael was writhing in his own sweat, choking as he fought the man, but Eddie was too strong for him. He was face down on the bed and with the whole of Eddie's weight holding him there, there was no way he could escape.

I'm going to die. He could feel the man inside him, could feel every movement. He squirmed again, trying to get free and only succeeded in receiving a crashing blow round his head.

'Mikey, keep *still*. You're only making it worse for yourself.'

Worse? How can this ... possibly ... be any worse? Michael stuffed his fist in his mouth and bit his hand, trying to distract his attention as Eddie made a final thrust, grunted again and relaxed. Michael felt a warm wetness inside him and he had to fight to keep back the vomit as Eddie withdrew and stood up.

Michael eased his legs out from under him. *Kill me, somebody. I want to die.*

Eddie flicked the light on. 'That wasn't so bad, was it? You'll get used to it.'

I don't believe this man. People this evil don't exist in real life, do they? Michael buried his face in the pillow, still shaking. The lower half of his body was on fire, a deep throbbing ache that seemed to penetrate through to his very soul. He didn't dare move. It felt like he'd fallen apart, as if Eddie's weight had been all that was holding him together. He was floating in little pieces, each one burning with a fierce indignation. *Nothing has ever been this bad.* Hearing Eddie leave the room, he reached out gingerly with one hand and switched off the bedside light.

The darkness was soothing. Still face-down on the bed, Michael gradually stopped trembling, although he was too exhausted even to turn over. The pain slowly subsided, leaving behind a numbness, a vacuum that could never be filled, and eventually, as sleep finally started to overtake him, he began to shiver with the cold. Only half-awake, he drew his legs up and rolled onto his side, screwing up his face as his body protested. He pulled the duvet over himself, curled up into a ball and cried – huge heaving sobs like he hadn't cried since he was a child.

Then he heard a door open and close. Soft footsteps crossed the floor. The duvet moved and he felt a body sliding into bed next to him.

An arm snaked around his shoulders. The touch alarmed him, but he didn't have the energy to pull away. Movement hurt too much.

'Don't cry, Mikey. It's over.'

Lee? His mind was still fogged by sleep. *Oh Christ, not Lee as well?* Michael was at the end of his strength.

But Lee didn't want sex. Instead he simply held Michael close and stroked his hair gently. And eventually Michael slept again – a deep and exhausted sleep with no dreams.

He woke with a start some time later, eyes wide in the darkness. He was sore and stiff; the sheet underneath him was wet and sticky and he didn't know whether it was semen, blood, or whatever else Eddie had used. His nose and throat were thick with snot and mucus, and his eyes felt itchy and swollen. *No nightmare could ever be that bad*

It hadn't been a dream. There had never been so much pain before, not ever in his whole life, never so much complete and total humiliation. Michael wasn't entirely sure whether he could stand up, never mind walk to the bathroom and he just didn't have the energy or willpower to even try. He knew now that the last time it had happened had been many days before he'd woken – last time his body had healed itself and he'd been cleaned while he slept. This time, he was not so lucky.

But what about the other bit? He'd dreamed that Lee had been there too, holding him; Michael felt across the bed and touched a warm and naked body. He recoiled violently and almost cried out at the pain.

Lee sighed in his sleep and turned over, flinging out an arm in a careless gesture. Michael lay awake for a long time.

NINE

'It will do, I suppose. It's about as good as we're going to get.' Derek sat back and passed the E-fit picture across the desk.

Kate had a look. It didn't seem much like a person – more like some kind of cartoon character, all square angles and mis-matched features. Was this the best chance they had of finding whoever it was Michael had been talking to? 'I guess Jenny had other things on her mind,' she commented, tossing the picture onto the desk.

'It's not that bad, honestly. I've seen a lot worse.'

'And did you find the face that fitted?' asked Kate acidly. Derek looked at her for a moment and shook his head. She sighed. Things were looking bleaker every day. Mum had started talking about Michael in the past tense and it annoyed Kate intensely. If they couldn't do anything to help, they could at least try to be positive.

Kate had telephoned Marsha the previous night. It hadn't been much of a success. Miss Adventure didn't have enough money to come home and the extent of her concern had been for Kate to call her again and let her know what happened. Kate didn't know what to do if nothing did happen. She was well aware that they might never know any more than they did now – that the weeks could turn into months and then years and they would never know where Michael had gone that night, or even if he was still alive.

And then what would she do? Could she, in all conscience, uproot her life and move to Carlisle with Colin? She wasn't sure if she even wanted to go through with the wedding at the moment; she didn't think she could walk down the aisle with a glaring space in the front pew where her brother should have been. It wasn't fair to Colin of course – after all, it wasn't his fault that any of this had happened and he'd put as much of an investment into this wedding as she had, both financial and emotional. Her parents liked him too; they had no objections to the wedding and why should they? Colin worked hard, had money and would no doubt be able to afford to keep his new bride in suitable style. With no family of his own to worry about, he was welcomed with open arms into hers. No, it was only the move they were trying to talk her out of and with Michael's recent vanishing act, she wasn't sure whether or not they'd succeed. And yet, if there was one thing that Kate did know, it was that she couldn't stay at home and be Michael's substitute for the next few years.

'I'll have some copies done of this and get them circulated.'

Attention drawn back to the DI, she glanced across the desk at him. He was wearing a black T-shirt this morning and Kate could see a gold cross nestling in the hollow of his neck. She wondered if he was religious. If praying for Michael would help, she'd do it, but she was frankly sceptical in that department. And how could she believe in a God that had allowed Michael to apparently vanish off the face of the earth?

'Do you want this picture?' Derek held it out to her.

'Is there any point?' She didn't mean to sound so bitter.

Derek leaned forward and touched her wrist. 'There's always a point,' he said gently. 'Don't give up hope. If *you* don't believe, who will?' He stood up. 'Keep trying

Michael's mobile; get his mates to check out the chat rooms online. Hell – get a blog going if you know how. Or a facebook page. I'll get this picture sent to you electronically if you give me an email address. Somebody, somewhere might see it and know something. I'll call you later in the week.'

'Yes, you go and enjoy a game of squash, why don't you?' She'd seen the sports bag and racquet in the corner of the office and couldn't resist throwing it into the conversation. 'You go and play games and I'll go back and tell my parents that the sodding picture could have been drawn by a two year-old, for all the resemblance it bears to a human being!' She grabbed her handbag and reached for the door handle.

Derek knocked her hand away. 'That's not fair.' He turned away. 'What do you want from me, Kate? What more do you want me to do? Don't you think there are other people working on this case, too? Never mind all the other crime victims I'm responsible for.' He grabbed a stack of files from his desk and peeled off the top one. 'Shall I tell this family that I can't look into their burglary? Or this one?' He pulled out one further down the stack. 'She was raped a month ago and left for dead behind a chip shop. Shall I tell her I don't have the resources to investigate, because another case has priority?' He threw the files onto the desk and stalked away to the window. 'I'm sorry,' he said quietly after a moment. 'That was unnecessary and uncalled for. My problems, not yours. I shouldn't have spoken like that.'

But Kate wasn't in the mood for consolation. The E-fit picture had been their only lead and the thread of hope had suddenly stretched too thin. She waved a hand at Derek, mumbling some sort of an apology before she half-ran out of the office, daring any of his staff to comment.

She drove round to Colin's house in West Ealing. He was working from home and wasn't expecting her; he was wearing glasses instead of his usual contacts and had a pencil behind one ear. Colin's house was immaculate, so presentable and predictable that sometimes Kate wanted to introduce just a hint of variety, a note of dissonance in the carefully rehearsed symphony which was Colin's daily routine. She'd bought him a set of shocking pink mugs last Christmas, just to add a bit of contrast to the blue-and-white kitchen and although he dutifully brought them out every time she visited, she could tell they offended his sense of colour co-ordination.

Colin was surprised, but pleased to see her and Kate instantly regretted the way she constantly picked at him in her mind. He put the laptop away and poured them both a glass of Chablis.

'How's it going, Kate?'

She took the glass. 'Bloody awful.'

'Is there anything I can do?'

'No.' She showed him the picture. 'It could be anyone. Half the population of London look like that.' *Assuming that he's in London. He could be anywhere in the country.* She took a sip of wine.

'Which means that half of them don't.'

There was no answer to that, so Kate changed the subject. 'Colin, make love to me.'

'Now?'

'What's wrong with now? What's wrong with right here and now?'

'Well, nothing I suppose.' He glanced at the window and Kate suppressed a laugh. Who cared what the neighbours saw? He took her hand and pulled her close, kissing her gently. She put the glass down and returned the kiss with a hunger that surprised her as much as it did him. Removing his glasses, Colin slipped a hand inside her shirt, found her breast and squeezed the nipple gently. Kate closed her eyes and let him lead her to the sofa.

Colin was a gentle lover, if conservative. He undressed her slowly and carefully, as if she was a piece of china which might break if he moved too fast. He made her feel fragile and delicate, but Kate wasn't at all sure that in the present circumstances it was a good feeling to have. She needed to be strong – she had to be strong for Michael's sake. She had to make something of this picture they had of the man in the night club as it might be the only clue they would ever have.

She gasped and wriggled slightly as Colin entered her. *Come on, Kate. Pay attention – this was your idea!* She forced thoughts of Michael from her mind and tried to concentrate on her fiancé. She loved him, she really did; he was everything a potential husband should be, caring and considerate, a friend as well as a lover. Colin would never stay out late with the lads and come home drunk. He'd never hit her or cheat on her and he'd never ever forget a birthday or anniversary. He was perfect. So why was she having second thoughts about the whole thing? Was it just because of Michael, or was there more to it?

Colin withdrew without coming. Kate had changed her mind and was grateful, although it annoyed her that he couldn't just get on with it. She dressed quickly, ashamed of herself, but Colin didn't seem embarrassed.

'They'll find him, Kate,' he said, kissing her cheek gently. 'He'll be home soon, I'm sure of it.'

Will he? Kate stared at the spider plant on the window sill. Colin had sensed her unease, her preoccupation during their lovemaking, and had put it down to worry about Michael. But Kate had other things on her mind as well. Above the television, coexisting in perfect harmony with the Laura Ashley decor, hung a large Salvador Dali print. *The Crucifixion*. She didn't care much for surrealism, preferring more classic art, but the image was startling, all the more so for the echoes it set up in her mind. Images of crosses led both ways. Crucifixion was associated with death, but all she could see was the gold cross which had been around Derek's neck earlier that morning.

Rachel assured her it was normal. 'You're bound to have

second thoughts,' she said that evening, curled up in the armchair at Kate's house. Kate's parents had gone to bed and she'd discovered half a bottle of Bailey's in the back of the sideboard.

'Am I?'

'I certainly would.' Rachel twisted the stem of the glass. 'Do you love him?'

'Of course I do.'

'Are you sure? Or are you just in love with the idea of getting away from home? There are other ways besides buying a house, you know – you could always flat-share, if it's that important to you.'

They'd never understand. Why should she want to leave home for any other reason than to get married? Wasn't home good enough for her anymore? Was she *ashamed* of them? She knew the questions would be endless.

'What happened last time?' Rachel reached for the Bailey's bottle.

'What last time?'

'When you were engaged. To what's-his-name.'

'Oh, Mark?' Kate shuddered at the memory. Mark hadn't wanted a wife at all – just somebody to cook his meals and wash his clothes. She hadn't believed it when she'd heard he was seeing somebody else and then she'd found them in bed together one night. They'd both been nineteen at the time and Kate counted it as a lucky escape. But perhaps Mark had simply been too scared to tell her he had second thoughts. Maybe getting caught with the other woman was the only way he had of showing her that he couldn't go through with it. And wasn't that *exactly* what she was trying to do to Colin? Were all these thoughts of Derek simply her own subconscious trying to tell her something?

Rachel agreed with her. 'I'll have to meet him,' she decided. 'Then I can tell you whether he really is as gorgeous as you make out, or whether you're just using him as an excuse to dump Colin.'

'Oh, and you'd know, would you?' She wasn't really annoyed. It was just that Rachel's psycho-analysis was cutting too close to the bone and Kate didn't need any more upheavals in her life at the moment. She couldn't think about Colin until they'd found Michael. *If* they found Michael.

TEN

Michael was floating in a sea of pain. Lying on his back, he could feel a dull ache throughout his entire body and when he sat up, it increased to a sharp jolt where Eddie had torn freshly-healed wounds. His head was throbbing and there was blood on his hands.

He didn't care. Alone in the room, he was too devastated to cry any more. Detachedly, he examined himself, but beyond the semen stains and dried blood on the sheets and on his skin where he'd lain in it, there was little external evidence of what had happened.

For the first time, he wondered how long it would be before he could get another shot of heroin. He wanted to be out of it, to escape from this place and if he couldn't do it physically then there was no other choice than to escape into his own mind – float away into another reality and leave this one behind. *Perhaps I'd be better off if I just killed myself and had done with it?* He wondered if he could, if he had the strength of character to do it and he wasn't sure. There was still a chance of getting out of here – there had to be. If he could just hang on for long enough, they'd have to let him go outside eventually, wouldn't they? Lee went out, so why not him? Michael didn't know if he could wait that long.

He climbed out of bed carefully, every movement sending shimmers of pain vibrating through his body. Leaving the bed for someone else to clean up, he found himself a robe and went out into the hall.

'Mikey?' Lee was there instantly; he'd obviously been alert for sounds of life. 'You OK?'

Michael looked at him but didn't say a word. Pushing Lee to one side, he shuffled down to the bathroom, intending to have a long hot bath.

'They were Joss' instructions – I'd have stopped him if I could. Honest I fuckin' would.'

Would you? Michael doubted it. Lee was too dependent on the two men to contemplate disobedience. Joss controlled the heroin and in Lee's eyes, that made him one rung down the ladder from God.

Michael reached the bathroom in a daze. He started the bath water running and turned to look in the mirror. It took him a moment to recognise himself. His face seemed pale under the newly-streaked hair, his eyes were still red and puffy from crying and there were huge dark circles underneath. Where was Michael Redford now? This reflection wasn't him – at least not the him he remembered. This was a street kid, living from day to day. Surviving.

'Say something, Mikey.'

'What do you want me to say? Would anything I said make a difference?' He was surprised how level his voice sounded, when all he wanted to do was scream himself awake from this nightmare.

'Are you all right? Does it hurt?' Lee sounded concerned.

Michael snorted and shook his head, wondering how he could possibly convey the pain – and worse, the humiliation – he felt. 'Yeah, it hurts,' he said after a moment. 'It hurts more than anything I've ever known. It hurts everywhere. It hurts that some fucking queer can do that to me, while other people just sit by and let it happen.

It hurts that my family probably think I'm dead, and it hurts that I can't get out of this fucking flat. Now fuck off, Lee and leave me alone.'

Lee nodded. 'Eddie's gone out,' he said after a moment.

'So?' Michael turned away. 'You think I should be breaking the door down, or something?'

'You'd have a job. Door's reinforced steel.' Lee hesitated. 'I just thought if you knew we were alone, it might help you to chill. That's all.' He turned in the doorway. 'I'll make some tea.'

Fucking tea? Michael shut the door after him. Christ, he was even starting to sound like Lee. Emptying half a bottle of Radox into the bath, he turned off the taps, stirred the water with one hand and inhaled deeply; the steamy fragrance was calming and he slipped off the robe and lowered himself gently into the water.

It hurt. Badly. Michael leaned back and clenched his teeth, determined not to cry out as warm water touched raw flesh and brought tears to his eyes. When the stinging stopped, he didn't move, but lay there and stared at the ceiling and thought about whether it would be possible to drown himself in a bath. He could hear Lee in the kitchen next door, and if he closed his eyes he could almost imagine he was at home, except that the acoustics were wrong. But home was the last place he wanted to be, right now. Dad would never forgive him for what had happened – what he'd *let* happen. After everything they'd done for him, all the sacrifices they'd made, he'd screwed it all up by letting himself be taken in by a smooth-talking bastard in a club. Christ, his father had escaped the Iraqis and he couldn't even get out of a fucking East End flat. Some son he'd turned out to be.

Well screw you, Dad! What's done is done and I've got to get on with my life. It's for my own good. He laughed hollowly and wondered what he was going to do. Last night was just for starters – he had no illusions about that. And yet he was still alive, wasn't he? Bruised maybe, but still alive and the pain would go away. Lee seemed happy enough. But Lee was gay. *Is he?* Michael had made that assumption from the beginning, before he'd known what was going on, but perhaps Lee had been like himself a year ago. Maybe that was why he was trying to make the transition easier for Michael, because he'd been there before. Either way, Michael couldn't afford to alienate him as he was the only person in this place who seemed to have any consideration for his feelings. Remembering how Lee had held him last night was somehow almost as embarrassing as Eddie's attack – he'd had a choice with Lee. He could have pulled away, left the room even and Lee wouldn't have stopped him. But he hadn't – he'd let himself be comforted and it had been a good feeling. Michael could feel himself blushing even now.

He washed himself carefully. Touching his body didn't fill him with disgust any more, not like it had done before and he was rapidly learning that he couldn't be responsible for events beyond his control. Instead it left him empty, sad that his life had changed irrevocably and his childhood gone forever. He'd liked being a teenager; it was fun being on the edges of both worlds and able to dip into each when he chose. Being a child could have its advantages. Sex with Emma had been an adventure, one step into the adult world; then there'd been Jenny, and now he'd been thrown the rest of the way.

There was a knock at the door and Michael jumped, startled. He hadn't heard the front door, so it could only be Lee.

'Can I come in?'

Michael sighed. 'Go on, then.' He made a half-hearted effort to cover himself, but gave up. *What's the point? He's seen it all before.*

The door opened slowly and Lee poked his head around. 'Do you want some tea? Or should I leave you alone?'

'You might as well come in.'

The door opened further and Lee brought two mugs in, pushing the door shut with one foot. He balanced one mug on the tiles at the end of the bath and retreated to the toilet seat with the other. 'Feeling any better?' he asked after a moment.

Michael nodded. 'A bit.' He reached for the mug.

Lee smiled slightly. 'It does get better, you know – things won't always seem so fuck-awful.'

'Won't they?' Michael wasn't convinced.

'You get used to it after a while. If you chill, it'll stop hurting so much.' He paused. 'And Joss and Eddie aren't so bad.'

'He's a fucking sadist!'

'Eddie? Not usually. I don't know what it is about you that winds him up.'

Michael shook his head; he thought the answer was fairly obvious. But Eddie did as he was told and maybe Joss had other plans.

'Pass me a towel, would you?' He sat up, wincing, and levered himself out of the bath. Lee handed him a towel and he wrapped it around his waist. He sat down on the edge of the bath to finish his tea, but it hurt too much and he stood up again quickly, wondering whether what Lee had said was true.

Michael was thinking long-term and it worried him. He had no intention of staying here long enough to get used to Eddie's attentions, never mind other peoples'. But even if he did escape, what then? He was under age, he'd end up back at home and the whole world would know what had happened to him.

Lee was watching him and Michael smiled weakly, then frowned as they both heard the sound of a key in the front door.

'Don't, Mikey.' Lee put out a hand as if he expected him to make another run for it, but Michael didn't move. There were footsteps in the corridor and then the bathroom door opened slowly. Michael gripped the towel tightly. Eddie had grown to nightmarish proportions in his mind and no matter how hard he reasoned with himself, the man terrified him.

Eddie stuck his head round the door. 'Excuse me. I don't want to interrupt anything, but I need a piss.'

Michael froze. The sound of his voice and the way the man moved as he came into the bathroom brought memories of the previous night flooding back in glorious technicolour. And as Lee stood up and Eddie calmly unzipped his fly in front of the toilet, Michael really didn't want to watch him get his dick out and urinate, but he couldn't move; his eyes were riveted on the man and he stared as Eddie did just that.

'Mikey?' Lee took his arm.

'What?' He shook his head, but didn't resist as Lee led him out of the room. He dried himself off in the bedroom and got dressed hurriedly, the carefully built wall of composure perilously close to collapse.

'Mikey, don't let him win.'

'Huh?' He swung round. 'You think I want to? He scares me, Lee. He *screwed* me last night!' His hands were shaking and it wasn't anything to do with heroin.

'And he'll do it tonight as well!' said Lee brutally. 'And tomorrow and the next fuckin' night. He'll keep on doin' it while he gets such a reaction out of you! It's what he gets off on, Mikey – haven't you worked that out yet?' He grabbed Michael's arm. 'Don't give him the fuckin' satisfaction.'

Michael couldn't help it. He was lonely and scared and for the first time in years, he'd have given anything for his mum. Parents were good at shutting cupboard doors and making the world a safer place. But he was an adult now and there was nobody to close the door against these monsters – nobody except himself and he wasn't strong enough to do it on his own.

Eddie had him again that night. This time, Michael was

prepared for it and although it was every bit as painful as it had been before, it didn't seem so bad somehow. He managed to bury his head in the pillow and survive the ordeal and Lee came in afterwards with tea and sympathy, which embarrassed Michael more than Eddie's invasion of his body. But Lee couldn't stay with him – Joss wanted him to work – and Michael was left alone for most of the night. Surprisingly, he slept.

The days began to blur into weeks and Michael had difficulty in telling them apart. From time to time, he worried about the routine he was settling into, a routine that was delineated by the evening fix when Joss arrived each evening, doing the rounds like a visiting doctor before he left, usually within a couple of hours. Three or four nights a week there were visitors and Lee would take them into Eddie's room, sometimes for an hour or two, sometimes for most of the night; Michael got used to sharing the second bedroom with him when he'd finished. Sometimes Eddie slept on the sofa. It didn't seem to bother him and the atmosphere in the flat while not exactly relaxed, was at least liveable with.

Michael didn't care anymore. The heroin helped him get through the nights and his body was adjusting to new ways. He still checked the front door regularly, not really expecting it to be unlocked, but it would be stupid not to try. He even re-examined the windows, testing the bars and scraping off the paint at the base to see how they were attached to the window frame. He contemplated pulling out the nails, but he'd never seen anyone to call to and he had the feeling that Eddie would take great delight in having a reason to punish him.

Eventually he gave up altogether, when he realised that he wouldn't leave even if he could. It made him cry and he hadn't cried since the night Joss had dyed his hair, but they were tears of nostalgia now, memories of another life when he'd been a different person. He couldn't remember much about Michael Redford anymore and he wondered whether it was the drugs which were screwing up his memory. Once, when Joss had turned up close on midnight one night, he'd been as wound up as the other two at the thought of missing a fix, although afterwards, he suspected it had been a deliberate ploy on Joss' part, to reel in the line every now and again, and show them who was in charge. It was psychological as well as physical – he knew that much – and he knew he was hooked as securely as Lee was. He needed Joss.

More than two months since he'd left home and even the sex didn't bother him. There were others as well as Eddie now, but it was just a part of the routine – mostly, the visitors had better manners and more consideration for his personal comfort – and he'd learned to switch off, not let them get to him. Sometimes he couldn't even remember their faces.

Apart from the first guy, of course. Ten nights of Eddie's attentions and Michael was past caring, then Joss had told him to take a shower as he was expecting his first client. Michael was less bothered about this new development than he'd expected to be, but this man had been nervous, jumpy even, and Michael had wondered if it had been his first time too. Sex with a stranger, sex with another man or possibly both? Michael could remember his face all right – the rabbit-in-the-headlights look about him – and he'd given him a double shot of scotch and undressed without a word. 'You're much more experienced,' the man said, and for a moment, Michael wanted to tell him the truth. Except he wasn't sure exactly what the truth was anymore and somehow it was just easier to go along with it all, easier to let the man carry on thinking he was a pro and had been doing this for years.

Easier for who? And he'd said nothing, let the man leave and never seriously considered asking him to go to the police or contact his family. The battle was over and Michael wasn't sure who had won – he wasn't even sure whose side he was on.

But while nights were for other things now, days were largely his own. There was nobody telling him when to go to bed and nobody to make him spend entire evenings studying. This was a world without exams and careers, where you were taken at face value and treated accordingly. And apart from the fact that he was still effectively a prisoner in this place, life was bearable and even fun on occasion. Lee had a Playstation, not to mention a whole cupboardful of games and models, and he introduced Michael to the world of wargaming; they set up the dining table with hundreds of tiny figures and when they weren't painting them, they were running battle scenarios which sometimes went on right through the night. Even Joss had got involved, bringing a model tank back to the flat and telling them how it was used. Michael had been amazed at his military knowledge, but once he'd questioned Joss, the man had backed off quickly, saying only that his brother had been in the army.

He didn't want to go home anymore. At home he'd be a junkie, a heroin addict of whom his parents would be ashamed. He could hear the voices now: *How could you let this happen? After everything we've done for you?* And if the shock of it all didn't kill his father, the knowledge of his sexual activities certainly would. In the past, his behaviour had always been metered according to how it would affect his father's health, with dropping out of college at the top of the scale and getting pissed somewhere in the middle – although to be fair, the shock value of alcohol had worn off a little over the past year, since he'd started drinking in pubs more regularly. But drugs and gay sex would shoot off the top of the scale altogether and that would be the end of family life as he'd known it. There were photos of him on the internet, for fuck's sake. Adverts on some sicko website. It wouldn't be fair on any of them and Michael didn't intend to put it to the test.

And then Eddie left the door unlocked one afternoon

and Lee suggested they went out for something to eat. Michael wasn't sure. His whole world had been within the flat's four walls and he hadn't been outside since his birthday nearly three months earlier.

Eddie looked at his watch. 'Where are you going?' He was filling in a pools coupon at the kitchen table. Michael couldn't imagine why – what the hell would he do with half a million pounds? *How many kids could he buy with that?* And just what was the guy's relationship with Joss anyway? Free gear and sex in return for minding the flat? It was unlikely. Joss might be running the show, but Eddie always seemed to get what he wanted – including Michael.

Lee pulled on a denim jacket. 'Probably McDonald's down the High Street. Maybe the arcade. Got any money?'

Eddie handed him twenty pounds. 'Two hours. Or you don't get a shot tonight.'

Michael knew the last was for his benefit. They were testing him. Lee would be under strict instructions not to let Michael out of his sight and no doubt Joss would want a report later that night as to how he'd handled the situation. It was a clever touch – if they could convince him that he wasn't a prisoner, he would have no reason to escape. And yet he didn't feel like a prisoner any more.

Michael was given a jacket like Lee's and he wondered if it had been bought especially for him. Eddie returned his shoes – the grey suede ones he'd bought for the club which seemed like years ago now when he'd been just a kid. It made him think of Jenny again and he hoped she hadn't been too upset by what had happened.

He followed Lee down three flights of stone stairs. The place was deserted and badly in need of decoration, although the front door at the entrance to the building itself was solid steel. Lee had a key for it, although Michael hadn't seen Eddie give it to him. The thought crossed his mind that perhaps Lee had always had keys, but it didn't seem important any more. Outside, the air was damp and the concrete was wet in the shadows where the sun hadn't reached. The sky was overcast and it looked like more rain was expected, but Michael thought it was wonderful. At the end of the alley, he took several deep breaths, stretched and felt like he'd finally woken up after a long sleep.

Lee laughed. 'It's been a long time, hasn't it? I know how you feel.'

'Was it the same for you?' Michael felt like a child out on his own for the first time.

'Pretty much.' Lee nodded. 'Only we had Eddie as an escort.'

'We?' It had never occurred to Michael that there had been anyone in the flat other than Lee and Eddie.

Evading the question, Lee shook his head. 'Come on. We've only got two hours.' He led Michael up the street and took a right turn into a wider road which was deserted. Disused factories and warehouses were decorated with rotting boards and awnings. Faded notice boards had been warped by the weather and there were few signs of life other than the occasional parked car or light behind a dirty window. The gutters were full of crisp packets and old cans and the walls bore traces of rain-washed graffiti. Even the vandals had moved on and left the area to the grass and bindweed which were already reclaiming their territory, pushing up between cracks in the pavements. Ivy tendrils clung to railings, strangling the fences and smothering the brickwork until eventually the buildings stopped breathing altogether and collapsed into rubble.

At the end of the road, Lee led him through a maze of alleys and cut-offs, eventually turning onto a main road from a tunnel under the railway. Michael blinked. From rotted signs and peeling paint, the shops here bore gaudy dressing, carnival colours of red, green and orange. Windows displayed swatches of turquoise and ruby fabrics swathed round dark-skinned female models with almond eyes and heavy jewellery. The people were dressed the same – Asian women in bright saris pored over unidentifiable vegetables arranged in displays which seemed to stretch the entire length of the street, broken only by shops full of exotic yellow gold with four-figure price tags.

Michael was drowning in colour and noise. There were people everywhere, buying and bargaining, pulling children along behind them. He couldn't understand a word of what was being said. The air smelled of spices and fruit, mixed in with the scent of wet tarmac and car exhausts. It was like being on another planet.

They walked down the street for maybe half a mile until they came to McDonald's. In between an Asian butchers and a sari shop, it looked oddly out of place, the logo absorbed into the surroundings. There were potted plants in plastic window boxes and several bicycles chained up outside.

Michael ordered a Big Mac, Lee the same and they found a table near the window. On the wall was a chart detailing the nutritional value of the various ingredients used and a sheaf of leaflets in a plastic box which you could fill in if you wanted to comment about the service or food. A couple of chewed pencils were balanced on the ledge next to the display.

Michael ate his burger. Lee was watching him closely and it annoyed him. What did Lee think he was going to do – get up and run for it? He didn't doubt that Eddie would be hanging around outside somewhere, close enough to monitor the doors just in case. He wasn't stupid enough to believe they'd let him out with just Lee for company, not until they were sure about him. The irony was, of course, that it was wasted effort on Eddie's part. Just thinking about not getting his fix that night was enough to bring on a mild panic and he knew he wouldn't dare risk it by attempting to run. And even supposing he got away, what was he going to do then? *Hi mum, I'm home. Oh, and by the way, I'm a smackhead.* Not to mention trying to explain to them that his body was no longer entirely his own.

Lee went to the toilet. *Test number two?* Michael watched the queue at the counter lazily. Then he sat up and put the burger down. There was a young woman talking to them, showing them a photo. The people shook their heads and she moved on, asking the staff wiping tables and then making her way around the restaurant. Michael sat very still. She was looking for someone – a missing boyfriend perhaps, or even a brother or son. She passed his table and he glanced at the photograph of a boy of maybe five or six years old. He shook his head and she nodded her thanks, on the verge of crying as she left.

Oh shit, Kate! It could so easily be Kate. Trailing round Chiswick or wherever, still desperately praying that he was still alive. Three months of nothing – no news, no phone calls and no hope. He couldn't do that to his family, couldn't let them go on not knowing. Surely it wouldn't do any harm just to tell them he was alive and safe. He didn't need to give them any details.

Michael glanced around the restaurant. Lee had been a long time and then he saw him queuing again, presumably for more coffee or maybe a dessert. Michael had two, perhaps three minutes to do something – something which wouldn't be noticed until they were long gone from here, but would provide enough information for his parents to know he was safe.

With Lee's back to him, Michael reached for one of the pencils and questionnaires. Opening the leaflet, he scanned it quickly and carefully filled in his name and address in the appropriate boxes. Somebody must read these things, surely? The text said something about mailing lists and future surveys. He added his phone number for good measure and wrote URGENT – PLEASE CALL across the top in capitals, underlining them twice. He glanced up at the queue and saw Lee was being served. Quickly he replaced the pencil, refolded the leaflet and stuffed it back into the box, two from the front just in case anyone else decide to fill one in before they left.

Out on the street again, he didn't want to go back just yet. There was an internet café on the corner and suddenly he wanted to be Michael again, just for half an hour; the old Michael had loved online gaming – the one bit of the tech college he enjoyed was the access to the computer labs and seemingly limitless messing around on the net. He'd tried to interest Lee, explain that table-top gaming was even better in the virtual world of the web, but Lee had barely seen a computer beyond his Playstation, and wasn't that bothered either.

'Can we? Please?' He indicated the café. 'Just for ten minutes or so?'

Lee looked around and confirmed Michael's suspicion that they weren't alone. 'I don't know—'

'Oh, come on. It's tons better than table-top stuff. I'll show you.' He grabbed Lee's arm and steered him in the right direction.

'I told Eddie it'd be just McDonald's.'

'He doesn't have to know.' *Unless he's watching.* Lee wasn't going to tell tales, was he? Not when he had a stake in the outcome.

The younger boy gave in. 'Just ten minutes, then.'

Michael pulled him inside the café and plonked him down at a terminal. The girl in charge looked them up and down and insisted they paid a fiver deposit before they even started; Lee emptied his pockets grudgingly while Michael called up his webmail. He had some great links from an American friend he'd met once on holiday in Florida and the two often met up in cyberspace and played some campaign or other – whatever was flavour of the month. Michael was itching to see if anything new had come in since he'd been away.

Lee wasn't so sure. 'What are you doing?' He was uneasy, glancing at the doorway and Michael realised he was still watching for Eddie. He said nothing, but checked his inbox on the screen, then froze as he saw the list of new messages. Lee wasn't paying attention, so he opened one surreptitiously.

... We love you, Michael. We don't care where you've been. Just call us and let us know you're safe ...

Shit. He didn't need this. Reality came crashing back in and he realised this was a mistake. Eddie would be in here in a moment, judging by the way Lee was fidgeting and the man still scared him. And he couldn't go home – not anymore. Home belonged to Michael Redford and he was Mikey now ...

Lee was looking at the screen. Michael hit the disconnect button but it was too late.

'What—?'

'Nothing.' He stood up. 'Let's go.'

'That was—'

'A mistake. Come *on*.'

And on the walk back to the flat, he never knew if it was Eddie or his conscience that was following them, eyes boring into the back of his head and clouding the day with the smell of danger.

ELEVEN

'Kate, don't get your hopes up too much, but I think we may have a lead. Can I come round?' Derek's voice on the telephone. It was the first time the DI had sounded enthusiastic since he'd taken on the case, and Kate had had enough contact with him by now to know that he didn't say anything he didn't mean.

'Yes, of course.'

'Be with you in twenty.' He hung up abruptly, and Kate switched the television off and went upstairs to put on some make-up. It was a Sunday afternoon in mid-June, and the first day it had really felt like summer was on the way. Mum and dad were round at her aunt's house, some fifteen miles away, so she'd have Derek to herself and in any case, Kate reasoned, it was better to see what the man had to say before telling her parents.

So Derek had a lead. She wondered what it was. They'd given up on the picture of the man from the club – Derek had drawn a complete blank on that one and Kate hadn't the heart to blame Jenny, who was as upset as the rest of them. She'd been ringing Kate every few days for news, but even that had trailed off as the weeks had slowly passed. What other lead could Derek possibly have? Kate had spoken to all Michael's friends now, conducting her own private investigation. It wasn't that she didn't trust Derek or the police, but she'd already proved that Michael's mates were more open to someone of their own generation. She'd been updating a facebook page daily too; it made her feel like she was doing something useful, instead of giving up on her brother as everyone else seemed to have done.

She needed to keep occupied. Relationships were strained, both with her parents and with Colin, and Kate didn't want to do or say anything she was sure she'd regret later. Colin was being more than patient with her, but her moods and sudden tempers were wearing him down and she didn't know how long he'd keep bouncing back.

Derek's dark blue saloon drew up about twenty five minutes later. Kate had the kettle on and handed him a coffee as he walked in. She was determined not to get too excited until she heard what he had to say.

Sitting down on the sofa, he opened a scruffy black briefcase, removing a small clear plastic bag and a piece of paper. He handed the bag to Kate. She frowned. It was sealed with a plastic pull-through tag showing a six-digit number and inside was what appeared to be a neatly folded McDonald's questionnaire.

'I don't understand.'

Derek smiled and handed her the piece of paper. 'This is a photocopy. The original's been fingerprinted and will go off tomorrow for handwriting analysis – I just thought you might like to see it first.'

She looked at the paper. There were various boxes for ticking in answer to a set of questions and at the bottom was a space for filling in a name and address. The name was Michael's and the address was her own. He'd even written across the top, asking the reader to call urgently.

She looked up, eyes wide, but Derek laid a hand on her arm. 'Yes, Kate. It looks real enough. But is it Michael's writing?' She didn't know. There was nothing distinctive about Michael's handwriting and she couldn't say one way or the other, although it looked similar. 'Do you have something with his handwriting on?' he continued. 'Something I can take away for comparison?'

'I'm sure there's something lying around.' She jumped up, finding one of his college books under the coffee table. It was one of the hated maths study books and it was carefully buried deep in a pile of magazines. Michael had wanted to do arts, but the parents had exerted their influence again and taken him out of school, sending him to a sixth form college. To do science. *Better job prospects*, dad had said. *Better for whom?* was Kate's unspoken reply.

Derek flicked through the book quickly and smiled. 'It certainly looks the same. I'll get it booked in for analysis tomorrow morning as soon as the lab opens. They owe me a few favours.'

'So where did you find this? Why didn't somebody call here – it's this number on the form?'

'In a minute. I also need your permission to have Michael's room fingerprinted. We've got several sets of prints from the leaflet and it's possible we may get a match. Unlikely, but possible.'

'Of course. Anything.' She felt like jumping up and down and shouting.

'Good. I'll arrange for a CSI to call round this evening. Where are your parents? We'll need prints from them and you as well for elimination.'

'At my aunt's. I haven't told them yet. I wanted to hear it first.'

Derek nodded and picked up his coffee. 'The leaflet was found in the East End, stuffed in behind some blank forms. Assuming it *was* Michael who wrote it, it would seem that he's alive and in London.'

She didn't understand his reticence. 'It might not be him?'

'It's possible.' He shrugged. 'You've no idea what sick jokes people like to play. But I think we can assume that it was Michael, for the time being. It can't do any harm and we'll know one way or the other in a few days.'

'What's he doing in the East End? Why hasn't he called? Why didn't he ring himself instead of leaving messages?'

'There are all sorts of reasons. He may not have access to a telephone. And I think you should face the fact that he may not want to speak to you.'

'May not *want* to speak to us?' She was incensed. 'Why wouldn't he? Why wouldn't he want to come home?'

'He may not be being held against his will.' Derek's voice was quiet now. 'He's left no clues to his whereabouts – nothing that would enable us to trace him. Why, Kate? Why didn't he write his current address on the form? He must know we're looking for him.'

'Perhaps he didn't have time,' she argued, not wanting to believe what he was saying.

The DI smiled. 'You may be right. It's also possible that he doesn't know where he is. I just want you to see the picture from all angles. McDonald's doesn't really fit with a kidnap theory, does it?'

Kate re-read the paper and tried to picture Michael sitting in the restaurant and writing on the form. What had he been thinking at the time? Perhaps he was trying to tell them something, something he didn't want whoever he was with to know about.

Derek picked at the seal on the polythene bag. 'Believe it or not, the assistant manager fancies himself as some kind of amateur detective. He was tidying these up, when he noticed that one of them was out of line as if it had been replaced in a hurry. So he had a look and found this one – most of the prints we got off it were his, unfortunately. He took it home with him, showed it to his girlfriend and she recognised the name from the story we ran in the *Standard* – remember? Just goes to prove that publicity has its uses. Once they remembered where they'd seen it before, they decided it would be better to call the police instead of your number.'

'So what are you going to do now?'

'Confirm it's Michael's handwriting and then go and have a look at this McDonald's.' He hesitated. 'I don't suppose you'd be free to come with me, would you?'

'When?' Kate wondered why on earth he wanted her along. Not that she was objecting – anything to help Michael and besides, spending time in Derek's company had other attractions.

'Tomorrow afternoon. You'd be useful as cover – we could go along as a couple – and you'll be much better at recognising him than I would. I don't want to attract too much attention as it may be dangerous for Michael.'

'All right. You can pick me up at the surgery if you want. I won't tell mum and dad as yet.' Kate wondered how finding her brother could possibly be dangerous. Surely it was just a matter of locating him and bringing him home? What wasn't Derek telling her?

He didn't give her the opportunity to ask. 'One o'clock?' He drained his mug and gathered up the evidence, ready to leave.

'Fine.' It wasn't fine at all. Derek knew something that he wasn't letting on, although she didn't know what deductions he could have made that he hadn't already told her. Perhaps there was other news, something from the picture, maybe. Whatever it was, she wanted to know – nothing could be worse than this awful vacuum.

Kate decided she'd have a headache by lunch time tomorrow.

Derek arrived outside the surgery at five to one and Kate was already waiting. She'd made some feeble excuse to the supervisor and knew that the other two receptionists would be gossiping about her already. No doubt words would be said and probably in a loud voice when Colin was in earshot. They'd be watching her getting into the strange car and wondering just what she was up to, but she didn't care. Right now, finding Michael was more important than her job. She'd told Rachel the real reason for her leaving and her friend had made a coffee between patients and offered her own support and assistance for what seemed like the millionth time. It wasn't that Kate was ungrateful, but offers of help weren't results.

Back in the black jeans and polo shirt, with Red Hot Chili Peppers blaring from the speakers, Derek looked for all the world like he was picking her up for a date. Only the serious look in his eyes gave the game away and Kate found herself hoping she'd be able to find an excuse to carry on seeing him after Michael had come home. The thought disturbed her, but more disturbing was the idea of never seeing Derek again once her brother was found.

The handwriting analysis had come up positive. Derek had pulled strings and got a quickie job done that morning. He had some blow-up photographs of both sets to show her and she could see the comparisons. They'd made transparencies – overlaid characters from one sample onto the other – and the matches were clear. Although they'd never swear it in court, the lab could be reasonably certain it was Michael's writing. The fingerprinting had proved a useful exercise as well; although there had been so many prints on the questionnaire, it had been difficult to get anything conclusive, but the CSI's had established a partial match.

But there was another piece in the puzzle now as well – that confirmed beyond reasonable doubt that he'd been in the area that day.

'He's been on the net,' Derek said, pulling up at a set of traffic lights. 'We had a trace on his internet account and we got a hit on the same day as the McDonald's link.'

'He's been sending *emails*?' It didn't fit with the mental image Kate had of him – alone and scared somewhere, being held prisoner. Not playing on the internet.

'From an internet café that co-incidentally is in the same road as McDonald's.' Derek was cheerful. 'Don't think he actually sent any messages, but we'll check it out while we're there. Sorry – is this music too loud?'

The traffic got heavier as they drove into the city. It was the start of the tourist season, the good weather had brought people outdoors and all along the Embankment, the parks were alive with lunch time visitors; Tower Hill was crammed with coaches full of Japanese tourists, and foreign students swarmed like bees around the Tower itself.

How could Michael be out on a day like this and not be thinking about his family? He'd never been a teenage rebel, never one to storm out of the house with threats of retribution. No, Michael had always fought the quiet fight, the subtle debate with the parents and although he hadn't always won the argument, he'd never seemed to mind.

Round Whitechapel and down Commercial Road, Derek slowed the car, occasionally consulting the A to Z on his knee. Another fifteen minutes and finally he pulled into a side street and parked up. Pulling off his seatbelt, he turned to her.

'I need your help, Kate, but I also need you to do exactly as I say.'

'OK.' She didn't see what he was getting at.

'I mean *exactly* what I say. No arguing and no questions – no matter what you think nor how unreasonable it may seem.'

'I'm not a child.'

'I didn't suggest you were.' The reply was curt and she backed off. This was business, not pleasure.

'Sorry. I understand.'

'Good.' He opened his door. 'Then let's go.'

She couldn't see any sign of a McDonald's until Derek explained that he'd parked some distance away. Walking gave him a feel for the area.

It was a predominantly Asian community – exotic shops teeming with colourful people and bursting with life in the sunshine. Kate felt distinctly out of place as she followed Derek and he took her hand, leading her through the street market. It made her jump; her palm was tingling and she felt like a sixteen year-old, shy and embarrassed at the contact. This was ridiculous – the man was probably twice her age and besides, she was engaged to Colin and supposedly getting married in less than two months. It reminded her that she had a dress fitting the following weekend and suddenly she knew she wasn't going to show up. Not at the fitting and not at the church. She couldn't do it, couldn't go through with the wedding. Not now. Michael was a convenient excuse for it all, but in reality, Kate realised there was more to life than comfortable and safe Colin. Her world had turned upside down since Michael had gone, but it had made her take a fresh look at herself and now her priorities had changed.

'Kate?'

'Sorry?' She looked up at him and he stopped walking and pulled her towards him.

'Pay attention. This isn't a game and Michael's life may be at stake.' He sounded irritated and she wondered if the attraction was one-sided or if he felt anything too. Derek was pointing down the street. 'There you are. See? Next to the butchers.'

She could just make out the sign, surrounded by a riot of colour. Would Michael be there, though? Just because he'd been there once was no guarantee he'd show up again, today or any other day.

'All right, Kate.' Derek paused just before the glass frontage. 'I want you to have a quick look around and tell me if you see him. Keep your head down and your eyes open – I don't want him to see you. You're not to approach him nor make any kind of contact. Understand?'

She nodded. 'Aren't you going to talk to the manager?'

'Later. I want to be a tourist first – it's a little less showy. You have to think of this as though every single person in there is the opposition.'

Kate followed him into the restaurant. *The opposition?* Just what were they up against here? Derek sounded like he already *knew* what had happened to Michael. She did a quick scan of the occupants, but nobody bore the slightest resemblance to her brother. Disappointed, she shook her head, but Derek smiled and squeezed her hand.

'Don't give up. We've got plenty of time and if we don't see him today, I'll have somebody else out here tomorrow. We'll keep going until we do see him. Now what do you want to eat? I hope you're hungry,' he added with a grin, handing her the A to Z he'd been carrying. 'We need to make this last as long as possible. You go and find a seat in the corner and look at this. Don't stare around the room and for heaven's sake, don't look obvious.'

She found a seat in the corner, half-hidden under the staircase which dominated the back end of the restaurant. Obediently, she opened the A to Z and glanced at it, keeping an occasional eye on the door. Derek returned a few moments later, laden down with a tray full of food and drinks.

They ate slowly, Kate looking past Derek to the entrance. She had to admit that watching Derek was more interesting as he chatted idly about the job and the hours he worked. She was about to drop his social life into the conversation, when three men entered the restaurant, laughing and pooling their change. The man in the middle was much older – the other two teenagers, really – and she frowned. He looked familiar, but she couldn't quite place him.

Then it came to her and she almost jumped from her seat. 'It's him.'

Derek didn't react. 'Who?' he asked mildly. 'Michael? Don't watch him, Kate. Look at me.' He leaned over the table and blocked any view they might have of her by taking both her hands and kissing her quickly. Kate was startled for a moment, but Derek pulled away, keeping his face close to hers. There wasn't a trace of emotion in his eyes, just a calm determination which was unnerving. 'Come on, Kate,' he said. 'Talk to me. Tell me what's happening.'

'The man from the club! I swear it is! I recognise him from Jenny's picture.'

'Any others?'

'Three of them altogether. Him and two youths. The smaller one's got long brown hair, and the other's hidden behind the man – he's about five nine or ten with shoulder-length blond streaks. Both very thin. Wait – he's moving—'

'Michael?'

Kate's eyes widened. '*Yes*. God, it *is* him.' Yet he seemed much older than she remembered; his hair was the wrong colour and his face was different somehow – she couldn't quite identify the changes. *Was* it Mike? Or just another teenager out with his friends? But in that case, why had she recognised the man he'd met in the club, the night he'd disappeared? It was too much of a coincidence for them both to be here.

Derek caught her gaze. 'Kate, I want you to go upstairs. Go into the toilets and stay there until I send for you.'

'Why? Where are you going?'

'To get a better look. Listen in to the conversation if I can.' Derek pursed his lips. 'Go on. Now.'

She pulled up the collar on her ski jacket and stood up. Head down, she walked quickly round the table and up the stairs into the ladies' toilets where she sat on the edge of the sink for what seemed like an eternity before there was a knock at the door.

'Kate? It's me.'

She was out in seconds. 'Well?'

Derek stood at the top of the stairs. He still had half a burger in one hand. 'It's him.'

'Michael? Or the mystery man?'

'Both.' He stepped forwards. 'Kate, he didn't exactly look like he was in trouble.'

'I don't understand.' He'd looked so different. Had he changed so much in a few weeks? Dyed his hair, even?

Why, Mike?

Derek finished the burger in two quick bites. 'Christ, this isn't easy. Kate, he looked to me like any other teenager out with his friends. He didn't seem upset and he certainly wasn't trying to escape.'

It didn't make sense. Michael was missing. He was supposed to be kidnapped or even dead – he was seventeen, for Christ's sake. And yet he appeared to be perfectly happy with this new life he'd found. She shook her head. 'Derek, something isn't right. He simply wouldn't do this. At the very least he'd have telephoned to let us know he was safe.'

'I agree. And that's why I've let him go.'

'You've done what?' She was aghast. They'd found him after all this time and Derek had done nothing about it.

'I've let him go. You're right, Kate – something's wrong with this. And besides, Michael is still under age, which means I'm obliged to sort this one out.' He hesitated. 'They came in for a take-away. The conversation I overheard seemed to indicate they come in here fairly frequently, so I took a gamble—'

'You took a *gamble?* With Michael's *life?*'

'I took a gamble that he'll be back again – at which time I intend to have a full team out here. We'll take him back to wherever he's living and *then* we'll get to the bottom of this little mystery.' He smiled. 'You'll have him home, Kate – I'm certain of that. What you need to face is the fact that he may not want to stay.'

TWELVE

Michael had just about got the hang of mixing his own shots, when Joss stopped him one evening. All four of them were in the kitchen; Joss and Eddie were both drinking and Lee seemed restless and edgy. Michael wondered what was going on. He could cope with the drug rush now, and while his body could still appreciate the high, he'd built up enough tolerance to retain his self-control. It made life a lot easier, not to mention safer.

He'd also acquired the knack of pretending to do one thing, while thinking about something totally different – something he'd never quite managed to do when he'd had the Saturday job in the hardware shop. It would have been useful then, to be able to serve a customer while planning his strategy for the night ahead. Now, the ability was put to far different use – closing off his mind completely and shutting out the pain and humiliation, although to be fair, there wasn't really even any pain any more. At first it had been difficult – near impossible – but since the situation hadn't changed, he'd had no choice but to accept it and find a way of dealing with it.

Lee made up his own fix and passed the hypodermic to Joss, who checked the level of the liquid in the syringe, before nodding and performing the injection. Lee sighed out loud and closed his eyes, but he remained where he was at the kitchen table and didn't disappear off into the lounge as was his usual habit.

Michael glanced round the table. He knew the other three well enough now to pick up on the tension in the air and he wondered what was about to happen. Maybe his pathetic attempt at contacting the outside world had finally been noticed. It had been three days since he'd scrawled the note in McDonald's, three days since he'd seen the email and three days of imagining somebody telephoning his parents to give them the news. And Michael had nearly panicked when Eddie had decided to accompany them earlier. The whole time they'd been in the restaurant, he'd consciously made an effort to be a part of the group, talking loudly with Lee and terrified that somebody was going to come over and announce that they'd seen him filling in the leaflet the previous day. And if some employee said anything like that with Eddie in earshot, Michael knew he'd be in serious trouble and God alone knew what Joss would do. Fortunately, Eddie had decided on a take away and he hadn't had to keep the act up for too long. Perhaps that was it – maybe they'd seen through his acting and realised what he'd done.

Joss selected different weights for the scales as he made up Michael's fix. He looked up and Michael saw the speculative expression on his face.

'What's going on?'

'You get a little extra tonight, Mikey. Special treat.'

'Why?' He had a feeling that he wasn't going to like the strings which Joss was about to attach.

'You're working. Big night, tonight.' Joss watched his reaction carefully as he added the powder to the distilled water in the glass ampoule.

Michael didn't reply. He'd been working for weeks – at least he assumed Joss was getting money for it. *So what's so different about tonight?* Sometimes his attitude frightened him and he wondered how much he'd changed. Would he even recognise himself anymore? But without the shell of indifference he'd created, he wouldn't have survived this far – he'd have used the kitchen knives for other purposes than attacking Eddie and slashed his own wrists long ago.

Lee was watching him. 'It's my punter, Mikey. Joss' mate, remember? He's asked for you tonight.'

'So? He likes it rough, doesn't he?'

'You don't seem very concerned.' Joss drew the mixture up into a syringe and swapped the needle for a sterile one.

Michael shoved up his sleeve and laid his arm across the table. 'Would it make a difference if I was?' It shocked him that he could be so cold about it. 'No, I thought not.'

Joss shrugged. 'I'm trying to make it a little easier for you, Mikey. This won't give you much more of a buzz, but it will last for longer.'

'And you should know,' said Eddie. His voice was deathly quiet and Joss glanced across the table, syringe in one hand. He looked startled, but recovered himself quickly.

'I'm sorry?' The words were questioning, but the tone suggested he knew exactly what Eddie meant.

'You know what I'm talking about.'

'Do I?' Joss laughed. 'Don't threaten me, Ed. It's neither impressive nor frightening.'

There was a sudden silence, thick and stifling. 'You shouldn't forget the old days, Joss,' said Eddie after a moment, pushing his chair back. He crossed to the door, but Joss was on his feet in an instant. Voice low and deadly, he caught Eddie's look and returned it neatly.

'And *you* shouldn't forget that Mikey here is not your personal property.'

Eddie was *jealous*? Was *that* what this was about? And yet there was more to it than that. Michael could sense the unspoken words, the challenge met and won, and Eddie backed down suddenly. He strolled out of the kitchen and Joss returned to the table, giving him his shot without a word. Michael felt the needle pierce his skin and forgot the strange conversation as the usual wave flooded his mind in a rush of satisfaction. Curling his fingers, he shivered with the sheer power of the drug in his veins. It was the nearest he'd ever come to a sexless orgasm.

Lee's client arrived at about nine. He was a big thick-set man with short hair and a greying moustache and Michael had seen him on a number of occasions. Lee didn't speak about him much – he never talked about any of his punters – and all Michael knew was that he was often viciously aggressive and Lee had emerged with bruises on more than one occasion. Joss claimed he'd sorted it. 'There'll be no violence in my house,' he'd said. 'Nobody abuses my boys.' Michael wondered who he was trying to kid.

Michael had already switched off mentally. Lying on his stomach in bed, he was watching a moth beat itself to death on the lampshade and he didn't even look up as the door opened and closed again. Sensing the presence in the room, he was about to make some comment when an almighty flare of red hot pain scorched a furrow across his back. Too surprised to cry out, his whole body jerked and thudded back against the mattress. Before he had time to wonder what had happened, his arms were yanked behind his back and secured with what felt like the thin leather belt that had just hit him.

It was over in minutes. From when the man told him he didn't like his attitude, Michael knew he was in for a bad time and he couldn't shut this one out. The lash of the belt had torn through his composure with his skin, and for a while he was a child again, young and terrified of what was happening to him. The heroin helped dull the pain, but by the time the man dressed quickly and left some ten minutes later, Michael felt as though he'd aged five years. He'd thought he'd done it, built a high enough wall around his soul that nobody could hurt him, but this friend of Joss' had cracked it as if he'd known exactly where to aim.

Hamelin's Child

He lay on his side, breathless and too shocked to cry. There were burns on his wrists and he could feel a ridge across his back where the belt had hit him. He felt empty, drained of all life and emotion and he wondered if he would ever feel normal or even human again.

The door opened softly. 'Mikey?'

Lee's voice. He didn't reply; he couldn't find enough energy even to move. It had been a while since he'd needed Lee's sympathy.

Lee closed the door and padded across the room. 'Did the bastard hurt you?'

He sounded concerned and Michael wanted to answer, but he was just too damned tired. All he wanted to do was sleep. Sleep forever, somewhere where the pain couldn't find him. He heard the sounds of Lee undressing and an arm reached over him and turned off the light; then he felt a hand touch his shoulder gently, hesitantly. It was comforting, Michael didn't shrug it off and Lee took no answer as encouragement, moving closer and snaking an arm around Michael's chest. Michael could feel the warmth of his body. It was a good feeling and made him smile, despite the evening's events.

And then Lee's hand began to explore. At first, Michael felt his whole body stiffen, but the touch was soothing and it helped melt away the horror of the evening as the hand moved lower, tracing small circles on his abdomen.

'Lee? Don't ... please. I—'

'Ssh.' Lee stroked his cock and Michael flinched, startled, but he surprised himself by not pulling away and he lay there, immobile, while Lee played with him. His eyes wide open in the darkness, he was tense and unresponsive. He wanted to push Lee away, but he didn't, he *couldn't*. He felt his balls being fondled, gently and expertly.

'Chill, Mikey. I'm not gonna hurt you.' Lee's voice was soft in his ear and accompanied by a delicate flick of the tongue. Michael shivered and to his complete surprise, felt himself beginning to harden at the touch of Lee's hand.

He was horrified at his body's response.

'Is that good?' He felt the tickle of Lee's hair on his face. 'Tell me if you want me to stop. I wouldn't hurt you, Mikey.'

Michael couldn't breathe. Lee's lips brushed his own and moved down to kiss his neck, his hand still not leaving Michael's balls. Feathery touches on his chest made him tremble and Michael realised there was a real chance he was going to come. He didn't know if he wanted to. In fact he was fairly sure he didn't.

'Lee, *please* …'

Lee raised his head. 'I want you to enjoy this, Mikey. So shut the fuck up.'

Michael couldn't answer and Lee resumed his exploration of Michael's body. His touch was electric; he was playing Michael like a musical instrument with a stroke here and a caress there – all carefully calculated to maximise the response and get the best out of the performance.

His lips touched Michael's cock and it was hard and ready. Michael gasped and immediately bit back the sound. *This isn't right*, his mind was screaming at him and yet his body said otherwise. This wasn't rape – something had changed. He knew Lee would stop the minute he said the word and yet his body had taken over now, blocking the words and preventing him from pushing Lee away.

Lee took him in his mouth. Michael could feel the touch of his hair trailing across his stomach and it tickled annoyingly. He'd never had oral sex before. Emma hadn't been *that* obliging and he hadn't got that far into his relationship with Jenny. It felt like his balls were about to explode.

Michael couldn't stop himself. He came violently, back arching and whole body shuddering with the release. It seemed to go on for eternity, but Lee didn't move; hands on Michael's hips, he rode the wave with him until finally he drew away and wiped his mouth with one hand.

Michael recovered his senses. 'Is that what you do to your punters?' he asked, without thinking.

'You *what?*' Lee pulled away sharply, vanishing into the darkness of the bedroom.

Michael said nothing. He felt guilty. Guilty that he'd allowed this to happen, but guiltier still that he'd actually enjoyed it.

Lee swung his legs over the side of the bed. 'Yeah,' he said softly, as he stood up. 'Exactly like what I do with my punters, Mikey. Just another fuckin' trick.'

Michael stretched out his arm. 'Lee, I'm sorry. I didn't mean …' But it was too late – the damage had been done, and Lee grabbed a robe from the back of the door and left the room. He didn't even slam the door behind him.

Lee didn't come back that night. By morning, Michael was lying awake and alone in the double bed and pondering the previous evening's events. His conscience could cope with the earlier incident, although the sheer brutality had shocked him and his back was sore from the belt – no, it was Lee's idea of comforting him afterwards which was giving him cause for concern. Up until then, Michael had simply been doing what he had to in order to survive, but he knew he could have backed out of the encounter with Lee. He hadn't. He could easily have stopped it or pulled away, but he hadn't. He'd let Lee carry on, led him to believe he was enjoying it and let him finish what he'd started. And, oh Christ, he'd *come!* Which meant he *had* enjoyed it – or at least his body had, even if his mind was telling him otherwise.

Michael couldn't understand his reaction. Lee had genuinely been trying to help and all he'd done was to take what was offered and throw it straight back. It wasn't fair. Not on either of them.

He yawned and scrambled out of bed. It was almost ten o'clock and the dull light from behind the curtains suggested it was raining. The weather suited his mood. He dragged on a robe and strolled down the hall to the kitchen, intending to make some coffee before showering.

'Mornin'.' Lee glanced up from the kitchen table. He looked like he'd been there all night. There was an empty half-bottle of scotch and the remnants of a packet of digestives next to him.

Michael couldn't reply. He didn't know what to say. What *could* he say? *Hi, Lee. Thanks for sucking me off last night.* Hardly your average morning greeting, was it? And in any case, he wasn't entirely sure he was grateful. Lee's actions had caused more problems than they'd solved.

'You OK?' Lee's voice was calm, but emotionless and he wouldn't meet Michael's eyes.

'Yeah.' Michael found his tongue. 'Don't think your friend likes me much.'

Lee snorted. 'He's no friend of mine. Some dealer that Joss buys from.' It explained a lot. In the same way that Lee and Michael couldn't afford to alienate Joss, Joss in turn depended on his suppliers.

'Does he hit you?' Michael took two mugs from the cupboard and dumped a teaspoon of coffee in each.

Lee looked up. 'No. I gave myself the black eye that time – what d'you friggin' think?'

'I meant with the belt.'

'Belt?' There was a trace of concern now, as Lee licked his index finger and stuck it in the bottom of the empty biscuit packet. He scooped up the crumbs and sucked his finger.

Michael dropped the collar of his robe and showed him the cut on his back in silence.

Lee half-choked on the biscuit crumbs. 'Fuck *me!* You're right, he doesn't like you.'

Michael pulled his collar back up, poured boiling water into the mugs, added some milk and put one on the table in front of Lee. 'Doesn't it bother you?'

'What difference does it make?'

'You could leave.'

'Oh, don't start on that one again. Haven't you learned

how it is yet? You leave, you don't get your shots. Think about it, Mikey. You want to do it?'

'No.' Michael shook his head as he sat down opposite. He didn't want to think about what might happen if he didn't get a regular fix. And it was harder for Lee anyway. Where would he go? Michael didn't know if he had any family other than Joss and Eddie. He never spoke of his former life and Michael realised he knew nothing about the boy at all.

Lee cradled the mug in both hands. 'About last night. I didn't mean to make you feel bad. I was tryin' to help.' He stared at the mug. It was the first time Michael had ever seen him look awkward or embarrassed and it made him feel even more guilty.

He couldn't reply. He wanted to tell Lee it was all right, but it wasn't and he didn't know what to do about it. Lee moved towards him and Michael pulled away instinctively. 'Don't—'

'*Shit!*' Lee thumped the table, spilling coffee and making a lake around the biscuit packet. 'Fucked up, haven't I? Let's face it, Mikey – I'm gay and you're straight. It ain't gonna work.'

'Are you? Gay, I mean.' Michael wasn't sure and he didn't really like to pry. 'Or is it just that you've been here too long?'

Lee didn't answer for a moment. He pushed his hair out of his eyes and took a sip of coffee. 'I'm fourteen,' he said after a while. It was an answer in itself and Michael wished he hadn't asked. Hell, no wonder Lee didn't know any other life than this place. No wonder he didn't want to leave.

Michael had had enough revelations for one day. He stood up and took his coffee through to the bathroom, meeting Eddie on his way out.

'How did last night go, then?'

'You should try him some time, Eddie,' said Michael. 'You've got a lot in common. You're both vicious bastards.' He smiled sweetly, closing the bathroom door before Eddie had chance to react.

He felt better after a shower and more relaxed than he had been in a while. As he lay on the sofa afterwards and idly flicked through the television channels, he wondered if perhaps Lee had the right idea after all. Maybe adaptability was the key to this life.

Maybe. Michael was tired and he fell asleep for some hours, not waking until Lee threw a cushion at him. The rain had cleared up outside and Lee was restless, pacing up and down the lounge.

'I'm bored. Talk to me.'

'What about?' Michael yawned expansively. He'd hardly slept during the night and the sofa hadn't made up for it.

'Dunno.'

Michael rolled over and winced as his sweatshirt rubbed the weal on his back. He sat up and switched the television off. 'Let's go out somewhere.'

'Where exactly did you have in mind?' Lee looked at him warily. 'Another trip to that computer place? I'm not stupid, y'know?'

'Lee, if I wanted to escape, don't you think I'd have done it before?' Here was the opportunity for Lee to say if he'd noticed the email, but he didn't. 'How could I go home like this?' Michael continued, pushing up his sleeve to reveal the needle tracks and bruises. 'I have as much to lose as you do.' For the first time he wondered if he'd done the right thing in trying to contact his family. Perhaps it would have been better to let them assume what they wanted, whatever was easiest for them to accept; maybe he was opening up wounds by making them realise he was still alive and well.

He couldn't go back to McDonald's – he was stupid to have returned with Eddie and Lee that day. If the message he'd left had got through to his family, it was a distinct possibility that there would be people looking for him now. All he'd wanted to do was to let them know he was safe. He couldn't tell them he was a heroin addict. And he could never in a million years explain what had happened last night.

Lee could have been reading his mind. 'I fancy a Big Mac,' he said, 'and a game of pinball.'

Michael shook his head. 'I'm not hungry.'

'I am. You can wait while I have somethin'. I'll get some money off Eddie.' Lee went through to the kitchen and Michael frowned. He didn't dare go back into the restaurant. If he was caught now, nobody – least of all Joss – was going to believe that it hadn't been all his idea in the first place. And Michael knew that if Joss thought that, both he and probably Lee too would suffer.

Outside, the clouds were still heavy and the early afternoon seemed more like early evening. Michael and Lee wandered down the main road in silence, Michael jumping at shadows and trying not to look concerned. When they approached McDonald's, he made a feeble excuse and waited for Lee in the park just down the road.

Kicking a stone along the path, he wandered three times round the artificial lake, hands in pockets and head down. It was the first time he'd been alone outside and he was nervous as hell. It was ironic really – the first real chance he'd had to escape and he didn't want it. In fact he was terrified of being found, scared of not being in the flat when Joss arrived on his nightly rounds. *Scared of missing a fix.*

'What's up?'

He jumped and spun round, but it was only Lee, watching him with a peculiar expression. He had a half-eaten burger in one hand and a bag in the other, which he passed to Michael.

'Thought you might change your mind if you saw me eating.' Lee hesitated. 'Mikey, what? You're so fuckin' jumpy.'

'Nothing. I'm just tired.' They sat down on a bench and Michael bit into the burger Lee had bought him. He was hungry after all, and eating took his mind off other things.

'You're embarrassed, right?' Lee looked away. 'I'm sorry. I won't do it again. It's just that—'

'It's nothing!' Michael repeated irritably. 'For fuck's sake, Lee, just leave me alone!' He glanced around the park guiltily, even more scared of being seen. But they were on the far side of the lake and the area was almost deserted – there was a woman and a dog in the distance and the man on a nearby bench was engrossed in his newspaper, an empty sandwich packet on his briefcase next to him.

Lee was watching him, and Michael didn't know what to do or say. He liked the boy and besides, Lee had been his lifeline during the first few weeks, without which Michael knew he'd never have survived. But things had changed since last night and they couldn't go back to the way things were before.

Lee finished his burger, screwed up the wrapper and tossed it into the bin across the path. 'Oh, I've fuckin' had enough of this.' He stood up. 'You know the arcade down the road?'

'No. How could I?'

'Turn left, past the pub and it's about three streets down. I'll be in there. Do what you like.'

Michael nodded. He needed to be on his own for a while to sort through his mind. This wasn't just about last night any more. That had been an introduction, a suggestion, maybe, of what could be. Lee was offering him something more than a cushion against this new life and Michael was worried, more so because he genuinely didn't know what to do. Three months ago – or even more recently – he'd have laughed derisively, and probably made some rude or sarcastic comment. Three months ago he'd had a girlfriend. But now the rules had changed. He couldn't imagine making love to a girl again, not even Jenny. Sex was inextricably linked to heroin now – heroin, Eddie and Lee – and with the choice between drugs and his old life hanging over his head, Michael had chosen the former.

Lee was around the far side of the lake, halfway to the gate. His long brown hair was loose down his back and from this distance he could easily be mistaken for a girl. Even as he thought it, a woman came out from the public toilets just behind Lee's path and Michael found himself comparing the two. She had shorter hair and was wearing jeans and a blue jacket, but looked much more feminine – something about the way she walked gave her sex away.

Something about the way she walked. Michael looked a bit more closely and felt the colour drain from his face. No wonder he could identify her so easily. Walking along the path about thirty paces behind Lee was his sister, Kate.

There was only one reason Kate would be here and Michael didn't have time to think about it. Jumping to his feet he sprinted the opposite way around the lake towards the exit, hoping he could get there before Lee did. There was no point in trying to pretend he didn't know him, trying to avoid implicating him in what was going on – if Kate was around, the chances were that other people had seen them together anyway. No, the only advantage they had was speed.

'Mikey?' Lee had stopped as the two paths converged just short of the park gates. 'What's going on?'

'Get out of here, Lee,' he said breathlessly, grabbing his arm. 'We're being watched.'

'What?' Lee looked confused and Michael swung round to see Kate about ten paces away with a look of horror on her face. She seemed genuinely surprised to see them, but he couldn't believe it. There was no way that Kate could be here, in this park, unless she was acting on his message from McDonald's.

'Lee, come *on!* We have to get away!'

Lee frowned and looked from Michael to Kate and back again. 'Who's she, Mikey? What have you *done?*'

'She's my sister. Now move.' Michael tried to push Lee towards the exit and finally he got the message. He shook free of Michael's arm, glared at him and bolted for the park gates with Michael close behind.

Out on the street, with all the side roads and traffic, Michael knew they could easily lose whoever was following them. And Kate hadn't even moved. He felt like screaming. He was close to his sister and yet he was leaving her like this, running off with some street kid back to a life of hell. *What's happened to me?*

There were figures at the park gates. Several of them stepped out from bus stops and parked cars. Lee skidded to a stop and turned quickly, his eyes flicking rapidly between Michael, Kate and the men. There were others from within the park now – the man from the bench next to where he and Lee had been sitting, and two more came out of the toilets. Lee finally met his eyes. He looked hurt.

'You set us up.'

'No.' Michael shook his head. 'I didn't, honestly. I didn't know this was going to happen.' He watched the approaching men. 'Lee, go. I'll hold them off.'

Lee didn't need telling twice. As the group converged on the two youths, he selected the weakest point and ran for it, with Michael following him. Lee cannoned into one of the men, who grabbed his shoulders, holding him away. Lee's response was a sharp knee to the groin and that coupled with Michael's teeth in his arm, persuaded him to let go. Lee sprinted through the gap in the circle, heading for the other park gate and freedom.

'Leave him,' one of the men said. 'He's not important.'

'They're *all* important,' said another. 'I wanted everyone involved. Jesus, Kate, I told you to stay in the car!'

'I wanted to use the toilet. How was I to know he was in the park? I thought you were in McDonald's.'

The second man shook his head. 'Well, I guess we've got what we came for. Anything else would have been a bonus. Hello, Michael.'

Michael stood in the centre of the circle. There were seven men around him, seven men and Kate all staring at him as if he'd just landed off another planet. What was he – some kind of fucking alien?

'We saw you go past McDonald's,' the man continued. 'Why didn't you go in?'

'Why should I?' He was suddenly defensive. He didn't want these people here. He didn't want to be rescued. He certainly didn't want to see Kate. And how the *hell* was he going to get a fix tonight? Michael could feel his hands starting to shake at the very thought of missing a shot.

He glanced round the group, looking for a way out, but the man was watching him curiously. 'What's the matter, Michael? I thought you'd be pleased to see us.'

'Well you thought wrong, didn't you?' The circle was closing in and the man stepped forward and took his arm gently. 'Let me go.'

'And have you run off again? I don't think so.' He hesitated. 'Come on, Michael, it's over now. You're safe.'

Michael wasn't convinced. It wasn't over. It hadn't even started.

THIRTEEN

Kate was stunned. Who was this total stranger who looked like Michael standing in front of her? The Michael she knew was seventeen, bright and intelligent with a warm personality and a future – this youth with the badly-bleached blond streaks was a wild animal, his eyes darting nervously around the group as if he might flee at any moment. His skin was pale and he looked ill, yet he was hopping from foot to foot as if he was desperate to be somewhere else – anywhere else. Was this person really her kid brother?

Sitting in Derek's car, she'd been bored. When he had asked her to go along, she'd been in two minds initially. It was more time off work which she couldn't afford and she couldn't see what use she could possibly be. Then he'd explained that if they picked Michael up, he could probably use a familiar face and she'd seen his point, even if spending the whole day in the car wasn't exactly her idea of fun. All morning she'd sat listening to Capital Gold and watching the rain on the windscreen, until when it had finally cleared up, she simply had to get some fresh air and find a toilet. As far as she knew, the hunt was on around McDonald's, half a mile or more from the car and she'd seen the park as they'd driven past. She only wanted to use the loo and find a newsagents to buy a paper.

Seeing Michael in the park shocked her. And seeing him with the other youth was worse. There was something about the way they looked at each other, a camaraderie that came from long hours of association – the closeness of an old friend and confidant. It made Kate shiver. Derek had warned her that Michael might not be pleased to see them, but she hadn't really believed him. She'd expected a fight of some sort, a confrontation with whoever was holding Michael against his will, and she'd thought that he'd be grateful to be rescued.

Derek was holding his arm and Michael was struggling half-heartedly, as if he knew there was no point, but felt he had to make an effort. Eventually he stopped and simply stood there in the circle of police officers as if he'd given up.

Tossing his keys to one of the men, Derek told him to fetch the car to the park gates. Kate noticed that he hadn't let go of Michael's arm and it annoyed her. Her brother was supposed to be the victim, wasn't he? Not the guilty party.

'Mike?' The circle opened to admit her. 'Are you OK? Are you hurt?'

'I'm fine.' He wouldn't look at her. She wondered where he'd got the denim jacket. He didn't own a denim jacket. Perhaps he'd stolen it and that was why he was so obviously scared of the police.

'What happened to your hair?'

'I dyed it. Are mum and dad all right? I didn't want them to be worried about me. I just wanted them to know I was alive.'

Kate caught his look and was shocked into silence. Had he really been away just a few months? He'd left as a teenager, but there was no child behind his eyes now. Michael had grown up and it didn't look like he'd enjoyed the experience.

'What happened, Mike?' She wasn't sure she wanted to

know.

'Nothing.'

'So where have you been all this time? Who was the guy in the club?'

Michael's head shot up, but he still wouldn't answer her and Derek shook his head.

'This isn't the time.' He asked one of the other men to hold Michael, and took Kate to one side, talking in a low voice. 'Don't push him, Kate. I don't like the look of this.'

'What do you mean?'

'He's not exactly pleased to see us, is he? If I gave him the chance, he'd run again.' He frowned. 'Shit! I wanted to take them back to an address. That way we could have nailed whoever is behind all of this.'

'Behind what? Derek, I don't know what you're talking about.'

'Kate, look at him. Does that look like normal behaviour to you? Somebody somewhere has convinced him that he doesn't want to go home, and I want to know who it is and why. I'd hoped we could get it first hand, but it looks like we're going to have to rely on Michael's version of the story. If he'll tell us.' He hesitated. 'I'm no psychiatrist, but it's obvious that something has happened to him. I think we should get him away from this environment, before we do anything else. And have him see a doctor as soon as possible.'

'A *doctor?* He's all right, isn't he?'

Derek hesitated. 'Probably. But it might be as well to have him checked over. Especially if he's been sleeping rough.'

Sleeping rough? Why would he want to do that rather than come home? They were supposed to have rescued him, brought him home and life would go back to normal, but Kate knew that only happened on tv. She'd been kidding herself in thinking it was all over, and whatever experiences Michael had been through were going to take a long time to work their way out of his system.

The cars arrived and the group began to disperse, Derek ordering everyone to report in to his office at five for a debrief. There were four of them left, and Derek got into the back of the car with Michael, leaving Kate to sit in the front with the driver. She heard Derek introducing himself, making conversation in an attempt to get Michael to relax and open up. But he wasn't playing and Kate could see him in the wing mirror, staring out of the window and absently picking a loose thread on his sleeve. Every now and again he chewed a fingernail and he kept glancing at his watch, as if he was late for something.

'Do you have to be back somewhere, Michael?' Derek tried a different approach. 'Is someone going to miss you?'

'No.' Michael shook his head.

'What happened to your wrists?'

'What?' That cut through the shell and Michael twitched visibly, letting the sleeves of his jacket drop. He folded his arms.

'Your wrists, Michael. Did you hurt them? They look sore.'

Kate couldn't see and didn't want to turn round, but she wondered what Derek had spotted. Why on earth would Michael have marks on his wrists? Christ, perhaps he *had* been kidnapped – handcuffed, maybe. Imagination working overtime, Kate strained to listen to the conversation in the back over the noise of the car engine.

'Do you want to tell me about it?'

No reply.

'If someone's hurt you, tell me. We can do something about it.'

'I doubt it.'

'What makes you say that?'

Silence.

'Do you want to see a doctor? Would you rather talk to him?'

'I don't want to talk to anybody! Why don't you stop asking me such fucking stupid questions and leave me alone!'

Thoughts were running through Michael's head so fast that he couldn't keep up. This was what he'd wanted, wasn't it? He'd left a clue in McDonald's, it had been acted upon and he'd been rescued. End of story. Sod Joss and whatever he would think – Joss didn't matter, because he'd never see the man again. It was over, finished, and he could get back to his old life. *So why am I not happy?*

He was aware that he wasn't exactly being co-operative with the detectives – what was the guy's name? Derek, or something? – but he couldn't seem to help himself. He didn't want to talk, not about any of it, and the most important thing right now was avoiding the questions while finding some way of getting a hit tonight.

Derek had spotted the marks on his wrists. Michael had all but forgotten about them and they looked much worse than they felt. The problem was that now they'd want him to see a doctor and once that happened, everything would be out in the open – the smack and the sex – and he couldn't handle that. OK, so it hadn't been his fault and he could tell himself he'd been the victim, not the perpetrator, but it didn't seem to make a blind bit of difference to the way he felt. And he felt guilty. Guilty that he'd been stupid enough to go with Eddie in the first place, guilty that he hadn't put up more of a fight, and worst of all he felt that he'd led Lee on right from the start. If he'd done things differently, perhaps it wouldn't have happened the way it had. He could have run when he'd had the chance, the first time he'd gone out and then the incident with Lee would never have occurred. *Christ, it's all such a mess!*

Some time later, the car pulled in at his local police station. He'd been there once before, when the police had run a cycling safety scheme years ago. Then there'd been a dozen of them, all eager to look around the place and experience being locked in a cell for a few minutes. At ten years old, it had been an exciting day out and the cycling had been all but forgotten in their tour of the place. This time it was just him and he knew that if they locked him in anywhere, he'd crack up. He could feel the eyes of the staff boring holes through him as if they all knew what he'd done. As if they knew he was weak, he'd given in to the drugs, let them take control of his life. *Yeah, I got screwed, all right. In more ways than one.*

'If you want to sit down, Michael, I'll have some tea sent in.' Derek led him into a small windowless room containing a table and two chairs. All the furniture was bolted to the floor, and there was a tape deck on the table and a cctv camera in a wire cage high on the wall in the corner. It made him feel even more like a criminal and he sunk into the chair, shoulders hunched and arms folded. Somebody brought two more plastic chairs in and Kate sat down on one of them. She didn't say a word, other than to tell him that their parents were on their way. It made him cringe. Part of him wanted them more than anything else, but the other part knew that he could never be the same son to them as he'd been before. He'd grown up now and they weren't going to like the changes. *And there's an understatement!*

Derek brought some tea in on a tray – polystyrene cups and sugar sachets with little white plastic stirrers. Michael watched the steam curl above the cup, but didn't touch the drink.

He glanced at the closed door and felt a tiny knot of panic blossom deep down in his gut. Even if it wasn't locked, there was no way he was getting out of here any time soon.

'I've sent for the doctor.' Derek perched on the edge of the table.

Michael looked up sharply. 'No doctors.'

'Michael, you're hurt. Don't you want it looked at?'

'No.'

'Why not? What are you afraid of?'

'Nothing! Why don't you fuck off and let me go home?

I've done nothing wrong.'

Derek frowned. 'Nobody said you had. I can't let you go home just yet, Michael. I need to establish that you're OK. We need to know what happened to you – where you've been all this time.'

'Mike, what's wrong?' Kate touched his shoulder gently, but he pulled away, glaring at her. Sympathy was the last thing he needed. Aggression was all that was holding back the tears, and if he gave in to them, he was finished. He *couldn't* let them know what he'd done. How many men had had him in the three weeks he'd been out of it? Or afterwards when he'd been conscious? Christ, he didn't even *know!* His mind wouldn't let him access the memories and he wasn't sure he wanted to anyway. Ignorance wasn't exactly bliss, but it was easier to live with – not like the night with Lee, which was shining like a beacon in his mind.

His parents arrived and were shown into the interview room, accompanied by another uniformed police officer. With seats all round the walls, Michael was beginning to feel like he was on trial. His mum put her arms round him and Michael tried his best to return the embrace, but he couldn't do it. Michael Redford was dead and they should be burying him, not trying for a resurrection. His mother sensed the unease and pulled away uncertainly.

'So what happened, Michael?' Derek tried yet again. 'Why don't you start at the club? You had an argument with Jenny, right?'

'You've obviously spoken to her, so why ask me?' he said sullenly. *Did she tell you she was shagging her dealer? Did she?*

'Because I want to hear your side of it,' replied Derek patiently. 'Who was the guy you left with? Is he a friend of yours?'

No, he's a homosexual pimp, Michael wanted to say. That would shock them. Instead he simply nodded. It was becoming increasingly obvious that he wasn't going to get out of here until he told them *something*, and he couldn't afford to be in this room too long. Once the shakes started, he wouldn't be able to conceal the real issues.

'So what's his name?' There was a pause. 'Come on Michael. I'm trying to help you. The sooner we get some basic details, the sooner you can go home. I don't want to know everything and I appreciate it might be distressing for you – all I need to know right now is enough to establish that you're unharmed and that you'd be safe at home.'

Just play their game. 'I'll be safe at home.'

'It's more than likely,' Derek agreed. 'But I have to be certain. Now what's this man's name?'

'Eddie.' There didn't seem much point in changing the name. It would only get confusing. The best lies were those which merely distorted the truth.

'And where did you go with Eddie?'

'To his flat. He's just a mate. We had a few drinks and I crashed the night. It's no big deal.'

'For three months?'

Michael shrugged. 'It seemed like a good idea at the time. I was bored at college. We had some laughs.' He couldn't look at his parents' faces as he spoke and he wondered what they must be thinking. He sounded cold and selfish, and yet it was better they think that than know the truth.

'You left your coat and your mobile in the club.'

'It was a crap phone.'

Derek sighed. 'You're not a very good liar, are you, Michael? I suppose the note you wrote in McDonald's was a joke too, was it?'

'Something like that. I just …' Michael hesitated. 'Sorry.'

'You saw the email we left for you.' It was a statement rather than a question, and Michael realised that they'd known his rough location from the internet café. His pathetic scribblings had just been a confirmation.

Derek shook his head and stood up, leaving the room. He came back a few minutes later and told them that the doctor had arrived. Michael gripped the edge of the plastic chair, but said nothing. Bullshitting the doctor would be even harder, and although it was patently obvious that Derek didn't believe a word of his story, there wasn't much he could do about it. A doctor was a different matter altogether and he couldn't hide the evidence on his arms.

'Do me a favour, Michael?' The DI sat down again and leant across the desk.

'What?'

'I'll make a deal with you. You spend ten minutes with the doctor and I'll let you go home.'

Ten minutes? What could happen in ten minutes? 'All right.'

'Come with me.'

Michael stood up and followed him out of the room, ignoring the rest of his family. It was easier that way. In a room further down the corridor was a short stocky man who looked more like a professor than a doctor. Derek left him and closed the door.

'Hello, Michael. I'm Paul. Why don't you sit down?'

First names already? Michael did as he was told. The man couldn't *force* him to be examined, could he?

Paul smiled. 'Don't look so nervous. The DI tells me you've hurt your wrists. Would you like me to take a look?'

Michael pursed his lips, wondering what else Derek had said. Perhaps if he let the doctor examine his wrists, it might satisfy them for the time being. But then he had a fair idea that Derek had already guessed at least part of the truth by now – Michael wasn't so naïve as to think he was the first rape statistic in the station, nor the first junkie. He held out both hands, carefully exposing only his wrists. 'It's not much, honestly. It doesn't even hurt.'

The doctor took one hand and turned it palm up, fingers probing the marks. 'Does that hurt?' Michael shook his head. 'How did you do it? This looks like a burn.'

'Just fooling around.' Michael withdrew his hand carefully. 'It was nothing.'

'Was it?' He sat back, absently clicking the end of a ball-point pen in the top pocket of his sports jacket. 'Michael, I can't make you talk to me. But I can guarantee that nothing you say will go beyond this room. If that's what you want.'

No? It was tempting, but Michael didn't believe him. He might not report back, but Derek would only have to ask a few well-chosen questions and the truth would be obvious without the man having to reveal Michael's secrets. No, it was better that nobody knew.

'Are you sure you don't want to talk? I'm a good listener.'

Michael nodded and forced a smile. 'There really isn't anything to tell.'

'All right.' He fished in his pocket and brought out a business card, handing it to Michael. 'This is my card. Off-record, Michael – this won't go back to the DI, I promise – if you find you *do* want to talk to somebody, give me a ring. Day or night. I won't even tell the DI you called.'

Michael glanced at the card. The name had a string of letters after it and Michael wondered if it he was some sort of psychiatrist. If Derek hadn't guessed the truth, then this doctor certainly had. He nodded and pocketed the card. *Guilty by association.* Talking would only make the situation worse now. Glancing at his watch, he stood up to go. The doctor sighed, but Michael didn't look back as he returned to his family.

Two cars took them all home. Kate sat in the front of one with Derek. Despite her mother's tears, she couldn't help thinking that things weren't this easy. Michael had been as responsive as a piece of wood to mum's hugs, but they hadn't really noticed. Not yet. And when they did, Kate wondered what would happen.

The lies were transparent. Kate wondered how on earth

he actually expected any of them to believe him. It was obvious that he was playing Derek along, saying what he thought the man wanted to hear, but Kate worried that it confirmed that something bad really had happened, and Michael either couldn't or wouldn't talk about it.

'Will he disappear again?' She was talking with Derek in the hall, while Michael had allowed himself to be taken into the lounge and fussed over. Kate was keeping Derek talking, only half-realising that this could be the last time she'd be alone with him. Now that Michael was safely home, she had no excuse to see him again.

Derek shrugged. 'What do you want me to do, Kate?'

'But he's under eighteen.'

'I can't stop him leaving. When I took this on it was a *missing person* case. He was missing and we found him. If Michael chooses to leave of his own free will, he becomes a runaway.'

'Don't split hairs. I thought you cared.'

A hesitation. 'I do care.'

'Well you've a funny way of showing it. You're treating Michael like he's the criminal.'

'I do care,' Derek repeated. 'About you, Kate. God knows, I shouldn't be even thinking this, let alone saying it. Can I see you again?'

'What?' The question was unexpected and she didn't know what to say. Of course, she wanted to see him, but there was still Colin, and she knew she'd have to decide what to do with her life. But Colin could wait. Tonight was Michael's.

Derek didn't give her chance to reply, as if guessing he'd moved too fast. 'Never mind. I have to go. I'll be round tomorrow to speak to Michael again – a night's sleep might make him a bit more co-operative. But go easy on him. I think he's going to need some time to readjust. And Kate,' he added cryptically, 'watch him. Don't let him near a phone and if he tries to leave the house, call me.' He was gone before she could get him to explain, and she had the feeling it was a deliberate move on his part.

Kate watched him leave. In the lounge, Michael was standing at the window, his fingers gripping the top of the radiator and Kate wondered what he was thinking.

'Are you glad to be back?' Even as she said it, she realised how inane it sounded. Yet he didn't seem remotely pleased to be home – quite the opposite in fact. Michael looked like this was the last place on earth he wanted to be.

He turned slowly and sat on the edge of the window sill, folding his arms nervously. His hair was longer, different despite the colour, and his face was much thinner and paler than she remembered. There were dark circles under his eyes. Nobody said a word. Mum was still crying, and her father was staring at his son as if he'd never seen him before. Perhaps he hadn't. It was like inviting a stranger into the house and Kate wondered if the old Michael was still there somewhere, buried beneath this veneer of indifference.

Mrs Redford went to make some tea. Somehow, Kate didn't think her mother's cure for all ills would work this time; it would take more than routine tea and sympathy to get through to her brother. She took a step towards him and he stiffened.

'Take your jacket off, Mike. You *are* staying, aren't you?'

He nodded slowly. For a fleeting second he let the guard down and Kate saw a black hollowness behind his eyes. There was pain there – pain and terror – and yet all the rough edges had been smoothed away and it was a part of him now, a part of who he was, who he'd become. And as soon as she saw it, it was gone; the wall was up again, reflecting her own curiosity and worry back at her, but he knew she'd seen it as he turned away quickly, pulling off his jacket. She saw the marks on his wrists, red abrasions on his skin as though he'd been wearing sleeves with very tight elastic.

Michael pulled the sleeves of his sweatshirt down hurriedly and sat down in one of the armchairs, curling his legs up underneath him. He took the tea his mother gave him, holding it with both hands and sipping it carefully. Too carefully, Kate thought as she watched. His hands were shaking and he seemed edgy and restless. She needed to get him away from their parents, she decided. Maybe he'd talk to her then, tell her what had happened to him – what was still happening inside his head. For the first time she thought that Derek might have been right when he'd mentioned doctors and psychiatrists. But Michael wasn't nuts, was he? Just a very scared teenager who'd evidently been through something he wasn't in a hurry to discuss.

Dinner was a strained affair that night. Michael picked at his food listlessly and pushed most of it round his plate. Nobody else felt much like eating either and they were all watching him, which only seemed to make him feel even more uncomfortable. He was fidgeting constantly, biting his fingers, eyes darting around the room as though he expected something to jump out of the shadows at any moment. When his father suggested a drink in an effort to calm him down, Michael jumped at the offer and downed the scotch in one go, pouring himself a large refill from the decanter on the sideboard. Nobody commented and he seemed to relax a little and eat a bit of the meal.

Their parents went to bed at about ten and Kate hoped it would give her the opportunity to talk more openly to her brother. He'd drunk most of the scotch by now, but it didn't seem to be having much effect on him and he was getting more and more restless, channel-hopping with the television remote control but not really watching the tv. Kate wanted to phone Derek, to ask him what she should do, but she didn't like to disturb him.

Michael was sweating profusely. He kept wiping his face with the sleeve of his sweatshirt and glancing quickly at Kate to see if she'd noticed. He was jumpy too, reacting to every sound in the house, and the neighbour's car starting up made him look round wildly. Sitting on the edge of the chair, he lost his balance, knocking the remote control off the arm. Regaining his seat, he swore loudly and reached for the remote where it had fallen on the carpet.

And suddenly Kate understood. *Oh, Mike! No!* The minute he stretched his arm forward and his sleeve fell back, she knew what all this was about. From her work at the surgery, she'd seen it before, seen the itchy restlessness of drug withdrawal, and drowning the signals his body was sending him with alcohol wasn't going to help. The only thing which was going to make Michael feel better was a shot of whatever it was he'd been taking.

She met his eyes and for once, he didn't look away. Leaning forwards from the sofa, she grabbed his hand firmly and pushed up the sleeve, trying to mask the horror she felt at seeing the mess on his forearm. Michael didn't resist – it was as if it was a relief to have the secret out at last – but when Kate let go, he pulled his sleeve down sharply, his face flushing bright red.

'So now you know.' He hesitated. 'Kate, I need money.'

'What is it? Heroin?' His behaviour was starting to make sense now.

He nodded. 'It wasn't my fault. I didn't want it to happen.'

'Oh, God.' She didn't know what to say. *If you didn't want it to happen, then why did you let it?* But that wasn't what he needed to hear, not now.

'It's a long story. I'll tell you one day, I promise. Please Kate, you've got to give me some money.'

'So you can shoot it up? Get real, Michael. You need professional help, not more drugs.'

His eyes were bright, mirror-shiny with his body's need for heroin. Kate didn't know what to do. If she gave him money, where would he go? Back out on the streets? Would they ever see him again? 'Michael, I can't. If you get caught, you could end up in prison.' She hesitated. 'Let me take you to the hospital.'

'NO!' He jumped up, backing away to the door. 'No hospitals. No doctors. I'll kill myself first. I will.'

He looked as if he meant it, too. She stood up. 'All right, Michael, I promise. No doctors. Now sit down and let's try to work this out.'

He didn't move. 'Kate, if you love me as your brother, you've got to give me some cash. Please!'

'All right!' Kate didn't want her parents to wake up and hear this. 'Just calm down a minute and we'll sort something out.'

'I don't want fucking sorting out! I want money!'

'Ssh.' She followed him through to the kitchen and watched him rummage through one of the drawers. 'What are you looking for?'

'Mum's purse. It's here somewhere. I *know* it is!'

'You can't steal mum's money!'

'I have to.' He found what he was looking for and opened the purse quickly.

Kate snatched it out of his hand. 'No, Mike. This isn't the answer. You need help. Let me help you.'

'If you want to help, then leave me alone!' There was a desperate look in his eyes and his breathing was quick and shallow. 'Give it to me.'

She backed away. This wasn't Michael any more, this was some crazy junkie coming towards her and she was suddenly scared, not knowing how far he'd go to get what he needed. But she couldn't give in and let him walk out of the house and back to wherever he'd been for the past few months. She couldn't give up without a fight. Somehow she had to get through to the real Michael, beyond the drugs and the pain. What was it Derek had said? *Call me if he leaves. Watch him.* Derek had known, or at least guessed what was going on. Why hadn't he told her? How was she supposed to stop Michael leaving? What did he expect her to *do*, for Christ's sake?

'Kate, I don't want to hurt you.' He was crying now.

'Please. Just give me the money.' Leaning against the worktop, he sank slowly down to the floor, his head in his hands and shaking violently.

She couldn't stand it. She crouched down on the floor next to him and put her arms around him, pulling her close to him and stroking his hair. Michael collapsed against her, all the fight gone and she felt him relax and lean into her. Then, before she realised what he was doing, he pushed his weight onto her, sending her toppling backwards onto the kitchen floor. By the time she'd picked herself up, he'd snatched the purse back, opened it and emptied the contents onto the slate tiles. Grabbing the notes, he ran from the kitchen, turning in the doorway.

His face was wet from tears. 'Kate, I'm sorry. I didn't want it to be like this. But I have to go. There isn't any other way.'

She didn't move. There was no point in trying to stop him – he was stronger than her and beyond reasoning with.

He'd been home less than six hours.

FOURTEEN

Fifteen pounds. *Fifteen fucking pounds!* It was hardly going to get him very far, let alone buy him any drugs. Michael stuffed the money into the pocket of his jacket and jogged down the street towards the tube station.

He wiped his face on his sleeve. Crying had worked wonders, although it hadn't been just for show. Sitting on the kitchen floor he'd finally realised that he'd cut his last ties with home and he could never go back. The evening meal had proved that to him. He was an alien in his own house. And they didn't even *know!* What would things be like when they did find out what had happened, when Kate told them he was on smack?

He'd been stupid to write the note in McDonald's, and he only hoped Joss would see it that way. Not that he was under any illusions about how Joss would react – he knew he'd have to do some begging to persuade Joss to take him back, but it didn't seem to matter, not when measured up against the image in his mind of a syringe full of heroin. So what if he had to grovel a bit; it would be nothing compared to what he'd gone through with Eddie and he'd survived that.

It wasn't until Michael got as far as Earl's Court on the tube, that he realised he didn't have a clue where he was going. All he knew about the flat was that it was in the East End, in an Asian area near a park and a McDonald's. He'd never known the address, he'd never needed to, but how the hell was he going to find the place without it? It had never occurred to him before and it made him panic. Sitting with his feet on the opposite seat, he wondered how he was going to get a fix if he didn't even know where to go. He shivered and wiped his forehead again; he'd already had one or two strange looks and the last thing he needed was to get stopped by the police. Michael was getting desperate and he wasn't sure himself just how far he would go to get a shot.

Come on, Redford. Think. OK, so he couldn't spend the night traipsing around the East End trying to find the flat – that much was obvious. He'd pass out long before he got anywhere. No he needed to get some temporary relief, which would hopefully give him enough of a clear head to start searching methodically, perhaps checking out McDonald's in the phone book, and finding them with an A to Z. *Why didn't I check them out before I left home?* There couldn't be that many in London, surely? But he couldn't do that tonight. He was far too strung out to think straight and what he needed right now, before anything else, was a fix. It was close on eleven and he was six hours overdue.

Michael got off the tube at South Kensington and changed onto the Piccadilly line. His feet knew where he was going even if his mind hadn't quite caught on to the idea. There was only one place he knew of where he was sure to be able to make a deal, and that was around King's Cross. He remembered seeing a recent documentary about the red-light districts of London, where anything was for sale if the price was right. Sex and drugs were there for the asking, if one knew the right question, and what he needed was the assistance of someone like Lee, someone who knew the streets and knew where it was safe to deal. But Lee wasn't here and he was on his own.

By the time he arrived at the station, he was shaking so

hard, he could barely keep a grip on his ticket and it took him two attempts to stuff it into the machine. Then he wandered across the concourse and looked around.

The main line station was eerily quiet. There were groups of youths hanging around and one or two businessmen in suits waiting for a late train home. A girl stood nervously alone, glancing at her watch every couple of minutes and an old woman ambled back and forth across the tiles, two carrier bags clutched in each hand. Most of the shops and kiosks had closed up for the night, except for one tobacconist which looked as though it was open twenty-four hours a day.

Michael sat down heavily on a plastic bench. He didn't know where to start. His head was aching and he felt like curling up in a corner and sleeping, but it wouldn't solve his problems and he couldn't afford the luxury.

'You OK, mate?' There was a boy standing in front of him, hair cut razor-short. Thin and wiry, he looked about sixteen and was dressed in skin-tight jeans and a leather jacket. He wore two hoop earrings in one ear.

He nodded. It hurt. It was getting difficult to focus.

'Suit yourself.' The boy turned to go.

'Wait.' Michael couldn't let the chance slip away. 'I need to score.'

The boy stopped and turned round slowly, raising his eyebrows. He looked Michael up and down for a moment. 'You for real?'

'What does it look like?' Michael glanced around the concourse and pushed up the sleeve of his jacket, showing the boy his arm.

'You got cash?'

He nodded again, hoping he wouldn't be asked how much. It was worth a go.

'Come with me.'

Michael stood up and followed him across the concourse. The main road outside was bright even in the dark; there were neon shop signs, cafes were still open and men drifted in and out with cigarettes in their hands. They crossed over Euston Road and down a maze of side streets; Michael wished he'd brought some kind of protection with him, a knife or something. Anything to give him a bit of confidence.

Halfway down the road, there was a group of youths sitting on a low wall beneath a streetlight and Michael was brought to stand in front of them. A mixture of white, black and Asian, they stared at him in amusement. One of them had an alsatian on a long lead; the dog was nosing around a split bag of rubbish on the pavement.

'Guy wants a fix.' The boy joined the jury on the wall. Behind them, the rows of terraced houses were dark and silent. Some were boarded up, their windows covered with peeling fly-posters advertising out-of-date rock concerts.

'Got any money?' A black teenager was rolling a joint. He lit it and took a long drag, then held it out. 'You wanna smoke?'

Michael shook his head. 'I've got money.' He wondered if he'd completely lost his mind. This was the kind of scene which shouldn't exist outside of films. What was to stop them taking his money and kicking his head in for good measure?

'How much?'

'A few quid.'

They howled with laughter at that. Even the boy who'd brought him. The joint was passed along the line and back again before anyone spoke. 'What d'you think you'll buy with that, kid?'

Michael stared at his feet miserably. There was nothing he could do without money. The boy and two others jumped down off the wall and came up to him, circling him warily, then the boy pushed up his sleeves and showed the other two his arms. Michael didn't react, not even when he felt hands going through his pockets and removing his money.

He felt a hand on his back and he flinched away from

the touch. It was still painful and he couldn't help himself. One of them studied his face and then lifted his jacket and sweatshirt. He whistled softly. 'You playin' with some nasty people, brother.'

They stepped away and picked over what they'd stolen. 'What's your name, pretty boy?'

Michael didn't answer, until he felt a blade at his throat and hot breath in his face.

'I'm askin' your name.'

'Mikey,' he said without thinking.

'And you want smack, do you, Mikey? How bad?'

'Please.' It couldn't get any worse. He could run, he shouldn't even be here, but his body wouldn't let him – not if there was a chance of getting what he'd come for.

'What wouldja do for it, Mikey? Look at me.' There was a hand in his hair, yanking his head back. The boy in front of him held a tiny bag of brown powder, a used syringe and a needle in the palm of his hand. 'You want?'

Michael reached out, but he stepped backwards teasingly. 'How far will you go, pretty boy? Wouldja take it up your cute little arse?'

He knew he would. It was no different from Eddie. He nodded and the group exploded into gales of laughter again.

The boy shook his head briefly. 'You ain't my type,' he said softly. 'Anybody else interested?'

They circled him again, hands on his hair and body, stroking and touching him. He clenched his fists, suppressing the urge to lash out as a finger traced a line down his crotch.

'You a queer?'

'No.' The words came out in a hiss.

'Fuckin' pansy rent boy? Huh?'

It was getting harder not to retaliate. 'No.' His self-control would have impressed him if his mind hadn't been on other things.

'Then what you doin' round here?' The voice was

challenging. 'You're not a smack-'ead, pretty boy. You don' look the part – even with these.' He stroked Michael's bare forearm. 'But someone's done you over, all right. What's your story?'

'I want,' said Michael, 'a hit. You've taken the money, so give me the fucking gear.'

'Money? What money?' He turned to the others. 'Anyone see any money?'

They shook their heads slowly. 'No money, pretty boy. Must've been mistaken. Now fuck off out of here, before your mummy wonders where you are.' The leader of the gang stepped up close to him and Michael was about to reply, when he saw car headlights turning into the street. A patrol car, cruising the area, but it scattered the gang like skittles.

'Time we was gone.' The boy with the bag tossed it and the syringe into the gutter, from where Michael just had time to retrieve them before the car drove slowly past him. Hands in pockets, he walked slowly back up towards the station, forcing himself not to run, but the car didn't return. Neither did the gang and Michael let out his breath, realising he'd had a lucky escape.

Kate took the phone into the lounge, closed the door and dialled Derek's mobile with shaking hands.

He answered on the first ring, voice thick with sleep. 'Yes?'

'Did I wake you?'

'Kate?' There was a pause. 'Sorry. Early night. I was up at four this morning.'

He sounded so calm, so normal, and Kate could feel the tears coming. 'Derek, he's gone. I couldn't stop him.'

'What happened?' He knew what she was talking about.

'Can you come round?' She didn't like to ask him, but she couldn't talk about it on the phone.

'All right.' He sighed. 'Half an hour.'

'Thanks. I'll be watching for you.' The line went

abruptly dead and she hung up. She wondered if she should call Colin too, but somehow, his comfort would only complicate matters and she didn't need it. For the time being, she could kid herself that Derek was coming because he had a professional interest. It was his case, after all, and still not closed – he had a right to know what was going on.

After what seemed like an age, she heard the car draw up outside and took her coat and a key before slipping out to meet him. With any luck, her parents would sleep through it all and at least she'd have something useful to tell them in the morning, something in addition to the real truth of what had happened while Michael had been away. *Michael's a drug addict, mum. It will probably kill him in the end.* She'd seen it before. The surgery had several registered addicts, coming in regularly for their supplies of methadone.

Derek leaned across and opened the car door. 'You want to go somewhere, or just sit here and talk?'

'Drive.' Kate got in and shut the door. 'Is there anywhere we can get a drink this late?'

Derek nodded and eased the car away from the kerb. Kate glanced at him. He was wearing a scruffy pair of tracksuit bottoms and an old sweater and was badly in need of a shave. He looked positively gorgeous.

They ended up at a small wine bar with which Derek was evidently well acquainted, judging by the reception they got on arrival, despite his clothing. Kate found herself wondering who he'd brought here before as he came back from the bar with two glasses of red wine. There were no more than half a dozen people and the art deco lighting was minimal. Soft music played from speakers hidden behind potted plants.

Derek squeezed into the booth opposite her. 'So what's all this about, Kate?'

'Michael.'

'Well I didn't think you'd dragged me out of bed to

discuss the weather.' He paused and took her hand. 'Sorry. I get scratchy when I'm woken. What happened?'

'He raided mum's purse, pushed me away and ran.' She twirled the stem of her glass. 'But it gets worse, Derek – he took the money for drugs. He's on heroin.'

He didn't seem surprised as he took a large sip of wine. 'That explains a great deal. It fits his behaviour earlier, not to mention his appearance. How did you find out?'

'I saw his arm.' Her voice caught. 'Christ, it was like looking at a map of the underground.'

'That bad?'

She nodded, blinking back tears. 'He was jumpy all evening. The atmosphere was awful. He looked so desperate when he ran off.' She hesitated. 'I can't tell mum and dad!'

'I don't see that you can keep it from them, Kate. If he's gone, they have a right to know why.'

'They wouldn't understand.'

'Do you?' He looked at her, his voice calm. Kate shook her head and rubbed her eyes. It was all getting on top of her, and she badly needed a shoulder to have a good cry on.

Derek was looking across the bar, at nothing in particular and Kate frowned. Something wasn't quite right. 'Derek, did you already know?'

'Know what?'

'About Michael? The drugs?'

He shook his head. 'Let's just say I had my suspicions.'

'And you didn't tell me?'

'Kate, they're only suspicions. Not facts. You get a feel for things in this job.'

She hesitated. '*Are* only suspicions? What else do you know?'

He shook his head. 'Nothing. Not yet.' He paused. 'I'm sorry. I got it badly wrong. I just thought he'd be better off at home than at the hospital. An ounce of TLC is generally worth a ton of medical advice and Michael has to *want* to be helped, before a hospital can do anything for him. Heroin affects the mind as much as the body, you know.' He sighed. 'My mistake, I'm afraid. I didn't realise it had gone that far – if I'd thought for a moment he'd do a runner, I'd never have let him go home with you.'

He had a point. Short of tying him up or locking him in, nothing would have stopped Michael leaving tonight. And Derek wasn't to know that tender loving care wasn't exactly the Redford house style. It wasn't her parents fault – they'd just never really been able to express their feelings. Military discipline didn't leave much room for emotions. There was plenty of love about, it was just that nobody ever verbalised it, and they'd got out of practice with hugs once they'd left childhood behind.

'So what do you think?' she asked after a moment.

'About what?' his voice was sharp. 'I'm not in the business of *thinking*, Kate. Not like that, anyway; speculation isn't my style. If I know anything, you'll be the first to hear it, but until then I'll keep my opinions to myself. Now drink your wine and I'll take you home.'

She didn't answer. It sounded like he'd made the mistake of thinking out loud before. Bouncing ideas off colleagues was all very well, but sharing them outside of work was a different matter and to be fair to him, it was something Kate could understand. She had enough problems with patient confidentiality herself and had once been accused of letting something slip outside of the surgery. Luckily, the matter had gone no further than a verbal warning, but she knew what she'd done and had since been careful to keep work and her social life separate.

She took a mouthful of wine. 'So can you find him, Derek?'

'Maybe.' He was twisting a gold ring on his right hand. 'But is that what you want?'

'I'm sorry?'

'Oh, Kate.' He pushed the ring back on his finger and took her hand again. 'Stop being naïve. I can't *make* him stay. I'm a police officer, not a social worker. If Michael's on heroin, you have to ask yourself how he's funding the habit. The chances are it's something illegal.'

'You're saying you won't help?' She drew her hand away and wished he'd stop talking in riddles.

'I'm saying I can't treat Michael as a missing person anymore.' Derek hesitated. 'Kate, I'm not dropping the case. There are other considerations – such as who the other kid was. Where the gear's coming from. And how Michael got those marks on his wrists.'

'So you *will* help?' She didn't understand what he was trying to tell her. Was he on her side or not?

Derek nodded. 'Yes, I'll help. I'll find him again. It will be harder this time as they know we're onto them, but there are ways. But I warn you, Kate,' he added gently, 'you may not thank me for it in the end.'

The station toilets were surprisingly busy for so late at night and Michael had to retreat into a cubicle before he got a chance to wash the syringe and needle under the tap. Terrified that the gang would catch up with him, he let the water get as hot as he could stand and rinsed the syringe several times, before finally filling it. By this time, his hands were shaking so much it took him a full minute to tear the corner off the polythene bag and he backed into a cubicle and sat down on the toilet. He couldn't afford to lose any of the precious contents as he carefully poured the brown powder into the syringe through a funnel made from toilet paper. It was fine and dusty and made him sneeze.

He was shivering now, a combination of cold, anticipation and a raw fear about what he was doing. Joss' first instruction had been never to use cheap heroin, but Joss had never expected him to be in this situation and if he wanted a fix tonight, this was all he was going to get. If this brown crap had been cut with anything, well, his body was just going to have to cope with it as best it could and to hell with the consequences. This was no time to be fussy.

Michael shook the syringe gently and squinted at the contents. He'd never administered an injection before – none of them had – it was the one thing Joss always did himself, even with Eddie. Pushing up his left sleeve, he studied his arm; it was difficult to see his skin properly as most of the inside of his elbow and forearm was covered in a mass of scabs and bruises. He was never going to find a vein there, not with perfect eyesight and a steady hand, never mind his own current inadequacies and he sighed, bending his hand back and examining several small veins in his wrist. That would have to do. If he left it much longer, he'd be incapable of doing it at all and he didn't want to be found here unconscious, discovered by a cleaner tomorrow morning.

Gritting his teeth, Michael pricked his skin over the vein, pushed and depressed the plunger slowly. It hurt more than he'd expected. Then he dropped the syringe onto the tiles and leaned against the cubicle wall, closing his eyes as the tide carried him out. It wasn't as vibrant or as sharp as the buzz he got from Joss' gear, but it was enough – enough to steady his hands and calm his nerves. Enough, he hoped, to give him at least a fighting chance of surviving the night and finding the flat.

Michael scrambled to his feet and carefully wrapped the syringe in several paper towels, before dropping it in the bin. The next task was to find somewhere to spend the night.

FIFTEEN

He was awake at dawn. Not that he'd slept much during the night, curled up in an office doorway behind a large bush in a terracotta tub. The branches had been some shelter from the wind, but the marble-effect portico was cold and uncomfortable and Michael decided that London was pretty miserable at night. The only doorways which appeared to offer any kind of decent shelter came complete with security guards, and he'd been threatened twice before he'd found this place.

As soon as it was light enough to see, he was on his feet, jumping up and down to ease the stiffness in his legs. He was hungry, but couldn't afford food. The gang had taken most of his money, but they'd left the change and he counted it out in the palm of his hand, digging into his pockets for any leftover cash from the times he'd been out with Lee. Unless he wanted to walk all the way to the East End, it was going to get spent on a Travelcard, which meant that breakfast was out of the question. He needed an A to Z as well, or a map of some sort which would enable him to locate all the McDonald's restaurants in the area and he'd also have to be on the lookout for the police. Back near the park would be the first place they'd look for him, and they had the advantage of local knowledge, not to mention transport.

The odds stacked against him were depressingly high. Somehow he had to find the flat without leading the police back with him. If they were waiting for him in the area, all they'd have to do would be to follow him and he'd never know who he was trying to avoid. It was an impossible task.

First things first. Michael made his way back to King's Cross and the toilets where he washed his hands and face and tried to make himself look a little more respectable. The circles under his eyes had reached bin-bag proportions and he looked like he hadn't slept or eaten in a week. He felt like it too. His head was pounding and there was an acidic taste in the back of his throat which he longed to wash away with a cup of coffee. He'd need to score again soon, as well – last night's fix had been adequate but wouldn't last much longer.

He browsed the maps available in the station shops. The cheapest A to Z he could find was a pocket sized version and he knew he couldn't afford it, not if he wanted to get the tube as well. Walking past a coffee shop and the smell was too much for him – he gave in to his thirst and bought himself a large polystyrene cup of milky coffee, savouring each mouthful as if it were the elixir of life itself. He sat down on the tiles, leaned back against a billboard and held the cup in both hands, feeling about three hundred percent more alive. He closed his eyes. Even the thought of having to walk the entire way didn't seem quite so daunting with a hot drink in his hands.

A sharp noise made him open his eyes and there was a fifty pence coin at his feet. Without thinking, he drained the dregs from the cup and held it out. The station was starting to fill up with the morning commuters and he was surprised how many people stopped and dropped a coin or two. But it wasn't more than a few minutes before he saw station uniforms approaching and he scrambled to his feet, feeling like the tramp he obviously looked like. He'd seen people like himself before and always despised them, wondering why they couldn't get off their bums and get a job like everyone else; now he was walking the other side of the line and it felt more like a tightrope. He was balancing by sheer will-power and it wouldn't take much to topple him off.

Losing himself in the crowds, he counted his spoils and bought a Travelcard before he got distracted by food. Then he hung around the shops, watching the stream of travellers buying their morning papers. He knew perfectly well what he was going to do, but couldn't quite bring himself to admit it just yet. Studying the pattern of people, he was putting off the inevitable for as long as possible, pretending that he was watching them out of curiosity and not because he was trying to identify any potential security agents, until finally he stood up and strolled into one of the walk-in kiosks, choosing the biggest on the concourse.

It was a new experience for him, seeing people refusing to meet his gaze and moving away as if he had some contagious disease. Yet eyes were on him from all angles, covertly – almost indecently – as if they expected him to steal, just because of his appearance. It made what he had to do even harder. He couldn't afford to get caught. Not now.

Michael wandered around for a while, trying to get them used to his presence. He picked up a magazine and leafed through it idly, carefully replacing it on the shelf and moving on until eventually he came to the maps and guide books. Standing in the corner, he selected one of the pocket A to Zs and he held it in one hand while he reached up with the other to get something off the top shelf. At the same time, he dropped the book into the inside pocket of his denim jacket. Retrieving the map from the top shelf, he opened it and studied it for a moment before shaking his head and replacing it. Then he turned and made his way out of the shop, forcing himself not to run.

It was so easy it was embarrassing. Outside the station, he stopped to examine his trophy and contemplate what he'd done. He wasn't proud of the theft, but shit, he had to find the flat somehow and he couldn't see any other way of doing it. He consoled himself with the thought that he'd come back some time and repay the money, although part of him laughed at the very idea. What they didn't know about, they weren't going to miss.

Cocky with success, he stole a pencil from a stationery shop. They were watching him from the minute he walked in, but they didn't stop him leaving and he wanted to go back inside and wave it under their noses. *Stupid fucking bastards.* If they couldn't catch him at it, he wasn't going to help them.

Michael found a telephone box. The telephone itself was out of order but it did have a set of directories in metal holders – at least it used to have; when he turned them right way up, there were just shreds of burned paper attached to the metal spines. But there was a McDonald's across the road, busy with commuters eating hasty breakfasts en route to their offices. He wandered in and found what he was looking for – a large wall chart of all the restaurants in London. He spent the next twenty minutes methodically marking his A to Z with all the McDonald's restaurants in the East End, chewing the end of the pencil and frowning when anybody got too close to him. He wondered if the staff were scared to approach him, if he looked as unstable as he felt and whether he actually would attack if cornered. But he wrote quickly, not wanting to give them a chance to call the police, as that would finish his search before it even started.

It took him most of the day to work through the map. By the third McDonald's he was so hungry he was contemplating rummaging through the bins outside. It seemed a cruel twist of fate that he was searching for a fast-food restaurant when he didn't even have the price of a coffee in his pocket; he'd spent the last of his change on chocolate, but it hadn't come to much and it had simply made him thirsty again. Back on the tube, he felt like he was wandering around in circles and there was a tight knot of fear in his stomach as he began to contemplate the thought that he might not find the flat today. There was no money for another fix tonight. Unless, of course, he really swallowed his pride – there were other ways of making money.

No! Michael jumped on the idea, trying to kill it before it had time to blossom, but it refused to die completely. He'd done enough over the last twenty-four hours – risked a kicking or worse for the last fix, slept rough and turned thief for what he needed today. But how else was he going to get a shot? He'd been prepared to do it with the gang – no matter how much he tried to convince himself he wouldn't have gone ahead with it, he knew he would. The heroin had too strong a hold on him to spare his feelings now and Michael knew that if it came down to it, he'd do whatever he had to in order to get a fix. *Don't even go there, Redford. There are a few hours yet.* But it made Eddie seem positively recreational.

Michael crossed off another address in his A to Z and jumped off the tube. Another journey where people had preferred to stand rather than share his seat. It hurt, but he couldn't blame them. The unknown could be frightening and he didn't even know himself any more.

This place looked more promising. The area even smelled right; the combination of Asian spices and exotic fruits made his stomach growl and the thought of food was now on a level pegging with the thought of shooting up. Michael wondered which of them would come out the winner. At least he could steal supper if he was in any state to do it by then.

Chewing the pencil again, he consulted the map. If he was right, it should just be a matter of a couple more turns before he was on the main road. Running a hand through his hair, he prepared himself for another miserable failure as he turned the corner and stopped when he saw the gate in front of him. A park. *The* park? He checked the map again, but it didn't make him any the wiser – there were enough parks with ornamental lakes and one looked much the same as another on paper.

Michael pocketed the book and leaned on the open gate in the late afternoon breeze. There was a laurel hedge in front of him and the path went both ways. Stepping forwards, he crept up to the left side of the hedge and peered around cautiously, looking for something familiar.

Ironically, it was the man that he recognised. Or not so much the man himself, but where he was sitting. Seeing the open newspaper on his knee, Michael felt cogs slipping into place in his mind as the scene slid into memory like a slide show. A different angle this time – he was *behind* the row of benches, looking past the man across the lake to the two exits in the far corners of the park. He hadn't known there was a way out here, it was too well hidden behind the hedge and he wished he'd seen it last time as it might have saved a great deal of hassle. Except that if he'd taken this way out, Lee would have been caught in his place.

Radio static made him jump and Michael realised the man wasn't just admiring the scenery. He was probably CID and making no real effort to hide the radio handset in his lap, not expecting anyone to come up behind him in this way. Then again, they might have called in the drug squad by now, which wouldn't have surprised him after seeing the expression on Kate's face when he'd left last night. Either way it meant that the hunt was on and somehow he had to retrace his steps back to the flat without being seen. Because it was the flat they were really interested in, of course. Michael was a means to an end, but he wasn't naïve enough to think that he merited this amount of resource input – surveillance on this scale implied that CID meant business. Arrests and seizures were the real objectives now.

Michael turned and left the way he'd come. Back on the side road, he pulled out the A to Z and from what he now knew about the local geography, he marked the other two park exits on the map and drew the route he'd taken back to the flat on previous occasions. Then he drew an alternative, taking him in a wide circle and avoiding all the main roads.

When he finally found the alley and the front door, he felt like sitting on the pavement and crying his eyes out with sheer relief. It had taken him the entire day and he'd compromised just about every code of ethics he'd had, but he'd finally done it. Shoving the front door open with one shoulder, he stopped for second as it registered that it hadn't been locked. Then he closed it carefully behind him and practically ran up the stairs to the top floor, pounding on the door with both fists.

There was no reply. Michael hammered again, wondering where the hell they were. The flat was virtually never unoccupied. Remembering Lee's comments about a reinforced door, he knew he'd never be able to break in, so he sat down in the corner of the landing. There was nothing else he could do except wait.

It was dark before he realised that nobody was coming back.

SIXTEEN

She knew they were about to have a row. She could sense it in the same way you can sense a storm brewing by the change in the atmosphere, the tension in the air. The look on Colin's face had been enough to spark it off and Kate had been fanning the flame for the last forty minutes, wanting to get it out into the open – knowing that she couldn't delay the inevitable any longer.

'They have to know, Kate.'

'No.' She shook her head. Colin wanted her to tell her parents of her latest discovery. But Colin didn't know them like she did, Colin couldn't predict their reaction the way that she could and Kate knew when enough was enough. She'd told them Michael had left during the night when she'd been asleep, and she'd replaced the money in the purse and said nothing more about the incident, other than to Derek and Colin. There'd be time enough for the truth if Derek could find him and if he couldn't, well perhaps it was better that they should remember him the way he had been. This time, Kate had no illusions that it was going to be easy – she was well aware that she might never see her brother again. And it would be *his* choice, *his* decision. Through work, she'd seen families torn apart over drugs; on a year's placement in a hospital, she'd witnessed the Jekyll and Hyde transformations which drugs could induce and she knew they had a time constraint now. If they didn't find Michael soon, he wasn't going to be worth finding.

'What gives you the right to play God?' Colin wanted to know. 'He's your brother, not your son. He's not your responsibility.'

'Isn't he?' Kate turned away, swallowing the last of the coffee and banging the mug down on the table; Colin immediately picked it up and carried it through to the kitchen. It made her want to scream. Weren't men supposed to be the untidy ones? Somebody should have told Colin that even in modern life, men were still the ones who made the mess while women cleaned it up after them.

He'd done nothing wrong, that was the worst of it. He'd stood by her these past weeks and refrained from commenting when she'd mentioned having a drink with Derek. It annoyed her – she wanted him to react, to show some kind of jealousy – anything which would give her a lever on him. But Colin was all shiny smooth composure, without a chink in the armour for Kate to break through.

She followed him into the kitchen. Colin was sitting at the pine kitchen table and fiddling with the pepper mill. Small grains of pepper spilled and he pushed them around with one finger.

'What do you want, Kate?' he asked without turning.

She wanted to put her arms around him, but she couldn't. This was it – the moment of truth – and she had a fleeting second of panic, wondering if she was doing the right thing. 'I don't know what you mean,' she said, knowing perfectly well. Shit, couldn't she at least spare him the indignity of having to spell it out?

'This isn't about Michael at all, is it? It's about us.' His voice was neutral, not a trace of emotion and suddenly Kate didn't want this at all.

Too late. 'Yes.' She sat down opposite him and tried to take his hand but he pulled away gently. There was no accusation in his eyes, just a calm resignation.

'Kate, I've waited for you for long enough and I think it's time you told me the truth. *Is* there something going on with this guy?'

'Colin, I think we should call it off.'

'You haven't answered my question.'

Damn you! Why won't you play the game? He didn't intend to make it easy for her, that much was obvious, and Kate was about to speak again when the phone rang. Colin glanced at her for a moment as if he thought she'd arranged it on purpose, before standing up and answering it. Shaking his head, Kate heard him say, 'Yes it is. Hang on a moment, she's here.' He handed her the receiver.

'Hello?'

'Kate? It's me.'

Derek. Such timing. It must be important if he'd tracked her down to Colin's house. She hadn't been home since leaving work and the battery on her mobile was flat again. 'What's happened? Have you found him?'

'Not exactly. Can you come down to the station? I want to show you something.'

'Now?'

'As soon as it's convenient.' There was a pause and the tone of his voice changed slightly. 'You got problems?'

'Something like that.' Kate sighed. 'All right. I'll be there as soon as I can.' She pressed the *talk* button to disconnect. 'Colin, I have to go.'

'I know.'

'Really, Colin. Derek wants me to go down to the police station.'

'Then you'd better go, hadn't you?' He turned away when she tried to kiss him and she shook her head, picking up her bag. She'd been granted a reprieve, but she knew it wouldn't change anything.

She got as far as the front door before he stopped her, a hand on her arm. She resisted the urge to shake it off, not wanting to hear whatever it was he was going to say.

'Kate, we need to talk. This isn't going to go away.'
She relented. 'I know. Later.'
He nodded. 'Good luck.'
Kate went straight out to the car.

Derek was waiting in reception for her, fingers impatiently tapping the counter. He kissed her cheek instinctively and then stopped, realising what he'd just done. Kate almost laughed, except there were other things on her mind.

'What have you found, if not Michael?'

'His friend.' Derek led her up to his office, sat down and pushed a photograph across the table at her. It wasn't very clear and taken from an odd angle, but was obviously Michael and the other youth sitting on the bench in the park the other day, just before she'd seen them. It was a disturbing picture and Kate couldn't quite put her finger on what wasn't right. She was beginning to wonder just what her brother had got mixed up in while he'd been away and yet at the same time, she wasn't sure she wanted to know.

'Who took this?'

'One of my men from the toilets. A bit out of focus, but he *was* standing on the washbasin at the time.'

'Who is he?' Kate studied the photo. It was sufficiently fuzzy for the other figure with the long brown hair to seem androgynous . 'Is this the best one you've got?'

Derek smiled and gave her another photograph. This one was smaller, a typical police mug shot. 'Lee Martin. Aged ten in that photo, which would make him about thirteen or fourteen now. What do you reckon from what you saw of him the other day? Same kid?'

'It could be.' It was difficult to tell. Four years was a long time at that age. And yet there was a definite similarity and she'd had the advantage of seeing him close up just before he'd bolted. It did look like the same boy. 'So who is he, then? How do you know him?'

One of the DCs brought some coffee in and Derek

took a sip before answering. 'Lee Martin was on our books a few years ago. History of abuse, mother on the game – not surprising he got his kicks out of drugs really, is it? Getting arrested was probably the first time anyone had ever taken any notice of the kid.' He paused. 'Lee got pushed around the system for a while – the way some do, unfortunately, and he wasn't doing himself any favours. He ran away from his foster parents two years ago and nobody's seen him since.'

'Until now.'

'Until now,' Derek repeated. 'But what the *hell* was he doing with Michael?'

SEVENTEEN

'Mikey? Wake up.'

Cold. Hurts.

More urgent now. '*Mikey!* For fuck's sake, wake up! We don't have *time* for this shit.'

A hand slapped his cheek and Michael opened his eyes blearily. There was a figure crouched in front of him.

'Jesus, will you *get up!*' Another slap and hands on his shoulders, shaking him. 'I don't know if they know about this place.'

Lee? It sounded like Lee. Michael tried to focus, but it wasn't easy. Somebody was banging his head with a large mallet and there were occasional flashes across hazy vision. His throat was so dry it was closing up and it hurt to cough. The sensation of cold identified itself as the stone floor on which he was sitting and he was leaning against an old radiator which was gouging holes in his back. It was dark outside and there were no lights on the landing.

'All right.' The voice calmed a little. 'Can you hear me, Mikey? Say something.'

'Lee?' Christ, he sounded awful. It hurt to speak, his throat was so dry.

'That's a fuckin' start. Can you stand?'

Michael felt hands underneath his shoulders dragging

him to his feet. Lee wedged him back against the wall and he put out a hand to steady himself, but it wouldn't take his weight. A bolt of pain shot through his wrist and he yelped hoarsely, somehow managing to keep his balance as he fell onto the window ledge.

Lee grabbed his arm. 'What the – *shit,* Mikey. Who gave you this stuff?'

He pulled away and examined his wrist in the street light from the window, forcing his eyes to focus properly. The skin was red and puffy, there was a dark bruise on the inside of his wrist and his hand hurt. It took him a moment to realise why, until he remembered the heroin he'd bought. Was it really only last night?

Don't ever touch smack – it fucks up your life.

'You stupid fuckin' moron.' Lee shook his head angrily. 'This is all I need. Come on, Mikey, we have to get away from here. I don't know if they're watchin' us, but I can't take the chance.'

'I ran away.' He got his lips round the words.

'Thought you might.' Lee was looking over his shoulder out of the window and down to the street below. 'Did you tell them about this place? Do they know where we are?'

'No.' He cradled his wrist in the other hand, feeling sick and dizzy. 'I didn't tell them. I didn't tell them *anything.*' As he spoke, his mouth loosened up a bit, saliva lubricating his throat. 'Lee, I didn't set you up. Well, not intentionally, anyway.'

'Didn't you?' Lee wasn't convinced. 'I suppose the pigs just *happened* to be there, did they?' He spat across the landing and wiped his mouth with the back of his hand. 'Fuck me, you really caused a riot. I've never seen Eddie move so fast.'

'So where is everyone?'

He laughed incredulously. 'You expected us to be here waitin' for the bacon? We was out within minutes.'

'I didn't tell, Lee. I didn't even want to go with them.'

Michael was painfully aware of the pleading tone in his voice. He wasn't entirely sure whether it was important for Lee to believe his story, or if Lee was just the means to find Joss.

'Joss sent someone back late last night,' Lee continued, without looking at Michael, 'jus' to check the place over and collect some crap. He says this place is red hot.'

'No.' Michael shook his head. 'They're out there, but they don't know where we are. I saw them in the park earlier.'

'They didn't see you?'

'Would I still be here if they had?' Now it was his turn for the sarcasm, but he could see that Lee was sceptical, wondering if he'd just walked into an elaborate trap. The boy was standing at the window, hidden in the shadows and staring out into the night; Michael could see the moonlight reflected in his eyes and he shivered. There was a hard calculating look on his face and Michael knew he was weighing up the odds. If Lee didn't believe him, he was finished.

Lee turned suddenly. 'When did you last hit?'

He checked his watch. It was eleven o'clock and he'd been asleep – *Asleep? Unconscious, more like* – for most of the evening. 'About midnight. I—'

'Save it. Can you move?'

Michael nodded, relieved. It sounded like the odds had come out in his favour, but Lee saw the look on his face and shook his head.

'It's not me you have to fuckin' convince, Mikey. Joss doesn't know I'm here. Come on.' He glanced out of the window again. 'Follow me and do as I tell you.'

Holding his wrist close to his chest, Michael followed him down the stairs. At the front door, Lee stuck out his arm and Michael stopped. Peering out from behind the shelter of the door, Lee looked back over his shoulder.

'If you get lost, meet me two roads down from the White Horse on the High Street. An' *don't* bring the friggin' pigs.' Without waiting for a reply, Lee issued another barrage of instructions. 'Down the far end of the alley – through the gate at the bottom – there's waste ground. Follow the line of the houses on the left and there's a burn-out on the other side of the playground. Give me two and join me. An' Mikey? If you get seen, I'll fuckin' leave you here, I swear.' He was gone as he finished speaking, and Michael stayed in the shadow of the doorway, repeating the instructions to himself. His memory wasn't as sharp as it used to be, and the man with the mallet had almost hammered through to his brain. His wrist was hurting now as well, and he could feel his pulse throbbing warmly in his hand; he wondered if he'd picked up an infection from the needle. A sudden vision of Maria flashed across his mind – a vivid image of bloodshot eyes as she screamed with the pain of whatever she'd taken.

Michael shook his head, wincing at the way his vision jarred with the movement. What was done was done and if he couldn't stay on his feet long enough to get to Joss, blood poisoning would be the least of his problems.

Out on the street, he felt like a thief, checking each way before jogging down the alley to the gate at the end. Running was beyond his capabilities right now and he didn't want to fall over as he wasn't sure he'd ever get up again.

The waste ground was deserted. Metal poles grew out of weed-choked tarmac like strange new life forms, twisted and grotesque as they reached towards the night sky. Michael stumbled across a derelict playground and prayed that the shadows weren't concealing watchers. There had been seven of them last time – seven that he'd seen, anyway – and that had been when they'd known where to start looking. Now they knew about the heroin, the game had changed and Michael wondered how many men were watching the area now, hoping to spot him. With any luck, they'd be concentrating their efforts around the High Street and McDonald's. They couldn't know about the flat

– they had no *way* of knowing.

Following the line of terraced houses as he'd been instructed, he slipped through a gap in the corrugated iron fencing and spotted the burn-out immediately. Lee was crouched on the pavement in the wreck's shadow.

He reached up and pulled Michael down to join him. 'Easy, innit?'

'What?'

'Avoidin' pigs. Used to hunt them years ago with some guys out on Brick Lane. A point for every set of pig wheels you could tag; ten if you could do the window without gettin' caught. Got twenty points in one night once.'

Michael couldn't be bothered to listen. There were bright flashes across his vision and his wrist was throbbing painfully. It was close on twenty four hours since King's Cross and it hadn't been much of a fix at that, whereas Lee looked like he'd recently hit and was fresh and alert. What the fuck was he doing here, anyway? He'd had a chance to escape, he *had* escaped, and yet he'd returned voluntarily. What did that make him? A fugitive, rather than a prisoner? The game had changed all right.

'Mikey?' Lee touched his shoulder. Dark eyes sparkled with reflected streetlight as he stood up, glancing down the road.

'Lee, they *don't* know about the flat. Believe me. If you weren't seen, then we're safe.' He leaned against the rusty wheel arch, sitting back on his heels and closing his eyes.

'Yeah, maybe.' Lee wasn't taking any chances as he ducked down again. 'If I lead the porkers back to Joss, he'll kill me first and *then* ask the questions. For fuck's sake, Mikey – what did you do?'

'Does it matter?' He really wasn't in a mood to make conversation and he'd have to explain it all over again to Joss anyway. If Joss would listen to explanations.

Lee arched one eyebrow. 'Dunno. Come on – I think we're OK to move.' He dragged Michael to his feet. 'S'not far.'

Michael leaned against the car unsteadily. He didn't know whether it was withdrawal, a crap cut, or whatever he'd done to his wrist that was making him feel so sick and dizzy, but he accepted Lee's arm under his shoulders without comment and allowed the youth to lead him down the street.

He lost track of time with his sense of direction and it seemed like Lee was taking them round in circles, or maybe it was deliberate. From time to time, he detached himself from Michael's side and sprinted back to the corner they'd just turned, peering both ways cautiously. The paranoia was alarming and Michael was beginning to realise just what he'd done by drawing attention to Joss' cosy little set-up. He wondered if Lee really was acting on his own initiative and what Joss' reaction would be to his return.

Eventually, Lee ducked under a concrete platform, led Michael through an underground car-park that stank of piss and into the service staircase of a tower block. Michael hadn't got a clue where they were; he had no more idea of their location than he had of the first flat and he didn't particularly care, either. His mind was narrowing, focusing on what lay ahead and whether he could persuade Joss to let him score. He wasn't much of an actor, quite the opposite, in fact; he'd never been able to lie convincingly and he'd always been the one the teachers at school knew they could rely on to tell them what the gang was up to. But he wasn't acting now. He needed a shot more than he'd ever needed anything in his life before. The throb in his wrist was pounding in time with his headache and his arm felt hot and heavy.

Fourteen flights of stairs later, Michael collapsed against the banisters as Lee fished for a key in his pockets. The sweat was dripping into his eyes and he wiped them with the back of his good hand as Lee unlocked the door.

This was it. The point of no return. He was walking into this of his own free will and there was no going back once he stepped through that door. And yet what else was there for him? He'd seen the look on his father's face, the disappointment in his son. Dad must have known he'd lied to the police, lied to everyone and there was nothing worse in the man's eyes than a liar – except perhaps a junkie and whatever else he'd become. And now they knew about the drugs, there was no way back to the person he'd been once before. *I'm sorry, dad. I can't be what you want me to be. Not anymore.*

From where he was standing, Michael saw Eddie in the hall as Lee pushed the door open. Beyond the capacity to be scared by the man, Michael just watched as Eddie shook his head slowly, a glass of scotch in one hand.

He looked past Lee direct to Michael. 'Hell, are you in the shit.'

Michael didn't care. It could have been judgment day in the flat, for all he was concerned. Joss controlled the heroin supplies, so Joss had to be faced. It was largely a matter of priorities. And after last night, nothing Joss wanted could possibly be any worse.

The man himself appeared at Eddie's shoulder and Eddie stepped to one side. Lee was still out on the landing and he glanced back at Michael with a touch of concern as Joss backhanded him hard across one cheek.

'Get inside. I'll speak to you later.'

Lee touched his face and hesitated momentarily before darting past Joss and into the flat without a word. Joss stepped outside and looked at Michael.

'Can I help you?'

'Joss, please!' His voice cracked slightly. 'I didn't mean—'

'Spare me the excuses, Mikey. Did you want something?'

'Lee said—'

'Lee had no business saying anything to you.' Joss closed his eyes for a second. 'Well, I suppose you'd better come in for a minute. We wouldn't want to draw any more attention to ourselves, now, would we?' His voice was soft and yet cold at the same time.

Michael pushed himself up off the banister and staggered into the flat as Joss closed the front door behind him. He leaned against the wall as Joss brushed past him and held open the lounge door. 'In here. Lee – go to your room and stay there.'

Lee's eyes were wide as he squeezed past Michael and disappeared down the hall. Joss shoved Michael forward into the room, followed him and shut the door. Michael took a deep breath.

'Sit down.'

He did as he was told, knowing better than to answer back. Neither Joss nor Eddie seemed surprised to see him and yet Joss' reaction had been to lash out at Lee – something in excess of his usual calm composure. He was wound tight and ticking. *Dangerous*.

'What do you want, Mikey?' Joss took a sip of scotch and swirled the contents in the bottom of the glass. 'Why did you come here?'

'I've come back.' It sounded pathetic and Michael tried to elaborate, but the words wouldn't come. He sat there stupidly, cradling his wrist in his other hand.

'I don't want you back. You betrayed my trust.'

'But—'

'I'm sorry, Mikey. It's over. Everyone gets one chance, remember? And you had yours. Shut the door as you go, please.'

'Joss, I need a fix!'

'Really?' Joss sounded surprised. 'So you thought you'd come here to get it?' He laughed harshly. 'Where did Lee find you?' The question was curt and Michael was surprised by the sudden ferocity in the tone.

'At the other flat.' He hesitated. 'Joss, I didn't tell. They don't know about the place. Honestly!'

'So how did they find you? Lee told me what happened in the park.'

'From McDonald's.' He explained the situation as best he could, feeling like he was bargaining now. His next shot depended on Joss' reaction to his story.

Joss didn't say anything for a while and Michael sat back and stared around the room, fighting off the tears. There were personal touches here – photographs on the sideboard and books stacked up on shelves. A large framed photograph of the Liverpool skyline hung above the mantelpiece, the Liver birds watching the Mersey ferry crossing the river. He wondered if this was Joss' real home, the place he came back to after making the rounds of his other houses.

'You got any money?'

'What?' He shook his head. It was getting hard to focus now and he couldn't concentrate on what was happening.

'Money, Mikey,' explained Joss patiently. 'If you're not working, you don't get it for free. Things are different now.' He shook his head. 'No money, no gear.'

Michael began to cry. He couldn't help it. He had less than twenty pence in his pockets and he'd turned thief to make the money last as long as it had. He'd gone through hell to get here and it didn't look like there was any way he was going to get a fix out of Joss. He didn't know what else he could do, where else he could go and if he didn't get a shot soon, he knew he'd end up unconscious in the gutter somewhere.

Eddie finished his drink and came over. He was wearing a dark blue sweater with an Italian logo on it. Sitting down next to Michael on the sofa, he put an arm round his shoulders. 'Why did you do it, Mikey?' he asked gently. 'Why did you go? I was worried about you.'

Michael cried even harder and Eddie pulled him close. It was comforting and Michael felt himself leaning into the man, trying to escape what Joss was putting him through.

'Are you hurting, Mikey?' Eddie pulled away slightly and lifted Michael's chin with one finger. Michael nodded miserably. It hurt so much, he couldn't think straight.

Waves of pain were running down his back and his stomach was tying itself in knots. 'Badly?' Eddie continued and Michael nodded again, unable to speak. Thoughts were jumbling around his mind, churning and fragmenting until he was no longer sure who he was or what he was doing.

'How badly?' interjected Joss from across the room. There was no sympathy in his voice.

'Badly enough, I think,' Eddie replied, looking up.

'Oh, I don't know,' said Joss airily. 'I think it could get a lot worse. I think it probably will. In a few hours or so, this will seem quite mild.'

Michael screwed up his eyes and made an attempt to fight back. 'If you throw me out, I'll tell the police.'

Joss laughed and finished his drink. He banged the glass down on a table and came over to the sofa, crouching down until his eyes were level with Michael's. 'Mikey, if I throw you out, you won't be telling anybody *anything*. Ever.' He noticed Michael's wrist then and reached out for it, turning the arm and examining it deftly. 'Ah. A bit of DIY. Made you appreciate how easy it was here, has it?'

Michael yelped as Joss touched his skin, snatching his hand back. He avoided the man's eyes as for the first time he realised that there was more than heroin at stake. The sudden panic cut through the pain as he remembered his initial impressions of Joss, when he'd made that abortive escape bid through an unlocked door. The man was a killer and he wasn't going to risk losing all he'd got to a scared teenage junkie. Michael would either get a second chance, or he'd be dead. Right now, he wasn't sure which option seemed the most likely.

'Well, Mikey?' Joss stood up. 'What's it to be? Are you worth the trouble? Do you realise how close you are to a body bag and a couple of bricks?'

He was crying again. 'I'm sorry, Joss. Please.' Eddie's arm round his shoulder felt like all that was keeping him afloat.

'Please what?'

'I'm sorry. I won't leave again. I promise.' It was coming out in great bursts now. 'I'll do anything you want, Joss. *Please*. Don't throw me out! Please help me.' His tongue had disconnected itself from his brain and he was babbling incoherently, aware only that he was still firmly pinned to Eddie's side and that Joss had left the room. Voice dissolved into tears again and he sobbed into Eddie's sweater as the man rocked him back and forth like a baby. Eddie was stroking his hair now and he felt his sleeve being pushed up. He opened his eyes blearily.

Joss was crouched in front of him again, a syringe in one hand. 'Remember this, Mikey. Remember how it feels in case you ever think about pulling a stunt like that again. You're mine, Mikey, and don't you ever forget it.' He shook his head, swore quietly and turned away; Michael felt something narrow and tight being fastened around his upper arm. He wriggled and reached for it, but his hand was smacked away.

'Don't touch.' Joss hesitated for a second. 'You're sure you want this, Mikey? There's no going back. Not anymore.'

'Yes.' Michael gritted his teeth and tried to hold his arm steady. He could feel his pulse pounding, speeding up in anticipation of the drug. 'Oh God, please …'

'Relax.' Joss injected him and Michael let his body go limp as the rush took him away on a wave of ecstasy. Sweet Jesus, he could *feel* the liquid roar though his veins like the tide. He could feel each blood cell moving round his body, carrying the power and energy with it, rebuilding him, making him whole again. He couldn't control it any more, didn't *want* to control it and he let the tide swamp him entirely, drowning him in pure sensation as he fell back onto the sofa and floated away.

Screw you all! This is my *life!*

EIGHTEEN

Derek was being evasive and Kate didn't know why. Three days after Michael had left and they had nothing more to go on other than the tenuous link with the runaway Lee Martin – at least nothing which Derek had told her, although Kate was still privately convinced that the man was keeping something from her. But he hadn't got to the rank of Detective Inspector without learning when to keep his mouth shut, and Kate knew there was no way she was going to get it out of him until he decided to tell her what was on his mind. All she knew was that the team out in East London was looking for both teenagers now and it was only a matter of time before they picked up one of them. She wondered how Derek could be so sure they were still there.

It was late on Saturday afternoon and she, Derek and Colin were sitting in her local pub. It was something of an achievement on her part, getting the two men together as Colin was still convinced that she and Derek had something going between them. He was being difficult and she couldn't really blame him, especially as there was more than a grain of truth behind his suspicions. But Derek was all polite professionalism today, pleasant but distant as if he could sense the undercurrents between Kate and her fiancé. In fact he was going out of his way to be friendly with Colin and it was Kate who was feeling distinctly out in the cold.

She was also feeling guilty. She'd been due for a fitting for her wedding dress that morning and she'd telephoned and cancelled it as soon as she'd got up. In fact, she'd cancelled the order for the dress, despite being told she would lose her deposit and possibly the entire cost if the shop couldn't resell the half-finished silk and taffeta creation. The assistant had been rather snotty about the whole thing, implying that Kate was both selfish and inconsiderate to have wasted everyone's time and money. With a reaction like that from the shop, Kate was nervous as to what Colin would say when she told him what she'd done. Despite everything, she still cared about him very much, but she couldn't in all honesty say that she loved him. And that was the problem.

Three glasses of wine hadn't improved her mood and Derek didn't seem to want to talk much either. They had more in common now – they both knew it – and Michael was fast becoming an excuse to be together. It wasn't fair on anybody and they were approaching the time when they'd have to make the relationship more formal or part company.

Having been coerced into coming along, Colin now appeared quite comfortable in Derek's company. The two of them were sitting opposite each other and discussing Michael's case amongst other things with a familiarity which Kate resented. Derek had already told him that they'd finally scored a hit with Jenny's E-fit picture, something he'd not mentioned to her before. Running the name *Eddie* through the computers had come up with numerous possibilities, which when compared with several stations' local records had thrown up a certain Edward Felsen with a photograph startlingly similar to Jenny's picture. Michael's so-called *friend* had a criminal record for sexual assault and violence. There was a warrant out for him too – for failure to notify a change of address for the Sex Offenders Register. And as he'd said it, Derek had glanced sideways at her as if to gauge her reaction.

So Mike was involved with some dangerous people. Had he gone back to them when he'd left? She wondered how on earth Derek had managed to pull the right photograph from police records, when all he'd had to go on was one name. The statistical probabilities were incredible and he must have had more information to have come up with the correct match. Which meant there were still things she wasn't being told – ideas and hunches which were nevertheless coming up with positive results.

Kate pulled her mind back to reality and realised that Colin and Derek had discovered they had something in common in that they were both fond of cooking. *Cooking?* She suppressed an incredulous laugh. Colin's meals were carefully prepared *nouvelle cuisine* fare, beautifully presented on bone china plates and – she had to admit – a delight to eat. She didn't know much about Derek, but she somehow saw him as a pie-and-chips man, or maybe lasagne on a good day and even then ready-made from the freezer. He didn't seem the type to stand over the cooker for hours on end, just to create the perfect cheese sauce.

This was bordering on the ridiculous. She was sitting at a pub table with two highly presentable men and they were talking with great enthusiasm about cooking. *What about Michael,* she wanted to ask. *Do you think he's eating well?* But she was being silly – nothing they did right now was going to make any difference to Michael, wherever he was, and even Detective Inspectors were allowed time off to relax.

Patience wearing thin, Kate was relieved to see Rachel coming through the door, hair damp from the rain. She threw her jacket onto a nearby chair and squeezed onto the bench next to Kate.

'Sorry I'm late. I did it.' She grinned. 'I finally got a date with him.'

'Him?' Kate couldn't keep up. 'Which him?'

'The hunk in the flat below me. Tim, his name is. Would you believe he knocked at my door to borrow a cup of sugar? It's the truth, honestly! Would I make up something as corny as that?' She ran a hand through blonde hair and turned to the men. 'Hi, Colin – how's the design business these days? And you must be Derek the detective. I've heard a lot about you.'

'You make me sound like a cartoon.' Derek smiled. 'Can I get you a drink?' He went up to the bar and Rachel nodded appreciatively.

'He's a bit of all right.'

'Rach ...' Kate tried to stop her but Rachel caught her eye. The look said *don't worry – I won't drop you in it,* and Kate grinned. Fortunately, Colin seemed to have relaxed since discovering he and Derek had something in common, and Kate began to think the evening might not be such a disaster after all.

'So somebody fill me in on what's been happening.' Rachel nodded her thanks as she took the vodka and coke from Derek's hand.

'Don't ask me,' said Kate, glaring at the men. She didn't want to stir up an argument, but she couldn't seem to help it. 'I'm only a woman.'

'Kate!' That was Colin now, an embarrassed smile on his face.

Derek sighed. 'I only found out this afternoon.' He explained what he'd done for Rachel's benefit. 'Seems like Jenny was paying attention after all.'

'You mean she was deliberately flirting with the guy to wind Michael up?' Kate suggested, wondering what on earth her brother had seen in the girl.

'Could be.' Derek nodded. 'Although from what others say, flirting would be a bit mild a word for it. For some reason, she really wanted to make Michael jealous that night.'

'And look what happened,' Kate mused. 'He goes off with some pervert who's done time for violence. And

Mike claimed he was a friend!'

Derek snorted. 'Michael barely said a single word worth listening to. I've never heard such a load of crap.'

Rachel stirred the ice in her drink with a finger and sucked it reflectively. It was a remarkably provocative action and Kate felt a fleeting moment of anger before she realised that Rachel was too good a friend to consciously make a play for Derek. And anyway, she was seeing this Tim guy.

'He went with this Eddie voluntarily?' Rachel pursed her lips.

'So it seems.'

'And when you found him, he was on smack and refused to see a doctor?'

Derek nodded. 'Rachel, don't—'

'Well, I can make a pretty good guess as to what's going on, then.'

Derek opened his mouth, but Kate beat him to it. 'What?'

Rachel hesitated, losing momentum, and Kate saw the angry flash in Derek's eyes. He'd wanted to stop her, but he knew it was too late. She'd said too much already. Rachel faltered, glancing between Kate and Derek and from the corner of her eye, Kate saw Colin shaking his head slowly.

'Go on,' she said. 'You're obviously all in on this.'

'I ...' Rachel fingered her glass nervously. 'I did my training in Liverpool. We had several addicts come in, for one reason or another. From some big housing estate – the name escapes me right now. You know where I mean?'

Derek nodded, a resigned expression on his face. 'One of the worst drug problem areas in the country.'

'Oh shit, Kate. I'm really sorry. I should learn to keep my mouth shut.'

'Will you *please* get to the point!' There was a long pause and Kate could sense the tension in the air. Rachel had guessed something and guessed right by all accounts – at least enough for Derek not to want her to continue. And Colin knew as well. Everybody knew except her. Little Kate. Stay at home and look after the family Kate, who doesn't need to know the gory details because they will only upset her.

Rachel had paled noticeably.

'Well?'

'Kids Michael's age came in all the time.' Her voice was toneless. 'Most of them kicked out because they were no longer young enough or pretty enough for the punters. Or they'd overdosed.'

Young enough? Pretty enough? Kate wasn't that naïve. She knew what Rachel was saying, but it was hard to believe. She'd worried when she'd heard that Michael's night-club friend was a convicted sex offender – what had never occurred to her was that his taste might run to boys.

Kate wandered down the street, hands in the pockets of her jacket. It was raining, a fine late-spring drizzle that looked set to stay for the rest of the evening and the roads were shiny. *God, how could I have been so stupid?* Derek had mentioned that there had to be a means of financing the drugs which Michael was using, and he'd obviously considered sex as an option. But Michael wouldn't be involved in something like that, surely? *Unless he had no choice.* He'd always been confident of his own sexuality, lost his virginity at fifteen and there had been no stopping him since then. Oh, he was careful enough – knew enough to avoid unwanted pregnancies and STDs – but Michael was young and active and determined to enjoy life. And with mum and dad so hard on him to produce good academic results, it made it all the more vital for him to let off steam somehow.

Kate realised why the picture of Michael and Lee had disturbed her so much; there had been an underlying sexual tension behind it and it made her want to throw up. *Jesus, Michael. What happened to you?*

'Kate?'

'What?' She swung round to see Derek behind her; he matched his pace to hers as he caught up.

'Slow down.'

'What for?' She wondered what had happened to Rachel and Colin. Why had only Derek come after her?

'So I can talk to you, damn it!'

'Feed me more crap, you mean.' Kate stopped and turned to face him. 'Any other little gems you'd like to share with me?'

'Hell, your mate's got a big mouth, hasn't she?'

'Oh, don't blame Rachel! You all knew – even Colin. I could see it on your faces. At least she had the decency to let me in on it.'

'Speculation, Kate, not fact. I've no proof Michael's involved in any of this. And Colin and Rachel drew their own conclusions – you heard her. It was nothing to do with anything I said.' He paused. 'Nobody's keeping anything from you.'

She met his eyes. 'Do you think it's true?'

'I don't know. The evidence is only circumstantial.'

'Is it?'

He took her shoulders. 'I don't *know*. When we find him, we'll hear the truth. Until then, all we can do is wait.'

'And at least he's alive,' said Kate sarcastically. 'Is that what you're going to tell me next? That I should be thankful for that?'

'No. I wouldn't patronise you that way.' He squeezed her arm. 'Come back to the pub. Colin's taken Rachel home.'

He didn't want to come after me, then? Or had Derek insisted? Unless it had been Rachel's idea. 'Shit, is she upset?'

'You could say. I think she's wishing she could turn back the clock twenty minutes. Colin will sort her out. He's not a bad sort, your fiancé.'

'No, he's not.' Kate took the plunge. 'I cancelled my

wedding dress today.'

'What?' Derek stared at her. 'Why?'

'Because I'm not getting married,' she said, with more than a hint of sarcasm.

'Oh.' He turned away and wouldn't look at her. 'Because of me?'

She glanced at the back of his head. He was certainly direct. 'Because the time isn't right. Because I don't love him. Because of Michael. And yes, because of you.'

'Oh,' he said again. He'd never been stuck for words before – but then she'd known him only a few months. 'What do you want me to do?'

'I'm sorry?' Kate couldn't quite believe what she'd heard.

'I don't know what you want me to say.'

You could ask me to go to bed with you, for starters. 'I don't want you to say anything. I just thought you might be interested, that's all.'

'Of course I'm interested.' He hesitated. 'Kate, I can't run your life for you. If you and Colin split up, then that must be your decision, not mine.'

'Don't back out of this now, Derek,' she snapped. 'That's not fair.'

He smiled slightly. 'I'm not backing out. But I won't be responsible for you breaking off your engagement. You think I want an irate fiancé down at the station, causing havoc?'

'Oh, right.' She was picking a fight, but she couldn't help herself. 'You don't want a messy domestic spoiling your career prospects.'

'Don't put words into my mouth.' He was getting annoyed now, jangling the car keys in his pocket as if he couldn't wait to be somewhere else. 'Incredible, isn't it,' he said after a moment, 'how history repeats itself.'

Now it was Kate's turn to look confused. 'What do you mean?'

'Kate, I'm not perfect. I don't know if I can find your

brother and if I do, I'm not sure you'll like what I find. Don't confuse what you think you feel with the real thing.'

'You sound like my father.'

'Maybe. I'm probably old enough. The point is that things may look very different in six month's time. Oh Christ, I'm not explaining myself, very well, am I?'

'No. Why don't you get to the point?'

It was still raining. Both of them were soaked, but Kate didn't care and Derek didn't seem to have noticed. He ran a hand through wet hair and sighed. 'You think you're the first young woman I've met through my job? I've made that mistake before and I don't want to repeat it.'

She wasn't sure she wanted him to continue, but she had no choice now. The cards were on the table and she had to count the scores. 'Go on.'

'What I'm trying to tell you is that I'm married.'

Kate felt her cheeks flush scarlet. But why *shouldn't* he be married? Just because he'd never mentioned a wife or family didn't mean they didn't exist – he was under no obligation to discuss his personal life with her, after all. She was only a client, a job. *A case number. An open file. A loose end – that's all.*

She didn't say a word. Without looking at him, she pulled out of his grip on her arm and strode away in the direction of home. It was raining harder now and the water disguised the tears on her face, so much that she wasn't sure herself if she really was crying and if so, who she was crying for – Michael, Colin or herself. All three lives had changed tonight, one way or another.

She didn't know if Derek was following her and she didn't care; embarrassment was giving way to anger as she realised how much he'd led her on. He'd had enough opportunities to tell her and he hadn't, which made it as much his fault as hers, surely?

He caught her in seconds, grabbing her shoulder. 'You didn't give me a chance to tell you what happened.'

'You lied to me. That's all I need to know.'

'I didn't! The subject's never come up.'

'You didn't tell me, did you? It comes to the same thing. You let me go on thinking that ... oh *shit*, this isn't fair!' She wiped her eyes with the back of her hand, determined not to give him the satisfaction of seeing her cry.

Derek didn't let go. 'Kate, I want to make love to you. Come home with me.'

'Oh yeah? A cosy little *ménage à trois?* With you and your *wife?*'

'No.' He was smiling now and she tried to pull away furiously. 'Just me. Don't jump to conclusions.'

'I don't understand.'

'Not surprising really, when you run off without doing me the courtesy of at least listening to what I've got to say. Kate, you idiot – I'm married, yes, but she walked out on me nearly two years ago. No kids – at least none that I'm aware of.'

'So? Does that make a difference?' She relaxed a little.

He let go of her shoulders and steered her in the direction of his car. 'We married for all the wrong reasons. Like you, she was a part of a case I was working on and we spent a lot of time together. Her lover was aggressive – put her in hospital twice and I gave her the courage to put him inside. One thing led to another and we ended up married. It wasn't one of the best decisions I've ever made, but it happened.'

'So divorce her.'

He grinned. 'I would, if I knew where she was. At least she's never asked me for maintenance.' He shook his head, more serious now. 'Helen was one screwed up lady. Not that I'm suggesting you're the same,' he added quickly. 'I just don't want to be responsible for any more lives.'

Kate was amazed. 'You really have no idea where she is?'

'Not a clue. I used to worry about it, but what can you do? Our relationship was long over by then and I know she was seeing someone else.' He stopped walking and turned to face her. 'Kate, don't leave Colin for me. I don't want that responsibility.'

She didn't answer for a moment. Then she smiled. 'Did you say something about going home?'

Derek's flat couldn't have been more unlike Colin's house. It was large with a picture window leading onto a wide balcony with views of the river; lined up in military rows outside was an array of very dead plants in cheap plastic pots. Inside, the lounge was spartan, but comfortable, with a huge and tatty sofa on which lay several different and out of date newspapers. There were numerous mugs on the coffee table and Derek scooped them up, mumbling apologies about the state of the place. Apparently the cleaning lady visited on Monday and Wednesday mornings, so by the weekend, the flat was a mess and he'd never quite worked out how to keep it tidy.

While Derek was in the kitchen, Kate was about to sit down on the sofa, when the only available spot was suddenly claimed by a large ginger cat, which eyed her suspiciously, before starting to wash itself.

'That's Trevor,' Derek called from the kitchen. 'It must be him that makes the place untidy. I'm never here long enough.' As if to prove the point, the cat calmly began to shred the nearest newspaper, claws curling and uncurling with obvious satisfaction.

'See what I mean?' Derek came in with two mugs of coffee and pushed the cat off the sofa with one foot. Trevor yowled meaningfully and slunk off into the hall in disgust.

Kate laughed and sat down. 'Are you really here that infrequently?'

He shrugged, pushing the newspapers onto the floor. 'It's a job with long hours. Time off is precious and I can't see the point in wasting it sitting around at home.'

What am I doing? The thought crossed her mind,

hesitated, and decided to stay. Colin had taken Rachel home so that Derek could explain the situation and whereas Rachel probably knew exactly what was likely to happen, Kate doubted that the thought had even occurred to Colin. He knew their relationship was rocky, suspected that Kate was going to call it off, but he trusted her enough to give them a chance.

She could still back out, apologise to Derek and get him to drive her home. Get a taxi, even. But was that what she really wanted? Her little brother was shacked up with some pervert druggie and she was about to sleep with the police guy in charge of the case? It didn't seem right, but then sitting at home and being miserable wasn't going to help anybody, least of all Michael.

'Why did you tell me about Helen?' asked Kate, changing the subject suddenly. She wondered why he'd deliberately brought the matter up earlier, as if he'd intended to force the issue.

Derek gazed into his mug for a minute before looking up. 'I wanted you to know all about me,' he said. 'I wanted to be straight with you from the start. No skeletons. They have a nasty habit of falling out on you at the wrong moment.'

He had a point. And if he wanted to be that honest with her, then maybe there was a chance for them, no matter what he'd said. Life was too short for prevarication. Ever since he'd kissed her in McDonald's, she'd known she was going to sleep with him sooner or later and it had just been a matter of waiting for him to realise it too.

When she kissed him on the sofa, nothing had changed, except that this time she had his full attention as well as his body. *Some body*. Kate felt firm muscle underneath the shirt. Running her hand down his side, she found the waistband of his jeans and traced it round to the front, where she unzipped his fly and reached inside. Derek tensed as she touched him, and then relaxed and grunted softly as he slipped his hand up her sweater and under her bra. He kissed her gently, then more fiercely.

There was nothing romantic about their lovemaking. Kate heard her sweater rip as she wrenched it off and both pairs of shoes and jeans rapidly joined it on the floor in an untidy pile with the newspapers. Derek expertly unfastened her bra and she ran her hands through his hair as he explored her breasts with his tongue, the touch making her shiver as she stroked the back of his neck. He turned away for a moment, unwrapping a condom and rolling it onto himself in one smooth motion. Kate's underwear went next and then he lifted his body and was inside her in one fluid action and they were moving together, her legs wrapped around his thighs. This was so far removed from Colin's careful considerations that it could have been a different act altogether – this was straight sex and Kate had never experienced anything like it. It felt like she and Derek were one being, the motion controlled by both and yet neither of them as if they had created something else entirely, something which was threatening to take them over and drown them beyond rescue.

She couldn't stop it. The tide was building with every movement and as it submerged her completely, she heard herself cry out as Derek's body tensed and jerked on top of her and he came seconds later. And then the sofa cocooned them both as they lay there for a good five minutes before either of them had enough breath to speak.

NINETEEN

Things were different this time around. Michael felt like he'd passed a milestone, made the transition from child to adult, or novice to expert. Nobody mentioned the night he'd returned, but they treated him differently now – although it wasn't so much that anyone forced him to do anything he didn't want to, but more that he just couldn't see any point in objecting. On the occasions he got to worrying about what had happened to him, he only had to recall the night at King's Cross and suddenly events paled into insignificance. He wasn't going to go through that ever again and if he had to work for a regular fix, well that was life.

Joss' treatment of his injured wrist confirmed his suspicions that the man had a strong medical background. Antibiotics appeared and the infection cleared up rapidly, leaving him wondering yet again what had made the man turn to crime and drugs for a living. On the window ledge in the lounge was a photograph of a young man in army uniform; it wasn't Joss but there was enough of a resemblance for it to be a relation. Its very presence established that this place was indeed where Joss called home; there were other clues in the medical journals stacked in the corner and military memorabilia high on the shelves and thick with dust. Michael was curious now – living in the same flat, it was difficult not to be, as Joss never went out of his way to volunteer information.

Joss was amiable enough these days. He refused to let Michael out of the flat *for the time being*, but beyond that, he was pleasant and even conversational at times and eventually Michael plucked up the courage to risk a few direct questions.

'Who's this?' he asked one afternoon, picking up the photograph. Lee and Eddie were out flat-hunting and Joss seemed in a good mood.

The man looked up from the paper. He frowned for a moment and Michael wondered if he'd said the wrong thing, but then Joss sighed. 'That's my brother, Sean. He was nineteen when that was taken.' He looked at the expression on Michael's face and smiled. 'You didn't think it was me, did you? Christ, not in the army!'

'Then all this stuff is his?' Michael swept his hand up to indicate the beret and photographs on the top shelf. There were medals pinned to a faded blue velvet backing and a rifle bayonet lay next to them.

'Some of it.' Joss put down the paper. 'The medals were my father's. They never gave Sean any medals. Only heroes get medals and it's hard to be a hero without any legs.'

Shit. He'd trodden on some raw nerves, judging by the sudden bitterness in Joss' voice and he wondered whether to continue. But it was nice to have a decent conversation, one that didn't consist of instructions or sexual innuendo. 'My father was in the air force in the Gulf War,' he said, sitting down on the edge of the chair.

Joss nodded approval. 'A brave man.' He hesitated. 'Sean was killed in Northern Ireland. Or as good as, anyway. He was only twenty and he lost both legs. His life was over when they brought him back.'

Like I thought mine was over when I realised what you'd done to me? Michael was tempted to ask, but didn't. Instead he kept the conversation going by asking: 'So what happened to him?'

Joss didn't reply. He stood up and crossed to the window, staring out at the view over the rooftops to the city skyline. In the distance was the landmark of the Post Office tower; from the bedroom you could see across to Canary Wharf and Docklands on a clear day. But it didn't look like Joss was admiring the view and Michael had the distinct feeling that he'd gone too far.

'Sean committed suicide.' Joss hesitated. 'He was addicted to morphine.' He turned round. 'You're full of questions today, aren't you? Not planning any more little surprises, I hope.'

'No, Joss.' *As if.* He couldn't contemplate a return to that awful strained silence over the dinner table with Kate and his parents on the night he'd run away. Joss, Eddie and Lee were his family now. There was no going back and he no longer wanted to. Here in the flat was a strange kind of security, and waking each morning with Lee's arms wrapped around him made him feel warm and safe in a way he'd never known before. By tacit agreement, it had gone no further, but it wasn't over – Lee was patient, but he wouldn't wait forever and it worried Michael intensely. He needed the boy and yet couldn't bring himself to take that final step over the line.

Lee didn't have any more information, only that Joss had once said Sean overdosed six months after being discharged from hospital. It explained the man's hang-up about correct procedures, but his involvement in heroin dealing didn't make sense. Surely anyone with a close relation who'd died from an overdose would be *against* drugs in a big way? At least Eddie was easier to understand – a small-time pimp who got his kicks out of free gear and apparently unlimited sex, although what Joss got out of this arrangement was beyond Michael's comprehension. It was a high price to pay for what was essentially a housekeeper. Still, Eddie's sexual demands had all but ceased since Michael's return and he was grateful, even if it had meant an increase in other work. Eddie liked to intimidate and with Michael's growing confidence, the enjoyment didn't seem to be there anymore.

Lee and Eddie returned with good news. They'd found the perfect flat – two bedrooms with panoramic views of the Thames in a quiet area and for a reasonable rent. A bit off the beaten track, but that was a positive factor in Joss' opinion, especially as this place was on the ninth floor of a tower block and boasted a large sunny balcony. No bars at the windows, but then it was a long way to jump. It sounded ideal and Michael felt himself getting caught up in the general good humour as Joss opened a bottle of wine to celebrate.

'It will take me a few weeks to get the place furnished. I'm open to suggestions, if there was anything in particular you wanted.'

'Big LCD telly?' asked Lee hopefully. 'Nintendo Wii?'

'I was thinking more along the lines of sofas and beds.' Joss poured the wine and handed one to the boy. ' But I daresay I could stretch to a tv.'

'What about the other flat?' Michael wanted to know. Did Joss intend to abandon everything there?

Apparently so. The man shook his head. 'Nobody goes back there. Not for at least twelve months, so if you left anything behind – tough.' He handed Michael a glass. 'This was your doing, Mikey, so you can count yourself lucky you got off so lightly. Now let's get down to tonight, shall we? God knows I'll be glad to get this place back to myself again.'

I bet. Don't like to crap on your own doorstep? He didn't dare ask, but watched as Joss poured the rest of the wine. Once everyone had a glass, he sat back and lit a cigarette.

'You two are working together tonight.'

Lee nodded, seemingly unperturbed. Michael was surprised. This was something new and he had mixed feelings about it, not wanting to put any more of a strain on his relationship with Lee. But Joss simply smiled at his reaction.

'Don't look so worried. Lee will look after you. It's about time you learned what this game's all about.'

There's more to it? Michael wasn't sure he wanted to know. He could cope with things as they were; he'd learned how to detach his mind and simply drift on a high through the worst parts. He took a large swallow of wine, wondering if he could get drunk enough not to worry about it. It couldn't be worse than what might have happened at King's Cross.

Surprisingly, it wasn't. Even so, when the man finally left, it was all he could do not to run to the bathroom and throw up. Instead, he kept as much of his dignity as was possible under the circumstances, slipped a robe around his shoulders and walked down the hall. He showered, then cleaned his teeth three times, making his gums bleed before he felt calm enough to sit down in the kitchen with the leftover scotch he'd found in a cupboard. He hated spirits, but being pissed was the next best thing to being high.

'That was OK, wasn't it?' Lee strolled in, still semi-naked with his robe untied and open. Michael tried to avoid looking at him and he wondered if Lee was doing it on purpose.

Lee shook his head in exasperation at Michael's silence. 'Grow up, Mikey. You came *back* here, remember?'

'What else could I do?'

'What else could I do?' Lee mimicked in a whining tone. He picked up the bottle and took a long swig. 'You've got another home, haven't you? With people who love you? You've got *choices*, Mikey, which is a fuck sight more than some of us have got! And you chose to come back here, so stop fuckin' us all about and actin' like some dumb kid.' Banging the bottle down on the table, he knotted his robe pointedly. 'Fuck me, I wonder why I bothered comin' to find you.'

'So why did you?' *Might as well get it all out in the open.*

'Fuck knows.' Lee hesitated. 'I got put into care when I was ten, y'know, when my mam threw me out.' He was twisting his belt now, chewed fingernails scratching in the silk. 'She had a new man – some guy who was into guns for a living.'

'Guns? What sort of guns?'

Lee half-smiled. 'Nothin' heavy. It was all legit – he had a licence and everythin'.' He shook his head. 'Shame he left really. He was one of the few blokes I got on with.'

'So what happened? Did you fall out or something?'

'Or somethin'. He decided he preferred me to mam.'

'Didn't you mind?' Michael was amazed at his attitude.

'He bought me comics.' Lee shrugged, wincing as he caught a nail in the silk. 'She was more upset than I was. I went back once, y'know. Just once after I ran. I found her shaggin' her dealer and the estate pimp. At the same time. That was the last time I saw her.'

'What about your dad?' Michael couldn't believe anyone could have such an awful childhood. He thought he'd had some bad times, but spending his weekends studying was nothing compared to what Lee had gone through.

Lee snorted. 'What dad? He was gone as soon as mam told him she was carryin'. I grew up wanting to meet him, so I could knife him.' He looked up suddenly. 'So don't give me all this crap about what else *you* could do, Mikey. Next time that punter will want to watch you 'n' me first – I know his type – so for fuck's sake, try to give it a bit more. I won't cover for you forever!' That said, he stood up abruptly and left the room, the mug of coffee untouched on the table.

Michael didn't move. Lee was right. He'd made the decision to return all by himself and it was up to him to deal with the consequences. And yet it was the only real decision he'd made in his life so far. Up until now he'd been playing a part mapped out for him by seventeen years of parenting and this was the first time he'd ever missed a cue and stepped off the stage. Oh, there'd been the usual teenage problems of course – alcohol, girls and the like – but nothing serious, nothing which had any major effect on his life. And if his old life had been a play, then he was writing his own script now.

He thought back to the photograph of Joss' brother. *The army would make a man out of you,* his father had once said, disappointed that his only son had shown no interest whatsoever in the military, not even in the school cadets. Army discipline would right most of the world's wrongs in his dad's eyes and he was a great believer in compulsory national service. No, there was no going back home; he'd come too far down this path to retrace his steps.

It was time to decide what to do. Stay, and take on this new life, which would mean sorting out what – if any – relationship existed with Lee, and in Lee's words *give it a bit more*. Or leave, and face the consequences of what he'd done.

Either way, it would be on his terms now.

TWENTY

'Kate, don't you think you should be going into work today?'

Probably, she agreed privately with her mother's voice from the landing, *but I'm not.* She couldn't face work today, couldn't face cheerfully listening to everybody else's problems – *can't face Rachel is what you really mean.* Which wasn't fair on her friend, as it wasn't her fault Michael was in this mess.

'Can I come in, love? I've brought you a coffee.'

'Of course.' Kate sat up and glanced at the alarm clock. Monday morning and Christ, was it really eight-fifteen? She'd been awake 'til past three, hearing Rachel's voice over and over again in her mind: ... *no longer young enough or pretty enough* ... And *God*, she felt guilty, for what had she done when she'd heard Rachel's theory? Jumped straight into bed with the nearest source of comfort, and he wasn't even her fiancé! Of all the stupid things she could have done, that one certainly came out top of the list. Not that – in all honesty – she regretted it, but the timing could have been better.

Getting home late on the Saturday night, she'd gone straight to bed, ignoring the message dad had taken from Rachel for her to phone back as soon as possible. There'd been no word from Colin and she wondered if he knew where she'd been, if he'd guessed what would happen. All day Sunday, she'd mooched round the house miserably, unable to pick up her mobile and call or even text any of them, and unable to confide in her parents. There'd been no news from anyone and she'd pictured them all going about their business: Derek maybe supervising yet another shift down the East End, Rachel waiting anxiously for her to phone back, and Colin – well, she didn't know what Colin would be thinking or doing any more. She still hadn't told him about the wedding dress, and sleeping with Derek had rather sealed the fate of the marriage that wouldn't be taking place. In fact her life was in complete disarray, and that was before Michael came into the equation. And how on *earth* was she going to tell her parents of this latest discovery? She hadn't even found the courage to tell them about the heroin.

She swung her legs out of bed as her mother came into the bedroom carrying a mug of coffee and a plate of toast. Sylvia Redford was wearing a lilac suit with a cream blouse. She was wearing make-up for the first time in weeks and her hair was neatly twisted up into a bun. Kate was surprised.

'Going somewhere nice, mum?' She took the plate and mug and bit into the toast, licking the end of her finger appreciatively. That was something she was going to miss when she left home – coffee and toast in bed every morning, another of her mother's rituals which usually meant the day had started well and was expected to progress in the same vein. It was like hanging seaweed out of the window and about as accurate. Since every day of Michael's disappearance had been a bad one so far, Kate knew that something had changed this morning.

'Your father and I are going to see the police. If you're not working, we wondered if you wanted to come along with us?'

'The *police?* Has something happened?' *Aside from the*

obvious?

Sylvia sat down on the end of the bed, smoothing her skirt more from habit than necessity. 'Nothing's happened, love. That's why we're going. Inspector Darwin hasn't been round since Michael ran away and we need to know what's going on.' Her voice was remarkably calm and Kate was amazed. This couldn't be the same woman who'd spent most of the last few weeks crying and asking everyone who'd listen if they knew what the family had done wrong to make their only son run away from home. After all, Michael was responsible for the Redfords of the future. *While I get lumbered with the ones of the past?*

And seeing her mum sitting there, still desperately trying to hold on to the pieces of the past, it was more than Kate could do to tell her what had happened to him. She wondered what Derek would say when he discovered that she hadn't told them anything. He'd be furious. As Colin had said, she had no right to keep the information from them. Michael might be her brother, but he was also their son.

'Well, what do you think?'

'What?' Kate shook her head. Her mother was waiting for an answer and she realised she was being invited to go along with them to the police station.

'Are you coming with us?'

'No. I'd better go into work, I suppose.' She made the decision, preferring to face Rachel rather than Derek. The last thing she wanted was to see her parents' faces when they heard the news.

'All right. I'll call you later.' Her mother stood up. 'Be careful, darling.'

What of? Michael was the one in trouble. Kate watched her mother leave and heard the car start up a few minutes later.

It was nearly half eight and she was going to be late again.

The telephone call came at ten-thirty. Kate was halfway up a step-ladder, hunting for a set of records and when the other girl spoke to her, she dropped the file in her hand. Papers went everywhere, medical confetti littering the carpet and she swore under her breath. It seemed like an omen of things to come.

It was Derek, his voice clipped with barely concealed irritation. 'What time's your lunch break?'

'One o'clock.' There was no point in social niceties. He evidently wasn't in the mood.

'Then I'll expect you at a quarter past.' There was the slightest of pauses, before he elaborated. 'No real news, but we need to talk. All right?'

'I guess so.' She didn't have time to carry on as the line went abruptly dead and she stared at the receiver for a moment before replacing it. Presumably he wanted to speak to her regarding her lack of communication with her parents – she couldn't think of anything else he'd want to talk to her about, unless he was regretting what had happened between them.

Rachel didn't agree with her. 'Anyone can see he fancies you,' she said later that morning, perched on the end of the table in the clinic's waiting room. 'You can tell by the way he looks at you – it's in his eyes.'

'Oh, crap.' Kate fiddled with the stack of magazines. It had been quiet for a Monday morning, the room was empty and there were no patients due in for another ten minutes or so. She'd spoken to Rachel first thing this morning; they'd met in the tiny kitchen and eyed each other nervously for a moment, before they'd both made their peace.

'So was it good?'

'What?'

'What do you think? I wasn't talking about the coffee he undoubtedly made you afterwards.'

Kate had to smile at her directness. With everything that was going on, Rachel wanted to know what Derek was like in bed. 'It was all right. What do you want – marks out of ten? Anyway, he's married.'

'You're kidding me? He doesn't look the type to have a wife stashed away.' They heard noises outside and Rachel got off the table hastily, smoothing down her uniform.

'They're separated.' Kate saw the door open and glanced at her watch as an elderly woman entered. 'I'm meeting him at lunch. I'll let you know what happens.'

She was on time, arriving at the police station just before quarter past one. Derek sent one of his officers down to meet her and he took her upstairs. Asking if she wanted a coffee, he deposited her at the door to Derek's office.

'Hi, Kate. I want you to meet someone.' Derek held the door open for her as he ushered her inside. The main room behind her was empty, the radios all out and the desks piled high with unattended paperwork. Pinned to the wall map with large red thumb-tacks were three photographs, closely grouped around the area where they were believed to be living. Michael, Lee Martin and Edward Felsen. It made her brother look as much a criminal as the other two – a photograph and case number was all there was of him. Not much to show for seventeen years.

Turning her attention to Derek's office, she saw his other visitor. It was the man she hadn't seen since the first few visits he and Derek had made to the house just after Michael's initial disappearance. She'd forgotten about him and remembered thinking he was a trainee of some sort.

'Miss Redford.' The man stood up and leaned across the table to shake her hand. 'I don't think we ever got introduced properly, did we? I'm Steve Peters from the drug squad.'

Kate shook his hand and smiled. So he was no trainee and the way he was sitting in Derek's chair implied that he held a certain amount of rank. What was this all about? Did it mean they'd found Michael? On the phone, he'd said *no real news*. Whatever was going on, it looked like she'd been wrong about the reason for her visit.

Derek handed her another photograph of the blond man. 'Edward Felsen. Did three years in Wandsworth for rape.'

'And one of our targets,' added Steve Peters. 'Albeit that we haven't seen much of him for some years now. He's changed quite a bit.'

She recognised him from the McDonald's visit. Jenny's picture had been a good likeness after all. Edward Felsen. Rapist. *And living with Michael*. But there was no proof of that, Kate told herself. The fact that they obviously knew each other didn't mean there were any other connections. *Don't be naïve, Kate. Mike refused to see a doctor, for Christ's sake!* But it still wasn't *proof*, was it? It was hard to believe.

'That's how I knew where to find him in the LIO records, Kate.' Derek took the photo back and pinned it to the wall by his desk. 'That and what experience tells me is a likely scenario.' He pushed another photo at her. 'Ever seen him before?'

Kate shook her head. It was a long-distance shot of a man in his forties leaving a Victorian semi in a leafy suburban street. His dark hair touched his collar and he was wearing jeans, yet there was a certain elegance about him, an aura of confidence apparent even from the photograph.

'You're sure? Not around the area where we picked Michael up?'

'Not that I remember.' She passed back the picture. 'Who is he?'

'Joss Harper. How about this one?' This was Steve now, showing her a photo taken from a similar vantage point and depicting an older man in a tracksuit. His face was red and he'd obviously been running. Kate hadn't seen either of them.

Steve shook his head. 'That's a pity. It would be nice to have a direct link.'

'Who are they? What's the connection?'

'Harper and this guy – Carl Phillips – are part of a drugs ring we were working on some time ago.' Steve paused as the door opened and a tray of coffee arrived. He leaned forward and stirred two sachets of sugar in one of the plastic cups as he continued. 'Felsen used to hang around with Phillips way back.'

'Before he went inside,' Derek added, passing a cup to Kate.

'Exactly,' said Steve. 'Which is why I never picked up on the girl's picture from the club. Felsen was a long time ago, before I got involved. Or so we thought. And Harper didn't appear on the scene until Felsen was halfway through his sentence.'

'Kate, you remember Steve was with me right back when Michael first went missing?'

Kate nodded, wondering what was coming next. Derek's speech was more formal now, more remote as if the night they'd spent together had never happened. She realised he had to separate work from his private life, but it was disconcerting to be a part of both.

Steve Peters took up his cue again. 'Derek asked me to sit in originally, because Michael's case bore some similarities to recent jobs of ours. Several teenagers vanished within a short period of time – we found out they were being recruited as drugs couriers and most were picked up coming back into the country.'

'But Michael wasn't.' This was getting complicated and she wondered where it was all leading.

'No,' said Derek. 'That became obvious fairly quickly.'

'Which is why I dropped out of the case,' Steve explained. 'Except that now Felsen's put in an appearance, I can't help wondering if he's working for the old crowd again.'

Kate was confused. 'But if you *know* about these people, why can't you just find them and arrest them?'

Steve laughed. 'I wish. Firstly we have to locate them.

It's been a long time since we've done any work on them and we've no solid evidence – nothing that'd stand up in court, anyway. As for Felsen.' He shrugged. 'There's a warrant out for him, but it's never been a high priority.'

'But if we can link them all to Michael,' Derek proposed, 'we'll have enough for convictions and maybe take out the whole gang. There've got to be more of them – finance people and dealers – never mind the couriers.'

Kate finished her coffee and began to squeeze the cup absently. It cracked suddenly and she put it down on the table, wiping her hand on her skirt. 'So you'd ideally like to find them all with Michael?' *You get all your people and we get Michael back?* Except that it wasn't just about him anymore. Now the police were more interested in this drugs ring than one teenage victim.

'Precisely. It also means that we can put more resources into finding him.'

Why don't I believe you? She wanted to, but there was too much enthusiasm in Steve Peters' voice and somehow she couldn't help but think that Michael was no more than a statistic to them now. 'Did you tell all this to mum and dad?' she asked instead, wincing at the inevitable reaction from Derek. She wasn't disappointed as his eyes darkened. She'd hoped his response might be muted by Steve's presence, but she was unlucky – the only concession he made was to refrain from discussing the events of the weekend.

'Not yet, no. Steve only came in an hour ago.' He glared at her. 'But rest assured that I *will* – just as soon as I get the opportunity. They're Michael's parents too, you know.'

'I know,' she said, her voice hard. 'Believe me, I know. It was for their sake I kept quiet.'

'Yes, well I don't have the privilege of being able to consider their feelings. It's my *job*.'

'So?' She scowled and Steve chose that moment to stand up, holding up his hands, palms outwards.

'Hey, count me out of this. I've got work to do.' He turned to Derek. 'You've got my mobile?' The other man nodded. 'I'll sort you out some troops when I get back – should give your team a bit of a breather. And yes, we'll pick up the tab, but you owe me, Darwin. Big time.' He smiled quickly at Kate and left the office.

Kate could hear him whistling as he left the main room and for some reason it annoyed her even more. She glared at Derek for a moment and he met her eyes.

'Oh, hell,' he said suddenly. 'Life's too short for this crap.' He paused. 'No regrets about the weekend?'

A drop of sanity in a sea of police procedures and formality. Kate shook her head. 'No. Why? Have you?'

'No. But you should realise the difference between work and off-duty.' He hesitated. 'Sorry – that was unnecessary. Helen never could get the difference.'

'Screw Helen.'

'I did – that was the problem. What about Colin? Screw him too?'

'Oh please. Haven't I got enough problems right now?'

Derek shrugged. 'It's your life. But I think you should tell him.'

'I will,' she agreed. 'I have to. But not yet.'

TWENTY ONE

It was two weeks before Derek phoned Kate again, suggesting a lunch time drink and Kate found herself checking her make-up before she left the surgery, feeling like she was going on a date. They hadn't spoken over the intervening fortnight and it didn't seem to have bothered him, if the telephone conversation had been anything to go by. Not that he'd been unfriendly – just off-hand and distant. Kate wondered where they stood now and whose move it was next.

She'd almost called Colin the night before, but chickened out at the last minute. He hadn't called her since that Saturday and he must know what was going on. Perhaps it meant he didn't want her – not enough to put up a fight for her. *Or more likely he's being the perfect gentleman and leaving me to make up my own mind.* Sometime she wished he'd stop being so perfect and be human for a change; it would probably do him and their relationship a lot of good.

Tonight. I'll go round there tonight and sort this out, she decided as she walked into the pub. It was only fair. This thing with Derek was already out of hand and even if it never went any further, she knew she could never go back to being the old Kate again – Colin's Kate. Too much had changed.

Derek was standing at the bar, a pint in one hand. Watching the horse racing on the television, he saw her as she came in and reached into his pocket, pulling out a five pound note as she approached him. She ordered a diet coke and they found a quiet seat in the corner.

'So how's it going?' She wanted to know why he'd called.

'OK. We're still covering the area. Steve's people are helping, so my lot aren't complaining too much.' He grinned. 'Actually, they're quite pleased to get the overtime.'

'But they haven't found anything?'

He shook his head. 'And we can't keep it up indefinitely – it costs too much, and it isn't fair on our other cases. I know it shouldn't be down to money, but this is real life and if I don't produce something concrete in the next few days, they'll pull the plug.'

Kate shuffled round in her seat and leaned back. She was tired. It hadn't been easy to sleep recently. Her parents had taken Derek's revelations hard and her mum had reverted to the crying stage, while dad was alternating between abject pity and disowning his son for allowing himself to be used in this way. Kate couldn't understand their attitudes. None of this was Michael's fault. Yet it had been his choice to return – if, indeed, he had returned to wherever he'd been before and wasn't scoring down some dark alley behind King's Cross station – so perhaps in a way it was his fault now. And maybe Michael wouldn't thank them for being rescued; maybe he didn't want to be rescued.

But if he *had* been sexually assaulted – if Derek's suppositions had some foundation in truth – then why the hell had he gone back to them?

'Do you want to hear about the other two?'

'Sorry?' She shook her head. 'What other two?'

'Joss Harper and Carl Phillips.'

'What makes you so sure they're involved?'

'I'm not. It's just that Felsen's a known associate and has a track record for abuse. He's also a known heroin user, or at least he was last time we worked on him. Besides he's not a loner. If he's involved with Michael, there have to be others too.' Kate didn't reply and Derek continued. 'Harper and Phillips are big-time dealers. Phillips had gangland connections and Harper got into business using army payoff money when his brother suicided with an overdose after returning from a tour in Belfast. Interestingly enough, Harper was a promising medical student, but got kicked out when he was caught supplying morphine to feed his brother's addiction.'

Kate frowned. 'His brother od'd and he's a *dealer?*'

'Odd, isn't it? I ...' He broke off as he was interrupted by a tinny chorus of *The Simpsons*. Reaching into his jacket pocket, Derek pulled out his mobile and grimaced at Kate as he fished a notebook from the other pocket and flipped it open on the table. It wasn't what Kate would have expected for his ringtone – she'd have seen him more with some archaic seventies rock tune, or maybe *The Sweeney* for a laugh. Michael's phone had played the theme from *Mission Impossible*.

Kate toyed with her coke. From having virtually nothing to go on, they were suddenly awash with possibilities. The thought that Mike was involved with people with gangland connections was alarming, but she persuaded herself that it was still speculation and until they actually found him, they'd never know the truth. She wasn't convinced about these other men, though – it seemed an easy way for the police to tie up their cases in neat little parcels, with no loose ends left over to complicate matters.

'Excellent.' Derek was making rapid notes, spidery scrawl across numbered pages, as he punctuated the call with curt affirmatives. 'You've got a floor?' he was asking, 'and a number? Good. Find me an OP if you can – three or four higher if poss. I want everything down there. Camera with zoom, digital video – c'mon, Joey, I know you've got another one stashed away – the works. Call me when you've got it set up.' There was a further spate of notes and he shook his head violently. 'Not under *any* circumstances. We go in at five tomorrow and I do *not* want this screwed up. Can you brief the local guys? Courtesy call – ask for Baz – let him know we're going in on their patch. Oh, and get me some uniforms on standby for the morning. And if the ARV is in the area … hope we won't need them, but they'll be pissed at us if we don't warn them. Briefing at 0430, then. Good work, Joey. Speak to you soon.'

He put the mobile down, grinning broadly. 'We've got them.'

'We have? Where?' Kate was sitting on the edge of her seat. Most of the conversation had gone over her head, but she'd understood enough to realise that somebody had been spotted and followed back to an address.

'About three miles from the previous plot. One of my DCs picked up Lee Martin early on today, and they've been on him all morning. Took him back to the sixth floor of a tower block.'

'So what happens now?'

'Now we establish who else is there. We get ourselves an OP and watch the place for a bit. God – the paperwork these things involve. I'll be signing authorisations all bloody afternoon.'

Kate frowned. 'And if you don't see anyone else?'

'We go in first thing tomorrow regardless. If we can confirm that Michael and Felsen are there, so much the better, but I want to see where Lee Martin is hiding out.' He looked up. 'Now if you don't mind, Kate – I'm going to have to cut this drink short. I have a lot to organise and I don't want …'

Me getting under your feet, Kate finished for him silently while Derek's voice trailed off and he smiled suddenly.

'It's coming together, Kate. I told you I'd find him again, didn't I?'

Yes, Kate thought. *You did. But what have you found?*

'Half-nine tonight, Mikey.'

Michael looked up at the sound of Joss' voice. He and Lee had set up a particularly intricate Napoleonic war game across the dining table, after Eddie had brought back half a model shop yesterday. Michael had been surprised at the gesture, but Joss had simply grinned, telling them to go ahead and use the table. It had kept them absorbed for most of the day so far.

He shook his head. 'Not tonight.' Out of the corner of his eye he saw Lee's head jerk up and his eyes widen; Michael doubted he'd ever contradicted the man before.

'I'm sorry?' Joss sounded surprised and Michael suppressed a laugh.

'I said *not tonight*.'

'You have something else to do?' Standing in the doorway, he'd regained his composure and his voice was sugar-sweet now. Lee winced at the tone.

Michael shook his head. 'Not especially.'

'Don't play games with me, Mikey. Half-nine and you'd better be ready.'

'Fuck off, Joss.' That got a reaction and he carried on blithely. 'You make enough money out of me to give me some say in the matter.'

Joss folded his arms, an amused smile on his face now. He looked like a parent indulging a petulant child. 'Rebellion, Mikey?' he asked softly. 'What happened to all those promises you made?'

Michael shrugged, ignoring Lee's look. 'So stop the smack,' he said belligerently. 'Where's your trade then? You gonna snatch some other dumb kid off the street? And take another chance at getting caught? One day you'll make one mistake too many and some kid will be too smart to be bullied. He'll leave the same way I did and this one will talk. And *then* where will you be? So give me a break.'

Joss didn't change his expression for the whole of Michael's outburst. 'Very impressive.' He turned to go. 'And you can have tonight off,' he called back from the hall, '*this* time.'

Michael was amazed. He heard Lee stifle a gasp. He'd challenged Joss and *won*. Perhaps it *was* possible to live here on his own terms.

Lee didn't think so. 'What the *fuck* are you playin' at?' he asked, the moment he and Michael were alone in the lounge. His eyes were dark with anger and Michael realised he was genuinely concerned.

He tried to explain. 'I'm standing up for myself, Lee. Don't you think it's about time you had a say in what you do?'

'It's not that simple, Mikey. Shit, don't you remember how you were when I brought you back here? You wanna go through that again?' He moved a row of figures on the table, misjudged the space and knocked one of the buildings over. An entire army went down like a row of dominoes and Lee thumped the table in disgust. 'Fuck!'

Michael stood up and went across to the window; pushing his hair out of his eyes, he gazed out over the estate and surrounding area. The sky was overcast and the Post Office tower wasn't on view today. He turned round and leaned on the window ledge. 'What are you scared of, Lee? Worried that Joss might think you feel the same way as me?'

'Just remember who saved your neck last time.'

'I know and I'm grateful. But you don't have to let them bully you. Have you any idea how much money you make for Joss? He can't *afford* for you to think for yourself. Besides, you could walk out of here and turn him over to the police.'

'Where the fuck would that get me? In case you hadn't noticed, this place is the only friggin' home I've got.'

Michael rolled his eyes. 'That isn't the *point!* I'm just trying to make this a symbiotic relationship.'

'A what?'

'Symbiotic. Where both parties benefit from the arrangements.' God, he could still remember his GCSE biology papers. That had been one of the questions: *Define the terms symbiotic and parasitic and give examples of each.* Or something like that. Fat lot of use GCSEs had been. 'The point is that Joss knows you could shop him. You could shop all of them – *and* the perverts who come here. Lee, you were the one who told me that Eddie got off on bullying me.'

Lee's expression didn't change and Michael gave up. He'd been here too long to look at life from any other angle, and there was no way Michael was going to make him see that he could stand up to Joss and the man might even respect him for it. It was too late.

He stared out of the window again and wondered if it was too late for him as well.

'There he is.' The camera clicked off several shots and Derek showed Kate the LCD screen attached to the camcorder on a tripod. She saw Michael standing at the window opposite; he seemed to be staring straight at them and she frowned.

'He's so close.'

'Don't worry, he can't see us through the nets.'

They were in an empty flat in an adjacent block, two floors higher than the one they were watching and with a superb view of the lounge window. Obscured by net curtains, the only way to see anything was via the camera lens or camcorder, both of which used tiny and carefully cut slits in the folds of the curtains.

Kate felt awkward. It was obvious that the two young officers on duty couldn't quite understand what she was doing there and Derek's explanations were more like excuses. They were Steve Peters' people and consequently unknown faces; it apparently wasn't normal practice to bring outsiders in and they resented her presence, keeping conversation to a minimum. The radios were silent and the girl not on watch was making notes in an exercise book. It was early evening and she'd used several pages already.

'So what's the body count, so far?' Derek leaned against the wall, folding his arms. They'd only been there a few minutes, checking on the progress of the operation and Kate couldn't see why he'd brought her all this way.

The girl glanced at her before replying, her voice abrupt and not giving away any details. 'Just Redford and Martin.'

'No sign of Harper?' He looked disappointed. 'What about Phillips? Or Felsen?'

She shook her head. 'No, sir. Not yet.'

'Ah well – too much to hope for. Any movements?'

'Nothing.' She glanced at Kate again. 'They've been in all day, ever since Martin came back.'

'I got someone,' came a voice from the window. The man currently watching through the crack in the net curtains adjusted the camera and ran off several shots from the remote shutter-release on the end of the cable. 'Time is nineteen-twelve. IC1 male leaving building. Blue jeans, red shirt and black coat. Carrying a black holdall.' He'd been speaking into the radio handset, then stopped transmitting and turned to Derek. 'Sir, he could've come from any of the flats. We need someone inside the building.'

'Let's see.' Derek crouched by the camera. 'That's Harper – I'd know him anywhere.' He took the radio from the officer and hit transmit. 'Echo 1. Confirm that's X-Ray 1 just left. Stay with him.'

There was a burst of static and a faint 'Ten-Four' came back over the air.

Derek turned to the others, handing back the radio. 'Wonder where he's off to at this time in the evening.'

'And what's in that holdall,' added the DC at the camera.

'Gear, I expect,' Derek suggested, 'if he's running the

same racket as before.'

'Then why can't we have him now, sir?' asked the girl. 'If it's gear, we can *Section 18* the flat.'

'Because we don't *know* it's gear – not for certain. And I want him without any mistakes. If we take him now, we could end up with nothing and scare them off again. It could be an overnight bag for all we know.'

'And if it is, you'll lose him.'

'He'll be back,' said Derek, with a confidence Kate wasn't sure he felt. 'I'd rather play safe than risk losing them all. If he's not there tomorrow morning, we'll wait for him. I wouldn't want him to miss the party.' He stood up. 'Are you two here all night, then?'

'Only 'til midnight, sir.' He scowled. 'We get to do the legwork and miss all the fun.'

Derek smiled. 'I think the repercussions of this will last well into your next shift. Thanks for helping us out. Come on, Kate – let's leave them in peace.'

Kate smiled at the two DCs, but they weren't looking at her. She followed Derek out of the flat and down all the stairs. Avoiding the front door, they went further down to the basement and came out in an underground car-park. It was gloomy, lit only by the fading daylight showing through fancy open brickwork in the walls, and it stank of urine and decaying rubbish. It was definitely not the sort of place she wanted to even walk through, never mind live anywhere near. There were numerous exits, but Derek didn't use any of them; instead they scrambled through a hole in one of the walls and came out in a narrow gully which circled the building. Eventually the gully became steps and they were out in the open air, on the opposite side from the tower block they were watching.

'Well, Kate.' Derek unlocked the car parked several blocks away. 'Do you want to go straight home, or shall we eat somewhere?'

So much for going to see Colin tonight. But she couldn't anyway. Not tonight. Not if they were going to get Michael back tomorrow. She realised she'd stopped using the word *rescue*, as if it was suddenly inappropriate. Now they'd confirmed the involvement of these gangland criminals, she had no reason to doubt the rest of Derek's hypotheses. Which meant Rachel had been right and Michael was caught up in more than just drugs. Skirting round the issue in her mind, Kate couldn't bring herself to consider that her brother was sexually involved with these men – it was too big a jump from the Michael she'd known all his life.

Derek took her to a pizza parlour in the West End, but the conversation was strained and she was relieved when he suggested they went home. He didn't offer her a coffee at his flat, nor did he assume she wanted anything else that night. There was too much tension between them and he was preoccupied with impending events.

One way or another, it would all be over tomorrow.

TWENTY TWO

Michael was bored. Joss had gone out during the early evening and Eddie had uncharacteristically offered to cook the other two a meal. He seemed in a good mood – but then he'd been asleep for most of the afternoon – and Joss left him to it, saying only that he would probably be gone all night. Michael knew he had other places, other kids; he wondered if any of them were like him, or whether they'd just had to choose between this life and the streets.

True to his word, Joss let him have the night to himself and he spent a quiet evening watching television. Every now and then he caught Eddie looking at him curiously as if Joss had told him of the exchange of words they'd had earlier. Perhaps he had; perhaps Eddie was seeing him in a different light and not as some kid he could push around. It didn't seem to matter anymore. Michael was revelling in his new-found confidence and nothing Eddie could do or say was going to spoil it.

Lee was working. He'd avoided Michael all evening, to the extent of going out himself, although he'd promised Eddie he'd be back for his ten o'clock appointment. He came home at about quarter to, mildly drunk and in a worse mood than when he'd left, and Michael listened to him banging around in the bathroom and obviously in a filthy temper about something. Lee raided the drinks cabinet before his client arrived and managed to drink a fair amount of Joss' scotch before Eddie realised what he was doing and put a stop to it.

Michael flicked through the television channels idly, until eventually Eddie reached over and took the control from him.

'Was there something you wanted to watch, or are you just being annoying?'

Michael shrugged. 'Not really.' He hung one leg over the arm of the chair and was about to speak when Eddie beat him to it.

'What's the matter with Lee?'

'Search me.'

'You two had a row or something?'

'Not to my knowledge.' Michael was aware that he was baiting the man, trying to see how far he could push him. It was an interesting exercise; he knew Eddie could sense something of his confidence and was testing him too.

The man was watching him again only this time the look had changed. There was something else in his eyes now – a lascivious leer which told Michael exactly what he was thinking.

'What's the matter, Mikey? It's just you and me.'

'Joss said I didn't have to work tonight.' He was on the defensive already.

'Who said anything about work?' Eddie sneered. 'You and Lee got something going, then?'

'What?' Eyes widening, Michael fought to control the embarrassment which would give him away. How come Eddie knew exactly where to hit?

'Is that why he's in such a mood?'

'I don't know what you mean.'

'Of course you do. He cares about you. He risked a lot to go back for you, even in the state you were in.'

Reminding him of the pathetic whimpering mess he'd been when Lee had brought him back to the flat was

Eddie's master stroke. With his self-assurance rapidly draining away, Michael remembered crying on Eddie's shoulder and it was worse than the man knowing about him and Lee.

'Gives good head, doesn't he?' Eddie grinned widely and Michael couldn't reply. 'Better than you – or so I'm told. Want to prove him wrong?'

Michael wondered how long he could stall for and whether it was worth the effort. After everything he'd done already, would it really matter if he just got on with it and gave Eddie what he wanted? At least the man would leave him in peace then. *Shit, give me a break, somebody!*

After a few moments, he glanced at Eddie with what he hoped was a bored expression. 'Whatever.'

The look on Eddie's face told him more than he'd ever wanted to know.

Kate couldn't sleep. After Derek had dropped her off, she'd sat down with mum and dad and filled them in on the latest news, as she'd promised him she would. It hadn't changed their attitude much, although mum had stopped crying and seemed more concerned with how they were going to prevent the newspapers getting hold of the story. Her dad was totally revolted by the whole situation and was expounding yet again on how an army career would have sorted Michael out years ago and prevented any of this nonsense from happening. Discipline was what the young people of today apparently needed, discipline and respect for society. Instead they'd got him doing subjects he hated in order to embark upon a career he didn't want, the result of which being that nobody won and everyone was miserable. Sometimes Kate thought that her father should have given Michael enough self-discipline to stand up for himself and do what *he* wanted to do.

Eventually she went to bed. They all needed an early night. There was a car coming at four o'clock in the morning, to take them down to the police station nearest to Michael's flat ready for when they brought him out of the place. It was like something off television – some police film drama – and there was a cloud of unreality hanging over everything. And would he thank them for putting his new friends behind bars, exploding his personal life across every newspaper in the country? Could he stand the inevitable scandal? *Can any of us?* She still hadn't spoken to Colin and was scared to, not wanting his name to be linked with what was about to happen.

The clock was ticking and the countdown had started.

Crawling into bed at one in the morning, Lee was doing his best to be quiet, but Michael wasn't asleep. He'd half-expected him to stay in Eddie's room overnight, and was surprised to hear the door creak slightly and light footsteps pad over the carpet. He hoped Lee's mood had improved; he couldn't face an argument, not now. Tired, he'd been glad when Eddie had finally left him alone, depressed at how easily his confidence had evaporated when faced with a challenge.

'You awake?' Lee's voice was soft and slurred.

'I am now.' It wouldn't hurt Lee to think he'd been asleep.

'Wanted to say sorry.'

'What for?' A sentimental conversation filtered through a veil of alcohol wasn't what he wanted right now.

Lee yawned loudly and stretched. 'Gettin' mad with you earlier. Guess you just piss me sometimes.'

'What do you mean?' Rolling onto his side, he propped himself up on one elbow, interested despite himself.

'Dunno.' Lee hesitated. 'You've been here – how long? A few fuckin' months? – and you've already got everyone figured, haven't you? You dissed Joss and survived.'

'Did I?' He supposed he had. Maybe that was why he'd felt so elated afterwards. Point scoring had never been his style, but he'd stood up for himself for once and Joss had backed down. So why had he let Eddie get under his skin?

Oh very funny, Mike. You'll be saying Joss gives you the needle next! It made him smile in the darkness and suddenly none of it mattered. If he'd faced Joss once, he could do it again. The principle was the same.

Lee reached out with one hand and Michael flinched instinctively before he relaxed. Lee was too pissed to do more than lie there and Michael wasn't about to initiate anything.

'You're so fuckin' ...' Lee was silent for a moment, evidently searching for the right words. 'So fuckin' *smart*. Things have changed since you came.'

Michael felt the mattress move as Lee shifted his weight and laid his head in the crook of Michael's arm. He tried to pull away, but instead ended up with his arm round the younger boy's shoulders.

'Why d'ya come back?' Lee twisted the ends of his hair. 'You don't belong here. You never will.'

'I needed the heroin.' He paused and added simply: 'Joss won.'

'Nah. Joss didn't win. You did – that was fuckin' obvious from this mornin'. It changed everythin'.'

'Changed what?' Michael didn't understand what he was getting at.

'*Everythin'*. I'm scared.' He rolled into Michael's shoulder.

Michael didn't move. It had always been Lee looking out for him, ever since Eddie had first found him. And now, the roles had reversed and Michael was the protector; it wasn't a position he wanted and he had no idea how to handle it – not that Lee seemed to expect him to do or say anything as he'd fallen asleep. Still half-lying on his side, Michael wondered what Lee had meant by everything changing, although he knew he was right. Things *had* changed, were still changing. There was something in the air and he knew another phase of his life in this place was about to come to an end. He wondered what the final outcome would be.

Four o'clock. Derek's car arrived with a driver. She'd thought it might be Derek himself or even Steve Peters, but of course they'd be busy organising things on the other side of London.

It was a crisp night and she grabbed her jacket from the banisters as she followed the man out to the car, her parents close behind. Mum and dad were silent; they'd barely spoken over the breakfast Kate had put together half an hour ago in an attempt to give the occasion at least some semblance of normality. She'd failed miserably.

Speeding down the A4, the car seemed to eat up the miles. Even Earl's Court was quiet in the deadest part of the night and the journey took on a dreamlike quality. It felt like they were driving through time and Kate wished it was possible. If they could only go back three months to before this all started, before she'd convinced them to let Michael celebrate his birthday in style. Before he'd met Eddie. *And before I met Derek?* Perhaps not.

She'd finally spoken to Colin. Late last night, she'd walked past the phone in the hall, picked up the receiver and dialled his number before she could change her mind. He'd been polite and concerned when she'd told him what was happening – polite, concerned and distant. He knew it was over. There was no need for words. He offered his help and support though, and for that she was grateful.

They were driven to a small but modern police station and shown into an unoccupied office. Coffee appeared on cue and Derek a few minutes later, who told them that everything was still running to schedule, although Joss Harper hadn't returned to the flat during the night.

Things became unreal and a fuzzy haze of confusion descended. Time jumped crazily off the rails with no apology for the derailment. Seconds stretched to minutes and then minutes condensed to seconds in a blur of people, telephones and radio transmissions.

It was twenty to five.

Michael was dreaming about Jenny. She was dancing for him, slowly and seductively, green sequins sparkling in the smoky strobe lights of the club as she spun and moved to the pounding rhythm of the music. He walked over to her and she twisted away from him. And when she looked over her shoulder, it was Lee's face that stared back at him.

Ten to five. Derek stood at the office window, a radio handset in one palm as the team checked in over the air, confirming their positions.

Michael woke briefly and rolled over, shoving Lee out of the way with one foot. Lee mumbled something in protest, but Michael was already asleep again.

Five o'clock. Two words spoken into the radio. It had started.

TWENTY THREE

'In here!'

Michael heard the voice in his sleep and didn't recognise it. He was in a corridor, but the walls were made of mirrors, bright and shiny glass above and below as well as all around him. Everywhere he looked there were thousands of Michaels endlessly reflecting themselves in all directions and all of them slightly different.

Which was the real Michael? And where was the way out of this maze? The walls stretched to either side and there were only two directions he could go – forwards or backwards. Shutting his eyes dizzily, he reached out, touching a smooth cold surface to one side of him and leaning against it gratefully.

And heard the voice again. 'I'll handle this one – you two take the other room.'

What room? Where am I? The wall abruptly dissolved into something warm and soft and he opened his eyes, realising he'd been dreaming. Screwing up his eyes against the glare of the lights, he wondered what had woken him.

The voice was still there. 'Two boys. I think one is the Redford kid.'

Redford? Nobody here called him by his real name. Michael was wide awake now and he rolled over onto his back, his outstretched arm finding Lee, who was curled up on his side in his usual fashion.

'Michael?'

He sat up, wondering what was going on and lurched backwards in the bed as he saw the stranger standing in the doorway. '*Shit!*' He clutched at the duvet protectively.

'You're Michael Redford?' The same voice again, and its owner crossed the room in long easy strides. Michael didn't answer, and he was saved from replying as Lee chose this moment to roll over and sit up, yawning sleepily.

Lee stared at the man blankly. 'Who the *fuck* are you?'

'Police,' came the reply. 'You must be Lee Martin. Just keep calm and we'll sort this out as soon as we can.'

'Like fuck!' Lee leapt out of the bed, tried to side-step him, but was stopped before he got anywhere close to the doorway. The man didn't react, but unhooked a robe and handed it to him, before calmly closing the door.

'Cover yourself up.' To Michael he said: 'You *are* Michael Redford?'

Michael nodded dumbly, cheeks scarlet.

The stranger was obviously surprised, but hiding it well. He had a radio in one hand. 'Redford and Martin so far.'

Michael heard sounds from the hallway, the door flew open and Eddie stumbled into the bedroom, eyes blazing. He was still pulling a sweater over his head and held a pair of socks in one hand. Close behind followed two more men and Michael wondered just how many people had managed to creep into the flat undetected. And for that matter, how had they got in?

'Looks like we got Felsen as well.' The man turned to the other two. 'Any others?'

'No.' One of them shook his head. 'Place is empty. Seems like Harper spent the night away from home.'

'Yeah, yeah,' said the first man. 'Don't rub it in – like you've never lost a target? I swear the guy vanished into thin air on Commercial Road last night.'

Michael was still hiding behind the duvet, watching the exchange in horror. If these men were police, then somehow they'd not only known how to find him, but who he was with as well. And all he'd told them was one name. *Eddie.* This couldn't possibly be down to him.

Eddie finished dressing and glared at Michael venomously. 'You little shit.'

He shook his head, not trusting himself to speak just yet. And who the hell was Harper anyway? Could they mean Joss? He'd gone out last night and presumably hadn't yet returned.

'Michael?' The guy in charge was speaking to him again. 'Michael, I'm Steve Peters. D'you want to put some clothes on? It might make you feel a bit more comfortable.'

He didn't answer, but looked over at Lee, who was standing backed up against the wardrobe, a black silk robe knotted around his waist. He looked tense and unhappy, long hair trailing over his face as he stared back at Michael.

'What've you done, Mikey?'

'He's shopped us all, the little *bastard*,' said Eddie in a low voice. 'That's what he's fucking *done!* Remember that, Lee, when you're in some fucking social services home. Remember it was this *shithead* who did it to you.'

'Eddie, I *didn't!*' Michael was quick to defend himself, forgetting that it really didn't matter what anyone – least of all Eddie – thought. And yet somehow he felt he had to justify himself to them, had to make them see that this hadn't been his doing.

Eddie moved towards the bed, a murderous look in his eyes, but was quickly intercepted by Steve Peters. 'You done the necessaries, Ross?'

One of Eddie's escorts nodded. 'Arrest and caution at five-eleven.'

'Then get him out of here, get him cuffed and start on a search of this place. With gloves, please. I'll get you some back-up in a minute, as soon as I've got these two sorted.

And watch out for sharps.' As the three men left, Steve took Lee's shoulders and gently shoved him in the direction of the armchair in the corner of the room, on which lay an untidy heap of clothes. 'Get dressed, Lee. And you, Michael. I want you both out of here as soon as possible. Michael, your parents are nearby.'

'And if I don't want to see them?' He didn't mean to be deliberately obstructive, but everything was moving too fast and he wanted to know how they'd got their information. What the hell were his parents doing here, anyway? *Oh yes, Mr and Mrs Redford. We found your son, and by the way he was in bed with another boy.* Shit, it didn't bear thinking about – there was no way on God's *earth* he was going to be able to bullshit his way out this time.

Steve shrugged. 'Up to you. Now get dressed.' Into the radio he relayed the arrest information and called in another two men to assist with the search of the flat.

Slipping out of bed, Michael was suddenly self-conscious despite the man's attitude. After the initial shock, Steve was acting for all the world as if finding two teenagers in bed together happened every day of the week. Perhaps it did in his job. But he tactfully turned away and stood looking out into the hall. Michael could hear raised voices from the kitchen, the sound of swearing and breaking glass.

Lee scrambled into jeans and sweatshirt, refusing to meet Michael's eyes and when Michael touched his arm, he pulled away violently. 'K'off.'

'Lee, for fuck's sake! I haven't *done* anything!'

'Haven't you?' He stared at Michael for a moment and resumed dressing in silence, sitting on the bed to lace his trainers.

Steve turned round as they spoke. 'OK,' he said, when they were both done. 'Before we go, I need to ask you something. Do either of you know a man called Joss Harper?'

'Joss?'

'No.'

Michael's reply beat Lee's by a fraction of a second and Lee scowled, shaking his hair from his face. 'Whose friggin' side are you on?'

'Nobody's.' *Fuck it!* He didn't have to explain himself to Lee. He didn't have to explain himself to *anybody*.

Steve had the radio up to his mouth and he paused, glancing between the two youths. 'How about Carl Phillips?' he asked after a moment. Neither Michael nor Lee said a word, and Steve shook his head and pressed the transmit button. 'Positive on Harper; negative for Phillips. Guess two out of three ain't bad, guys. Where the hell are the rest of my team?'

A burst of static followed and Steve shook his head. 'Bloody tower blocks. You both ready? Then let's get out of here. I don't want you two around when Harper returns.'

Michael could see his point. He had no desire to be anywhere near Joss when he came back to a reception committee.

Two more police officers arrived as they were leaving – a man and a woman who Steve instructed to assist in the search. In the hallway stood a uniformed constable and as they got out onto the landing, there were two more in plain clothes to escort them down the stairs to the basement. The police evidently weren't taking any chances on Lee running off this time and they positioned themselves one in front and one behind the trio.

'For your own protection,' Steve commented, seeing the look on Michael's face. 'Our friend Joss Harper isn't fussy about the company he keeps.'

Michael didn't understand what he was on about. Presumably they had the building under observation, so if Joss did put in an appearance, they'd have sufficient warning of the event. *Unless our people are in other flats in this block.* It made him stop and think for a second until one of the men walked into him from behind. *Our people?* Whose side *was* he on? The flat's front door was half-off its hinges and he wondered how come he hadn't heard them enter.

Feeling a gentle push from behind, he carried on walking. He'd forgotten how many flights of stairs he'd come up that night. *The night Lee came back for me.* He glanced covertly at Lee, but the boy had his head down, watching the steps with his shoulders hunched inside his jacket. He looked as taut as a crossbow, ready to bolt at the first opportunity, although Michael doubted he'd get one.

Down in the basement, they went out the same way Lee had brought him in, squeezing under the cracked concrete lintel and coming out onto a piece of grass between two tower blocks. It was eerily quiet in the grey light of near-dawn; even the birds weren't yet quite awake, although there were one or two soft chirrups from the line of straggly rowan trees which fringed the edge of the area. There was nobody in sight, other than one early-morning jogger and a man in a leather jacket at the bus stop across the road, whom Michael suspected might well not be all he seemed. Moving quickly across the open space, Steve led them down a slope and into the dark subterranean car-park for the adjacent block of flats, where it was a different story.

There were six cars down here, headlights on and doors open; groups of men and women were talking in low voices. Michael recognised Derek immediately and the man walked up to them as the group stopped by one of the cars. Steve nodded to one of their escorts and he moved to stand behind Lee, whose head shot up with an incensed expression on his face as the man took hold of his shoulders with a firm grip.

Steve smiled slightly. 'Sorry. 'Fraid you've got a bit of a reputation for running out on us.'

'Am I under arrest?' His voice was caustic and Steve shook his head.

'No, Lee. I'm just—'

'Then get your fuckin' hands off me.' He tried to jerk free, but the man wasn't having any of it. 'Let me go!'

'Lee?' This was Derek now. 'Lee, listen to me.'

'Fuck off. You can't make me stay if you're not arrestin' me—'

'Don't quote your rights at me, Lee Martin – I know them better than you do. I've seen your files and if I need the law to keep you here, I'll use it. Give me cause and I'll cuff you right now.'

'Is that how you like it?' Lee glared at him through the gloom. 'What do you want?'

'Your version of the story. What you've been doing with yourself since you ran away.'

'What, here?' He raised his eyebrows. 'You want all the friggin' details right here and now? I hope you've not just had breakfast—'

'For fuck's sake, Lee!' Michael interrupted him suddenly, convinced he was about to tell the whole world their secrets. If they backed him too far into a corner, Michael didn't know what Lee would say in order to take the heat off and divert attention elsewhere; if he told about the night they'd gone too far – the night which was etched in acid, still burning his mind as fresh as the moment it happened – Michael didn't know what he would do.

Lee tried to pull away from the man holding him. 'Let me go. I won't run.'

'Somehow, I'm just not convinced.' He turned to Michael next, looking him up and down appraisingly as if considering what to say. 'Hello again, Michael. You going to stop feeding me crap this time? Or are you still going to insist that Eddie Felsen is just a friend of yours?'

'I don't know what you mean.' *Eddie Felsen?* Derek knew his surname, something which Michael had been very careful not to let slip. He remembered that Joss had once said Eddie had a criminal record.

Derek shrugged. 'Have it your way.' He waved at the man still standing behind Lee. 'Get them back to the station. In separate cars, please. And you'd better contact social services – I think there's an emergency number somewhere on the board behind the custody sergeant's desk. I'll be back in twenty.'

'Guv.'

With the assistance of several more police officers, Michael and Lee were led to different cars. A woman climbed into the back seat with Michael and he shrank away, not wanting to be near anyone. The car doors wouldn't open from the inside and he watched the rest of the group morosely. There were a good dozen or so people still standing around the four remaining cars, huddled around the open doors like moths gravitating towards the light; they were talking in low voices and through the open driver's door of his car, Michael could hear the occasional burst of radio static. It looked like a large and carefully-planned operation and he wondered yet again how they knew so much about what was going on – more than he did and he'd been living there for months.

A young-looking man with blond hair and faded jeans jumped into the driver's seat, shutting the door behind him. 'Hi, Michael,' he said, twisting in his seat as he started the engine. 'You feeling OK?'

He said nothing. Why wouldn't he be OK? How much did they *know?* Glancing at the woman out of the corner of his eye, he saw she was watching him intently and he squirmed uncomfortably. It was like playing a card game with somebody who'd seen your hand, and he frowned as the car manoeuvred in the confined space, trying to think how on earth he could shorten the odds.

By the time they arrived at the local police station, the sun was up and the birds were out in full force. As a child, Michael had always loved early mornings – it had been a time when he'd felt like the only person alive, and he'd frequently gone for long Sunday walks in the park before the rest of the day caught up with him. Then the world had tightened its grip as he'd grown up, and morning strolls had been replaced by sleeping in after late nights. Now he felt as if it had strangled him altogether, caught him in a web of shame and deceit from which he couldn't break free.

They sat him in a small windowless room; it was stuffy and claustrophobic and the pale dawn light vanished into the glare of overhead neon. The woman from the car sat with him and for the first time in his life, Michael wanted a cigarette. He didn't even smoke, he never had done, but he needed something to do with his hands, something to ease the tension which was building with remorseless persistence in the back of his mind and spilling out into the atmosphere. And although his body had no physical need for heroin as yet, his brain was stubbornly counting the hours and telling him how long he had before he would need to score. A slight tremor shuddered through his body as he realised there would never be a chance to go back to Joss and Eddie now. This time it really was over.

Derek came in about twenty-five minutes later, pulling out the chair opposite him and sighing as he sat down. He checked his watch, leaning back to the woman. 'Get us some coffee, would you, Susie? And Michael might like breakfast. Or toast at least.'

He shook his head. Food was the last thing on his mind. He stared at the black formica table and ran a fingernail down the grooves, hearing the woman leave and the door close behind her.

'Do you want to see your parents?' Derek's voice had changed now; it was softer and calm, with a tone which suggested he had all day to spare.

'They're here?' He looked up and saw far too much in Derek's eyes.

The man nodded. 'Your mother, father and Kate. One of my men picked them up at four this morning. Do you want to see them?' He hesitated. 'You don't have to.'

'No.' He shook his head. Later. He knew he'd have to

face them at some point, but not yet. But he couldn't go home with them; he didn't have a home anymore, did he? Not now the police were probably trashing it even as he sat there, destroying the battle scenario he and Lee had spent so long setting up ...

'Fine,' said Derek lightly. 'How about Susie? You mind her sitting in? Or would you prefer a man?'

Oh yeah, I prefer men. Haven't they told you that yet?

Susie returned with coffee and Michael didn't refuse a cup. He yawned. How long were they going to keep him here this time?

'All right, Michael,' Derek began a few moments later. 'Are you going to tell me about it, or are we going to play twenty questions?'

'Where's Lee?' Michael asked instead.

'He's next door with one of my colleagues from the drug squad. Social services will look after him.' Derek leaned across the table. 'Have you been living with him all this time?'

Michael nodded. There didn't seem much point in lying any more.

'Was he there when Eddie took you?'

'Lee's my friend.' God, it sounded pathetic.

'Friends are good.' There was no sarcasm in the man's voice, only a quiet concern. 'Edward Felsen has a record for sexual assault and violence.'

'I know.' *Sexual assault as well?* Though why it should surprise him, he didn't know.

'And you still want to call *him* your friend?'

'No. Never.' He took a sip of coffee.

Derek gave Susie an *ah, we're getting somewhere* look, but didn't comment.

'Eddie took you back to his flat that night. Why did you go with him?'

'I was pissed. Haven't you ever done anything dumb when you're pissed?'

'More times than I can remember. So go on, Michael.

What happened next?'

'I don't know.'

'You weren't that drunk. You walked out of the club.'

I don't remember. It was a lifetime ago and somebody else's lifetime at that. Michael shrugged. 'He spiked my drink and I woke up three weeks later.'

'*What?*' Derek sat up straight and was about to continue when the door opened and a face peered round.

'A word, Derek?'

He swore softly and stood up, returning to the room a few moments later. 'Sorry about that.' He paused, perching on the corner of the table and folding his arms. 'Do you know anyone called Joss Harper, Michael?'

He nodded. 'Joss was the other guy. He was in charge.'

'Of what? The drugs or the prostitution?'

Michael's head shot up and his hand knocked the cup of coffee, sending liquid pooling across the table and dripping over the edge. They knew. That meant *everyone* knew. They all knew what he'd done.

'Talk to me, Michael.' Derek sat down on the chair again, moved the cups to one side and leaned forward, oblivious to the spilt coffee. 'Help me nail these bastards.'

There was a long silence. He stared at the man for a moment before his eyes focused. Closing his mouth, he couldn't speak for several minutes and Derek didn't push him, but let him sit there flexing his fists and clenching his teeth. 'How did you find out?' he asked finally, forcing the words out from behind the lump in his throat.

'I'm a detective, Michael. It's my job to find things out. The only sensible bit of information you gave us last time was Felsen's name, but it was enough to set the wheels in motion.' Derek glanced at Susie who was sitting by the door. 'Michael, nobody is blaming you for *anything* that happened, but I need you to tell me about it. Susie can leave, if you want privacy. Just you and me.'

'I can't.' His voice wasn't much more than a whisper. 'Oh, *fuck!*' He pushed the chair back and stood up, walking across to the corner of the room and leaning against the wall, his face resting on his arm. Closing his eyes, he was breathing heavily, his shoulders shaking. The plaster felt cool on his forehead. He kicked the wall a few times.

Derek looked at Susie again and nodded. She slipped out of the room, closing the door quietly. There was a long silence.

Derek tried a different tack. 'If you can't talk to me, then give me a word, Michael. One word. Yes or no. Did they – did Joss Harper or Edward Felsen – force you to have sexual intercourse? With them or anybody else?'

One word. That's all he had to give the man. But one word was answering way too many questions and it was never going to end, was it?

'Come on, Michael. Just one word. The rest can wait until you're ready.'

Ready for what? Michael took a deep breath, pushed himself off the wall and met Derek's eyes. He tried to speak but nothing came out, so he sat down on the floor in the corner, brought his knees up to his chest and buried his face in them. 'Yes.'

'That's all I needed, Michael. Thank you.' Derek paused, then went on relentlessly. 'They've finished the search of the flat. There were two handguns found with an impressive quantity of ammunition, over 5 ks of heroin and several thousand pounds in cash. Michael, it wasn't your fault. None of it was. These people aren't petty criminals – they're intelligent, manipulative men.'

Michael didn't move. Of course it was his fault. He'd been stupid enough to go with Eddie in the first place, full of a teenage bravado that made him shrug off the knowledge that the man had quite deliberately spiked his beer. He'd been determined only to prove to Jenny that he didn't give a shit and instead he'd given his life. And even when he'd had the chance of a fresh start, he'd thrown it away.

Yet it hadn't all been bad – that was the strange part.

He'd grown up away from home, made decisions about his life that only he had the right to make. He'd enjoyed the freedom of Joss' regime, the conversations he'd had with the man – adult to adult – and the friendship he'd forged with Lee, no matter what else had come with it.

He didn't want to turn his back on it all and go home. He couldn't. The line between Michael and Mikey was blurred and indistinct, and he was no longer sure on which side of it he belonged.

TWENTY FOUR

'He doesn't want to see you.' Derek gave it to them unsweetened. 'I can't force him. I *won't* force him. He's been through enough already.'

Sylvia Redford was as white as chalk. 'Is he all right?'

What kind of a question is that, mum? Kate wanted to ask. If he was all right, he wouldn't be here. Yet, despite the pale skin and worried eyes, her mother had that *coping* look about her again. Now she could do something more than sit at home and wait, Mrs Redford would hold her family together to the best of her ability. It was when there was nothing *to* do, that she went to pieces, as if she was saving her strength for when it could do some good.

'I don't know. He's not going to talk to me about it. It will be a while before he'll open up to anybody.' Derek held up his hands. 'Frankly, I don't want to get involved. It's outside of my experience and I'm just as likely to make matters worse. He should see people who are trained to help. Counsellors.'

'Psychiatrists,' said Charles Redford, Kate's dad. 'You think my son should see a psychiatrist.'

'Yes, if you like.' Derek stood at the window and turned to look out at the early-morning traffic. 'Mr Redford, I wouldn't presume to tell you how to deal with

Michael, but—'

'Good. I'm glad we see things the same way.'

'—but he'll need to see a specialist for the heroin. And get some blood tests. I can arrange both for you now, if you like. Find Michael somewhere secure to stay for a few days, somewhere safe and away from the press.'

'Yes, well I'm sure we know what's best for him. Thank you for finding him, Inspector, but why don't you get back to your job and prosecute these men? We'll look after Michael.'

'Dad!' Kate shook her head, apologising to Derek with her eyes. 'Derek knows what he's talking about – he's had cases like this before!'

'Derek, is it?' Her father gave her an odd look and stood up. 'We'll take Michael home with us now.'

Derek swung round. 'I really don't think that's a good idea. He needs—'

'*Thank* you, Inspector. Rest assured that Michael will get all the help he needs. Now, if you'd be so kind as to fetch him.'

'Wait here.' Derek's voice was clipped as he strode from the room, closing the door firmly behind him. Kate cast a backwards glance at her parents and followed him, ignoring her mother's voice behind her.

She caught up with Derek further down the corridor; his mouth was set in a tight line and his eyes dark. 'Derek, I'm sorry.'

He sighed. 'It's not your fault. Jesus, where does he get that Victorian attitude?'

'It's not like it seems. He loves Mike, believe it or not. It's just that he always wanted a son and he doesn't understand why Mike can't live up to his expectations.'

Derek leaned against the wall of the corridor. 'Kate, he's curled up on the floor back there, trying not to cry. He's so messed up, he doesn't know night from day. He ran last time – he'll run again. And this time there's nowhere for him to run back to. He needs professional help *now*, or he'll end up on the streets.'

'Then keep him here.'

'I *can't!* He's under age and he's done nothing wrong. If they want to take him away, I can't stop them.'

'Let me talk to them – see if I can persuade them. What do you think is best for Michael?'

'I don't know. The one thing he's adamant about is that he doesn't want to see any of you.' He pursed his lips. 'I've a contact in a drug dependency clinic I'd like to speak to. He might be able to suggest the best move, maybe find him a secure placement. Meanwhile I want to hear what Lee has said.'

Kate nodded. 'All right. I'll go and work on the folks.'

Michael was alone for the first time. The room seemed even smaller somehow, the air full of dirty secrets and stinking half-truths. Echoes buzzed around his head like angry flies, constantly bombarding his brain with questions. *Who? When? How?* He couldn't sort the thoughts into order anymore; they lay in his mind in an untidy heap, oozing a bitterness that would stain him for the rest of his life. He was marked now. A great sign hung over his head for all the world to see. *I let men fuck me!* Not *I'm gay*, which while it might not be true was still socially acceptable, but worse than that. He'd never be able to go out in public again, never be able to look a girl in the eye. And, oh God, how could he ever speak to dad again? What was Eddie compared to Saddam Hussein and he'd let it happen.

The walls were closing in. He didn't even know what time it was; having left his watch back at the flat, it could be morning or afternoon by now and with no natural light, it was difficult to judge the passage of time. He felt like he'd been here days. Standing up, Michael carefully opened the door. Outside, the corridor was empty, but a distant murmur of voices from behind the swing doors told him he had only seconds to get away before they'd be at him again, trying to persuade him to see a doctor. He didn't know how long he'd be able to resist them. How long before they stopped consulting him and went ahead and did it anyway? And a medical examination would kill him – or if it didn't, he'd kill himself afterwards. After all, they didn't care about *him*, did they? Not as long as they proved their own theories and gathered enough evidence along the way to charge Eddie and Joss. It didn't matter that by this evening he'd be a gibbering wreck and he wouldn't be able to stop himself telling them everything they wanted to know and a great deal more besides. No, he had to get away. Anywhere. Just away from the questions. Away from the looks and the sighs – and away from his parents.

'Michael?' Another stranger appeared from up the corridor. 'Sorry. I just had to go to the loo. Is there anything you need?'

God, they had a guard on his door. What did they think he was going to do? *Exactly what I'm doing. Getting out of here. Escaping.* But wasn't the escape supposed to have been from Joss, not the police?

More voices and Derek appeared through the double doors, closely followed by Kate and his parents. Much as he hated the idea, Michael realised he'd have to play along, get outside the building before he could make a run for it. But he'd need money to survive.

His parents approaching, Michael eyed the handbag his mother was clutching and an idea began to form. He forced a smile onto his face. 'Can I go home now?' he asked the group as they got within earshot.

'If that's what you want.' Derek sounded puzzled. 'I'll need to take a statement at some point.' Michael nodded. 'I can sort you a methadone prescription for tonight, and I'll have a hospital appointment arranged for you tomorrow.'

Michael gritted his teeth and nodded again. *Think money. Credit cards. Agree with them.*

They went through to the front office and Derek let them out into the reception area. 'Are you sure you'll be all right? I can find somewhere for you to go now to get help, or get a meth scrip written up by the duty GP in ten minutes—'

'We'll be fine, thank you.' His father answered as he opened the main door. Michael could smell freedom.

He took his chance. They were all preoccupied, nobody knew what to do or say and he stepped towards his mum as if he was about to embrace her. As she opened her arms, he grabbed her bag – for all the world an experienced street thief – and headed for the door, squeezing past his father. They were all so stunned they just stood there, and for a second he wanted to laugh.

'Michael, wait!'

He hesitated, standing in the doorway to the street. Outside he could hear the roar of the traffic on the main road as the day woke up. He didn't know which was worse – the pity in their eyes, or their revulsion over what had happened to him. They didn't know the half of it, thinking he'd been forced into it, raped and bullied into submission and maybe it had been that way at first, but not later, not after he'd realised that sex was just a means of survival, a physical act of no more significance than masturbation. Even Eddie hadn't really bothered him towards the end. Only Lee – and that was different.

'Michael?' This was Derek now, half a dozen paces away and waving a hand back at the family, trying to stop them coming past. 'Michael, it's OK. Nobody's going to make you do anything you don't want to.'

Oh yeah? He wasn't convinced. *Don't patronise me! I'm not stupid.* They knew as well as he did that in twelve hours time he'd be past caring anyway.

'You don't have to run. It won't solve anything.'

'Let me go.'

'Go where?' Derek stepped forward slowly, his eyes not leaving Michael's. 'It's over, Michael. There *is* no going back.'

'I can't stay here, either. Why doesn't anyone

understand?'

'I do understand.'

Michael hesitated. Was it possible? He looked beyond Derek to where his – *family?* – were standing and knew he couldn't do it.

He went down the steps backwards, still clutching the bag and nearly fell over the uniformed constable coming back to the station. The man made a rapid assessment of the situation and took the bag in one hand and Michael's wrist in the other.

Michael wrenched away, twisted out of his grip and ran straight across the road and into the path of a red Ford Ka.

TWENTY FIVE

'Other than the obvious problems, there's no reason why he shouldn't be awake.' The doctor at the end of the bed shook his head, making notes on his clipboard as he spoke.

Kate looked at her brother, knowing perfectly well why he'd rather sleep. Awake, he'd have to face the world, face the knowledge that what had happened to him had now been confirmed beyond any doubt. Conscious, he'd have to accept the past and make plans for the future. Could any of them really blame him for choosing to block it out with sleep? 'You think he's faking it?' she asked in a low voice. 'Pretending to be asleep, when he can hear every word we're saying?'

'I doubt it,' the doctor replied. 'It goes much deeper than that. I don't think it's a conscious decision at all, more of an instinctive reaction to the situation. It isn't unusual under the circumstances.'

You mean you've seen this before? Christ, did things like this happen frequently? 'So what can we do?'

'Just wait. When Michael decides he's ready to come to terms with things, he'll wake up. He's fine otherwise – he's a very lucky young man. His wrist will mend and as for the other physical ... issues – well, there are no real injuries, not anymore.'

'How do you mean?'

The doctor tucked his clipboard under one arm and adjusted his wire spectacles. 'Miss Redford, your brother has been sexually active for some time. There is evidence of anal intercourse, certainly, but any damage it did has long since healed. The human body is remarkably adaptable, you know.' He paused. 'Getting him off the heroin will be harder – but it's not impossible. Physically, I'd expect him to make a full recovery.'

But not psychologically. Kate watched him continue on his rounds and resumed her position at Michael's bedside. Asleep he looked so young, so vulnerable and yet he had to be strong, he must have been to have survived the past few months. His face was pale and his right wrist was encased in plaster, the hard shell only partially obscuring the needle marks still visible on the inside of his elbow. His other hand was attached via a venflon to a saline drip and he'd been catheterised too; she wondered how he'd react to that when he finally woke up. Not to mention the blood samples they'd taken for STD testing.

They'd given him methadone, which while it wouldn't give him the buzz he presumably got from his regular shots, would at least keep his body stable and prevent the awful debilitating withdrawal symptoms she'd seen in some of the surgery patients. Two of the GPs in her surgery were sympathetic to addicts, offering both physical relief in the form of methadone prescriptions, and counselling to reduce the dosage. It was a delicate and controversial subject which had already led to two of the other doctors walking out and setting up their practice elsewhere, believing that encouraging addicts with NHS funds was not the answer and the only solution was complete abstinence. She wondered if they saw the withdrawal process as some kind of penance for what in their eyes was clearly a self-inflicted problem. Kate had never really considered the subject before – it had never affected her beyond her job. She remembered one case where an addict had totally wrecked the waiting room, throwing chairs through the windows and sending the other patients running for cover; they'd had to call the police to subdue him and he'd been up in court the next day. The publicity had been awful and hadn't been helped by the fact that two days later the young man concerned had gone out, made a street deal and overdosed. They'd found him in somebody's front garden, curled up under a forsythia in the rain. He'd been dead for some hours.

She looked up, hearing movement behind her and turned to see Derek standing there. He looked tired and didn't smile when he saw her.

'How is he?'

'Apparently fine. Aside from a broken wrist and the drug addiction, of course. They say the only thing preventing him from waking up is Michael himself.'

Derek pulled up a chair and sat down. 'They've examined him?'

'You mean for evidence of abuse?' Kate shrugged. 'They won't confirm it's rape. Just sex. He's over sixteen and for all we know, he consented.' *And just maybe he did.*

It was all so formal. Kate couldn't believe she'd slept with the man. Somehow with Michael lying there, things seemed different and it was the family that was important now. Derek was too involved for her to be able to separate him as a detective inspector from them as a couple. It could never work.

'I have an idea,' said Derek after a moment, looking at Michael thoughtfully. 'You want him to wake up?'

'He has to sooner or later. Much as dad hates the idea, he needs professional help.'

'Michael's fallen off his pedestal, right?'

'Something like that. Mike could never live up to his ideals. He was never allowed to make mistakes, so he never learned how to deal with them. It's hard having a war hero for a father.' She hesitated. 'And it's hard for dad to be smacked in the face with the truth. So what's your idea?'

'I might know a way to get through to him. Or rather, someone who could.'

'You mean Lee, don't you? How is he?'

'Unhelpful and generally obstructive. I guess it can't be much fun for him, being dumped onto social services like an unwanted present. His mother laughed at me when I tracked her down, and told me in no uncertain terms that she would be more than happy never to see the kid again. I'd give him a week before he'll be off.'

'Back to the street?'

'It's the only life he knows.' Derek stood up. 'He's fourteen years old, for God's sake. What more can I do?'

'I don't know.' Something about Lee made her uneasy. The relationship he had with Michael might make matters worse, not better. But on the other hand, she had the feeling that Lee might be the only person he trusted right now. 'I guess it can't do any harm.'

'Do you want me to have him brought in?'

'Only if he wants to. I don't want him forced into it – who knows what he might say under those circumstances.'

'All right. Let him sleep tonight and we'll see what Lee can do tomorrow.'

Michael was in the corridor of mirrors again, but he understood why now. It was a choice he had to make – which of the images was really him and which of the two paths he was going to follow. It was a hard decision and he didn't appreciate the distractions. There were noises and lights, voices trying to push him in directions he didn't want to go and he fought them angrily, wanting only to be left in peace. Occasionally there was pain and when he looked down at his dream-body, his wrist was swollen and sore to the touch. He'd hurt it, hadn't he? Back when he'd been trying desperately to score out on the streets around Kings Cross. But this was a different kind of hurt, a sharper more acute pain and things weren't quite right. He couldn't make his version of events tie up with what he suspected might really have happened.

The confusion was numbing. He wanted to think, to puzzle out the situation, but all around him were these other Michaels, moving independently and laughing at him. Closing his eyes, he could still see them, pictures dancing on the back of his eyelids until he thought he might go mad.

'Mikey?'

A voice. Michael looked up and there was another figure among the images. Dark hair contrasted with blond and Lee stood there, motionless in the midst of the dancers. He was holding out his hand and Michael wanted to take it, wanted to step forward, but it was only a picture, only a dream and he didn't want to wake up. Not ever again. Moving would break the illusion and he continued to stare at the isolated figure as the surrounding images began to fragment, dissolving into nothing as they broke up.

'Come back, Mikey.' The hand reached out for him, growing in size until it filled Michael's whole field of view.

No. He stepped backwards, but the shiny wall was right behind him and there was nowhere left to go.

'You're safe, Mikey. I wouldn't fuckin' lie to you.'

But I don't want to go back. There was nothing there, nothing for him except more pain.

Then go forward, said one of the voices in his mind. Lee was standing down one of the mirrored corridors, fading now as he moved away.

Wait for me. Before he could change his mind, Michael pushed himself off the wall and ran towards the receding figure. And as he touched his shoulder, Lee took his right hand and the corridor exploded, shattered glass flying in all directions.

The pain was excruciating and Michael jerked his wrist away, which hurt even more as he opened his eyes to see Lee sitting backwards on a plastic chair by the bed. He looked round wildly, but the mirrors had gone and he was in what appeared to be a hospital. *Of course – the car!* He could remember it now, remember the look in his father's eyes as he'd pulled free. And then there was the car, the driver's face frozen in a mask of horror, as he slammed his foot on the brakes and the air was full of the screech of burning rubber on tarmac.

'Tryin' to kill yourself won't help.'

'I didn't,' he retorted, not knowing himself whether or not it was true. He'd seen the car, yes, but had his emotions got the better of him for the fleeting half-second it had taken to crowd out reason and leap into the road?

'Didn't you?' Lee arched one eyebrow as he folded his arms on the chair back. 'Live with it, Mikey.'

'Oh, tell me about it, why don't you?' said Michael irritably. His arm was throbbing viciously and Lee's presence was embarrassing, although fortunately there was nobody else around to listen to the conversation.

'Fuck me, we *are* full of self-pity today. Stop pissin' around – I know it wasn't your fault. It was me they followed back to the flat.' He hesitated. 'I was out early the day before. Couldn't sleep, so I went down to the river and the bastards followed me back.'

Michael didn't understand. It was unlike Lee to be so forgiving, never mind allow himself to be talked into coming here. Frankly, Michael was surprised he wasn't back out on the streets already, setting up house with some other pimp. From what he'd gathered about his previous life, Lee didn't have many other options.

He manoeuvred himself into a half-sitting position, wriggling up the bed in some discomfort and trying not to snag the drip they'd attached to a small tube in the back of his good hand. Back muscles protested as he leaned against the pillows. The clock on the opposite wall of the four-bed ward said it was ten o'clock; it was daylight outside, which meant he hadn't had a shot last night – so how come he was still lucid? Tired maybe and light-headed, but there were none of the awful desperate cravings he'd had last time.

'So what're you going to do now?'

'Dunno. Looks like I'm stuck with social fuckin' services.' He nodded his head towards the corridor. 'They watch me like friggin' hawks. I can't even have a bloody crap without someone askin' me what I'm doing.'

'What about scoring?' They couldn't be letting him shoot up, surely? And yet Lee would be crawling up the walls by now if he hadn't had some kind of fix.

'Methadone. Same as you. I have to go see some soddin' *counsellor* as soon as I leave here. Under escort of course. Jesus, it's driving me crazy!'

'You're a witness,' said Michael reasonably. 'They can't afford for you to do a disappearing act.'

'A *witness?* For what? Who the fuck's going to believe anything *I* say?'

You won't need to say anything. The medical evidence will be enough. Michael closed his eyes, wondering what was indelibly written on his own medical records now. They wouldn't have wasted the opportunity for a full examination. God, think of the court case. Even if they didn't want him to testify, there'd still be full reports and maybe even photographs. The whole world would know who he was. He could see why Lee wanted to get out now, stop the merry-go-round before it spun away out of control. And if they got Lee anywhere near the box, what would he say? He'd be just as likely to tell them of the incident with Michael, enjoying the shocked expression on their faces as he described everything in graphic detail.

He had to know. 'Lee?'

'Mm?' He was picking at a scab on his arm.

'Would you tell them about us?' He could feel his face redden even as he spoke.

Lee's eyes opened wide with a sudden scorn. 'What are you ashamed of, Mikey? You want to go back to your comfy middle-fuckin'-class life and pretend none of this ever happened? Pretend I don't friggin' exist? You're as bad as the rest of them, aren't you?' He stood up, pushing the chair away with one foot. 'Well, fuck you, *Michael* – I don't need you or anyone else.' He turned at the end of the bed, hands in his pockets. 'Oh, and don't worry. Your dirty little secrets are safe. Have a nice life.'

'Lee! I didn't mean …' But he had meant. He'd meant exactly what Lee had accused him of. He watched the boy leave the ward without a backward glance and wondered if he'd ever see Lee Martin again.

TWENTY SIX

'What can I do for you, Kate?' Derek looked harassed. 'Was there something you wanted?'

She leaned across the counter. 'Not exactly.' Did she have to spell it out to him? She wanted to talk – needed to talk – and if he wouldn't respond to her out of hours, she had no choice but to see him at work. 'You could try replying to my messages on your voicemail.'

'You want a call at one in the morning?' He ran a hand through his hair and glanced at his watch. 'Shit, I can manage a coffee, I guess. Come through.' Reaching down behind the counter he pressed the access button and she heard the soft buzz as the door lock released.

Don't put yourself out, Derek. I'd hate to disturb your work, she thought with more than a note of bitterness as she followed him through to the staff restaurant. Apparently she didn't even rate the privacy of his office any more.

'How's Michael?' he asked, as he paid for two coffees and took them over to a table by the window.

'So-so.' She shrugged. 'They let him out on Saturday afternoon.' Michael, it was always Michael. As if nobody else in the family existed any more. So they'd found him and got him back, but he was still centre stage and looked likely to remain there for the foreseeable future, especially if the police wanted him for the court case.

'How's he coping?'

'Difficult to tell. They've given him a supply of methadone and he's been seeing some guy at the hospital. He doesn't say much, really.' And that was an understatement, if ever there was one. Michael had barely said a word to them since he'd regained consciousness; he wasn't volunteering information and nobody knew the right questions to ask him. So he simply sat there – in the hospital bed at first, and later at home – watching life go by, and absorbing all the rubbish in the newspapers with a morbid fascination which was bordering on obsessive. Kate suspected the silence was deliberate, a way of pre-empting the parents' reactions with a kind of verbal stalemate.

Derek shrugged. 'I'm sorry.'

'You did the best you could.' There was too much finality for her liking in this conversation. They were winding up more than a case.

He seemed to sense it too. 'I didn't mean to be short with you earlier. I've just got a lot on at the moment. Felsen's got a bail application in and we're still looking for Harper and Phillips.'

'Bail?'

He shook his head. 'Highly unlikely, given the presence of firearms in the flat. And we're still reeling in the rest of the catch – looks like a big haul, too. Harper was fronting quite a number of smaller operations. There are several arrest warrants out.' He toyed with the cup. 'And then there are the finance links to consider. Money laundering. Enough work to keep us busy for quite a while, even if we don't get any more bodies out of it.'

It was another world. For a while they'd had something in common in Michael, but he was incidental now – a possible witness in a huge drugs and prostitution case of which they'd so far merely scratched the surface. How could she compete with a life she couldn't share with him?

What did they have left to talk about? There was no room for a relationship. For the first time, she understood what had happened with Helen; the attraction was based on the heat of the moment, the intense involvement in a case and all its peripherals. Derek was married to the job.

You're being unfair, she told herself, knowing she should credit him with more sensitivity than that, but it was difficult, watching him sitting opposite her and obviously itching to get back to whatever it was she'd interrupted. Besides, she was tired and she'd had enough of police and hospitals. Nobody knew how Michael was going to handle a return to normal life, and the strain of living with him – never knowing if he was going to do a runner every time he got close to the front door – was severely stretching her patience. Sometimes, she just wanted to grab him by the shoulders and shake him, make him see that he was tearing the family apart. But it was like sharing a house with a robot and several times she'd caught him staring out of his bedroom window at nothing in particular for hours on end. She wondered if he was looking for Joss Harper, if he thought the man might come after him since the police had failed to catch him after he'd not returned to the flat that day.

Kate didn't stay much longer. There was no point – Derek had told her what she wanted to know, although she doubted he realised it himself. She wondered if he expected her to go back to Colin, if indeed he thought she'd ever really left her fiancé. What was it he'd said? *Don't leave Colin for me. I don't want that responsibility.* He'd been right, but then she hadn't left Colin for *him*.

For the first time, Kate realised she was free. She'd drifted from man to man for as long as she could remember, trying to find the courage she needed to make the break from home, but she didn't need it any more. Leaving home didn't mean she had to abandon the family altogether. There could be compromise. She didn't have to jump straight from her parents to a husband; she could be herself first, perhaps share a flat with someone for a while until she either saved enough for her own place or met the right man to settle down with. And this time she'd meet him for the right reasons. It was quite a revelation and by the time she turned the car into the drive, she was practically grinning. It was a new start for all of them.

'Kate?'

She jumped, turning as she locked the car door to see Rachel standing at the end of the drive, her car keys jangling nervously from one finger and a newspaper stuffed under one arm. She looked upset. Kate hadn't seen her in the street and she realised Rachel must have been sitting in her car, waiting for her to come home.

'What's the matter, Rach? Are you OK?' She'd been all right a couple of hours ago at work, full of the weekend date she'd had with Tim, the man from the downstairs flat she'd been after for ages.

'Can I come in?' Rachel glanced behind her at the man lounging against the lamp-post across the street.

'Of course you can. If you can stand the atmosphere.' Kate waved a hand in the direction of the man. 'Don't worry about him. He's looking for another bit of scandal for tomorrow's paper.' They were everywhere, the reporters. Hanging around the street, hoping for a clear shot of Michael; sitting in cars down the road in case he went out anywhere – they popped up with a dogged persistence, despite the complete lack of encouragement from the Redford family. Michael was paranoid about them, both the doorbell and the telephone made him jump. *As if he wasn't jumpy enough already!*

'Coffee?' Kate unlocked the front door and dumped her handbag at the bottom of the stairs. 'Or stronger? I think there's some Chablis in the fridge.'

Rachel shook her head. 'I need to speak to Michael.'

'*Michael?*' She'd never seen her friend look so agitated before. 'Why? What is it?'

'Let me tell Michael first. I need to know if I'm right.'

Kate shook her head, puzzled, but went to the bottom of the stairs and yelled his name. He appeared a few moments later, sat down on the top step and watched them in silence. The light from the landing window reflected off the blond streaks in his hair and he looked so much older and less like the brother she knew. *What's going on inside your head, Mike? Why can't you share it with us?*

'Michael? Rach wants to talk to you.'

'Not here.' Rachel glanced at the lounge door. There were sounds from the television. 'Can we go upstairs?'

Kate led the way, squeezing past her brother who waited until they'd passed before he stood up and followed them into Kate's bedroom. Standing in the doorway, he shuffled from one foot to the other as if embarrassed by their presence. It was a warm evening and yet he was wearing a long-sleeved sweater, hiding the scars on his arms the way a child hides a guilty secret. His right arm was still in plaster, but he'd adjusted to it well enough.

Rachel sat down on the bed, picking at the strap of her handbag. 'Michael, have you read this? About Joss Harper?' He might still be free but the papers had the story anyway.

'Why?'

'Because I think I know him.'

He twitched at that, eyes darting around the room as if he expected the man to leap out of a cupboard. Then he looked back at Rachel and came across to pick up the paper, reading the article in silence before he screwed it up violently, crushing it against his chest with one hand and hurling it at the window. 'Fucking newspapers! Why can't everyone just leave me *alone!*'

Kate stared at her friend. 'What do you mean – you think you know him?'

'He trained at the same hospital I did. I was only a student at the time.'

'Oh *God!* You're not going to tell me you went out with him, are you?'

'No.' Rachel raised the ghost of a smile. 'Sorry. But there was a registrar called Joss Harper when I started my nursing course. Bit of a hunk, he was – a lot of the girls fancied him, but he was never interested.' She hesitated. 'We used to wonder if he was gay.'

Michael said nothing, chewing a fingernail and staring out of the window. Kate's bedroom was at the front of the house and she could see the man still standing by the lamp-post.

Kate prompted her friend. 'So what makes you think it's the same guy, Rach?'

'Well, look at him.' Rachel bent and retrieved the crumpled newspaper, glancing apologetically at Michael before smoothing it out on the bed. 'OK, so he's older, but this says he used to be a doctor.'

'You don't want to believe everything you read in the papers,' said Michael with such venom in his voice that it made both girls glance up. Neither said a word for a moment until Rachel continued hesitantly.

'Joss left the hospital under a cloud. Apparently he was caught nicking morphine. He'd paid off some of the other staff to cover for him. His excuse was that his brother was an addict who'd had a raw deal from the army and he committed suicide at about the time Joss left. There was an almighty scandal.'

'So what's your point?' asked Michael nastily. His expression was cold and Kate got the distinct impression that he was scared of what Rachel might say next.

'Because the inside story wasn't that his brother committed suicide. The story *we* heard said that Joss killed him. They were only rumours, though. I don't think it ever came out at the inquest.'

'But somehow Eddie found out.' There was a sudden silence as Michael leaned back against the bedroom wall. 'There was something between them – something that Eddie knew. *That's* why he had such an easy time of it. I never understood why he got everything his own way.

Why he got *me!* He stopped abruptly, as if realising he'd been thinking out loud and he turned away, stumbling from the room.

Kate stared at Rachel. 'I think you'd better go and see Derek. If we've got a potential murder count against Harper, he'll want to know.'

'I will. Don't know if telling Michael was a good idea, though.'

Kate smiled slightly. 'Don't you believe it. That's more reaction than we've had out of him since he's been home. Anything that makes him come alive has got to be a good thing.' She stood up. 'D'you want that coffee now?'

Rachel stood up. 'Let's go out for a drink. Come on. We'll go and speak to Derek en route, if he's still at work.'

'Oh he is,' said Kate darkly, not relishing the prospect of returning to the police station that night. The last thing she wanted was for him to think she was chasing him.

Rachel caught something of her mood. 'What's happened?' she asked with a sigh. 'Things not going too well with Derek? Come on, Kate – a drink is exactly what you need. Let me buy you a large Bailey's and you can tell aunty Rachel all about it.'

Michael opened the bedroom window and leaned out, taking a deep breath of the evening air. There were no reporters on this side of the house and the Redfords were fortunate in that the house they backed onto had a long and private garden. He supposed it would only be a matter of time before money changed hands and he'd see a photographer crouched in the bushes, zoom lens focused on his window.

Rachel's news had shaken him more than he wanted to admit. Not that he wanted to admit anything. Talking to Derek had been bad enough and the counsellor he was seeing had told him to take his time to sort himself out, before he spoke about it to anybody else. *As if I wanted to go out and discuss what happened with all my friends!* Though to be fair to the guy, he was calm and patient and Michael found himself saying far more than he'd intended to at the outset. But talking to trained professionals was one thing – talking to his family was quite another. Sometimes he wanted to, sometimes he really wanted to put his arms round his mum's neck and cry, but when it came down to it, he couldn't. He couldn't speak to them at all; the words got stuck and he found himself drying up into an embarrassed silence. It was easier to keep out of the way.

Joss killed his brother. The idea was racing out of control around his brain, sparking off loose thoughts and associations which were gradually falling into a pattern. It all made a horrible kind of sense. Joss had steered the conversation away when Michael got too close to the truth and said only that Sean had been addicted to morphine. Lee had elaborated, saying that he'd overdosed, but Joss knew too much for that to be credible. So Joss had killed Sean for some unknown reason – euthanasia maybe? *Or for his army money?* Perhaps it was from a genuine need to help his brother in any way he could, or maybe it *had* been an accident. Nobody except Joss himself would ever know the truth of that one.

Then Eddie had discovered his secret and used it against him, crime on both sides leading to an uneasy truce between the two of them. And while Eddie got a supply of clean drugs and his sexual needs satisfied, Joss was playing a far more dangerous game, proving to himself that he could control drug doses *without* killing his patients. Except that these days his patients had never been sick to start off with.

Michael sat down heavily on the bed, his arm aching again. It was Joss himself who was sick. Morphine had turned to heroin and there were no shortages of willing participants. Until Eddie had taken a fancy to Michael in a club one night.

How many others? There had to have been more people before him – street kids with nowhere else to go. *Boys like*

Lee. Joss had killed his brother and God knows how many others in his quest for perfection. Michael realised how close he'd come to losing his life. And he'd gone back *voluntarily?* He wondered if he was entirely sane, but knew it was the heroin talking, drowning out rational thought in a hazy chaos of compulsion and craving. It was hard even now; even with a daily dose of methadone, he found his fingers constantly curling with frustration, his mood swings unpredictable and his body itching for the high which never came. True, he'd not come anywhere close to the depths he'd reached out on the streets, but it was little consolation when his body was screaming at him, breaking his thoughts and confusing his mind. In the middle of the night he'd wake up, crying out and drenched in sweat; it was acutely embarrassing and had scared the shit out of him and his parents the first night it had happened.

He leaned back against the bedroom wall, drawing his knees up to his chest. He didn't know how long he'd last here, not under these conditions. It was only a matter of time.

TWENTY SEVEN

Kate was tired. It was the third night this week that she'd been woken by Michael's screams and although she didn't exactly blame him, it was becoming increasingly difficult to be tolerant. She didn't know whether it was memories or simply his body's reaction to heroin withdrawal; to be honest she'd got to the point where she didn't much care, if only he would shut up and let her get a decent night's sleep.

She'd driven Michael down to the East End, to look at the flat where he'd first been taken. He'd wanted to go back there and she could see his point – laying to rest a few ghosts would be good for all of them. It was the first enthusiasm he'd shown for anything for days.

'I need to go inside,' Michael had said on the stairs, climbing them two at a time.

'It'll be locked up, if Derek's finished with it.' She was disconcerted by the lack of any kind of police presence at the place. It was a rough area and even though she'd parked out near the main road, she was still worried about their safety and whether or not her car would still be there when they returned.

But Michael had already pushed the door and it swung open slowly.

'Mike?' She was suddenly scared. Something wasn't right. Why was the door unlocked? *What is this place?* Outside on the dirty landing, she couldn't contemplate what had happened to her brother here.

Michael didn't answer. His hand was still frozen on the door frame.

'Mike, you did *tell* Derek about this place, didn't you?' This wasn't the flat she'd see from the OP that evening and things were not adding up.

'Yes, of course.' Then he shook his head in confusion. 'No, maybe – I didn't remember at first. It was … different. This isn't the right flat. Joss lives in a tower block …' He took a hesitant step forward, but Kate was already reaching into her bag for her mobile.

'No, Mike – you can't. Not if they don't know.' She was dialling as she spoke.

'I have to. I have to see.'

She couldn't go with him. Not after what they'd done to him here, she couldn't make herself take that step over the threshold, so she watched as the door closed gently behind him and willed Derek to pick up the phone this time.

Michael stood in the hallway in a dream, not understanding how he could have not told Derek. God knows, he'd spent enough time drafting witness statements, letting the man interview him with and without tape recorders, and piecing together his life over the past few months. But he hadn't *remembered*. Realities were constantly shifting and even the counsellors were finding it hard to unravel the tangled threads of his mind.

And the doors were all open. The tough steel door onto the alleyway had been on the latch; the door to the flat itself wasn't even shut. The place was waiting for him, inviting him in. Expecting him.

The maroon room. *Eddie's room*. He hadn't forgotten waking here, but it had somehow become a part of Joss' flat in his memory. He frowned, wondering if he really was losing his grip on sanity.

And here was his bedroom, the one he'd shared with Lee for so long. Where Eddie had raped him and where Lee had …

No. *Don't even go there*. He moved on, fingers trailing down the wall and feeling like he was leaving a part of himself behind at every doorway.

And at the end of the hall, he knew he wasn't alone.

Laboured breathing came from the lounge and Michael hesitated, frozen outside the open door. But he'd come this far and had to see what ghosts were within. Chewing his lip, he felt for the comforting solidity of the packet of cigarettes in his jacket pocket – he'd been smoking for a whole week now and he wished he'd tried it months earlier. It was something else for his parents to condemn him for – something that didn't hurt so much as the rest of his life.

The room was exactly as he remembered – bachelor-pad smart with a leather suite and wooden blinds at the window. Except that he *hadn't* remembered, had he? Was it the smack that had fucked his mind so thoroughly? And there was Lee too, on the sofa, part of the tableau, but—

—It really was Lee. This wasn't his mind playing tricks. Sprawled across the sofa, his breathing was ragged and shallow, T shirt ripped and bloody, with one eye swollen shut and grazes across his face. On one exposed arm ran fresh and clumsy needle tracks etched into dried blood and blue-black bruises.

Michael was kneeling next to him in seconds. 'Lee?' Fuck everything else. Lee *mattered*.

Lee opened his good eye and focussed it with obvious difficulty. His pulse was racing and there was a thin sheen of sweat on his forehead.

'Mikey? What—'

'I'm here. What happened?' *Shit, Lee. Why didn't you stay with social services?* They'd all said he'd run away again and they'd been right. And it was Michael's fault that Lee had nowhere to go now, especially after he'd betrayed their friendship in the hospital.

'Fuckin' bastard didn't want to pay up. Needed the money. Needed— Mikey, it *hurts*.'

'I'll get help.' Kate could call, if she was still outside. He hadn't yet replaced his own mobile, not wanting to be contactable – not yet ready to be a part of the real world.

Lee grabbed his arm suddenly. 'I won't tell, Mikey. Promise.'

'I know.' He stood up. 'I'll be back in a minute.'

The lounge door had swung almost shut and he yanked at it hard. Kate could call an ambulance, and he could perhaps make it up to Lee in some way for what he'd done. But he didn't even get out of the room, because propping up the frame of the doorway opposite, arms folded and with a curious expression on his face, stood Joss.

'Shit.' Michael lurched backwards, almost tripping over his own feet. How long had he been there? *Where's Kate?* Of course, *somebody* had to have had the keys, didn't they? How else could Lee have got in?

'I'm flattered that the pair of you don't seem able to resist my hospitality.' Joss stepped into the lounge and closed the door firmly behind him. 'How are you, Mikey? Apart from what looks like a broken wrist, of course. Sorry, but I'm right out of smack thanks to your buddies in the drug squad.'

'It's Michael. Not Mikey.'

'Is it? Are you sure?'

Michael backed away to the sofa, remembering the first time he'd tried to escape from this place. For a second he slipped back in time and he shook his head angrily. *I am in control.* To mask his confusion, he took out a cigarette and lit it – smoking at least anchored him in the here-and-now.

'Did nobody ever tell you about the dangers of those things?'

'Not exactly my biggest worry, is it?' Michael sat down on the arm of the sofa, panic calmed by the nicotine. 'What are you doing here? I thought you'd have left the country by now.'

'I intend to. Just as soon as I locate my passport, which Eddie appears to have mislaid.'

Michael grinned suddenly. 'More insurance?' He'd been right about Joss and Eddie.

'Clever boy. You read the papers too? Not all crap, are they? How *is* your relationship with Lee, by the way?'

Despite himself, Michael couldn't help but turn scarlet, but Joss just laughed.

'I'm really not interested in your sex life, Mikey – or you, for that matter. I'm not looking for revenge. You were always too smart for this game, but I did think it might work for a while.' He hesitated. 'I was watching this place for days before today, but you never told them, did you? Why not?'

'I don't know. I wasn't sure it was real. That's why I had to come back …' Michael shook his head and changed the subject. 'I think Lee's overdosed.' He glanced at the boy on the sofa, but he'd lost consciousness.

'I know. Nothing to do with me. He showed up an hour or so ago – poor kid just came back home. You can call an ambulance when I've gone. I'll even leave you my mobile.'

'You killed your brother.'

'Years ago, Mikey. I had to – he was only half-alive.'

'Eddie knew, didn't he? Why didn't you kill him too?'

'Give me a break. This isn't tv. I just want to find my passport and we can all get on with our lives.'

Michael lit another cigarette from the stub of the first. He tossed the butt into the hearth carelessly and looked at Joss. 'Kitchen drawers, third one down in a blue envelope. Underneath the instructions for the microwave. And no, I can't remember what name it's in – I was too busy looking for ways out of this hell hole at the time.' *How could I remember that, and yet not remember this place existed?*

Joss glanced at him and went through to the kitchen, rummaging in the drawer at the same time as trying to watch the sofa through the archway. He pulled out a blue envelope and whistled softly. 'Nice one, Mikey.'

'Now piss off. I want to get help for Lee.'

Joss stuck the passport in his shirt pocket. 'You've grown up a bit, haven't you?'

'I had to, didn't I? You made me ...' He broke off as they both heard the wail of police sirens outside.

In an instant, the civilised veneer was gone. Joss was at the window and dropped the wooden blinds in one smooth movement. Then Michael saw him pull a gun out of the waistband of his jeans. In all the months he'd been held captive, he'd never seen any guns and he'd been genuinely shocked when Derek had told him of the firearms they'd found at the tower-block flat. But then Eddie had other ways of intimidation and Joss had the heroin. Guns had never been necessary.

'Shit.'

'Shit indeed, Mikey. And a bit too much shit for coincidence.'

'I'll just go, then.' He stood up.

'I don't think so. Sit down. Who else was here with you?'

It didn't matter anymore. 'My sister was outside.'

'She must have hit the nines as soon as you came in.' Joss lifted the edge of the blinds with the muzzle of the gun. 'Here come the ARVs. Stupid. There was no need for this.'

What have you done, Kate? Michael felt for Lee's pulse and it was faint and erratic. There wasn't time for this stuff anymore.

'Fuck this.' He strode across to the door. 'I'm going for help for Lee.'

'Sit *down.*'

'Joss, if you want to stop me, you'll have to shoot me.

It's nothing I haven't already considered doing myself since you fucked up my life. You'd probably be doing me a favour.'

'That bad, huh?' The man met his eyes and for a second Michael saw a trace of something that looked almost like guilt. He didn't answer and – hand on the doorknob – was about to leave when there were noises out on the landing. Heavy footsteps and doors banging.

Joss was by the lounge door in seconds and before Michael could get it open, he grabbed Michael's broken wrist in his free hand, jerking it hard up behind his back.

Plaster of Paris cracked and Michael screamed. Bright purple flowers blossomed across his vision and the ground swayed alarmingly. He dropped the cigarette on the carpet.

'Sorry, Mikey. Nothing personal.'

He could feel the muzzle of the gun in his side as Joss pulled him back off balance behind the door. Reaching out with the other hand, he tried to steady himself by grabbing the corner of the shelves; Joss jerked him back harder and he scrabbled to stay upright, knowing that if he lost his footing, he'd lose his arm as well. The pain was indescribable, great waves of it choking him so he could barely breathe, and with each wave came another bloom of purple in front of his eyes.

The door to the flat crashed open, but Michael barely heard the voices.

'Armed police. Stay where you are.'

More footsteps and the doorknob moved slightly. Another crash and the door flew back, rebounding off Joss' arm where he was backed up against the wall. Two Judge Dredd figures thundered through and Michael felt a hand in his hair forcing his head upright before the gun returned to his side, jammed painfully between two ribs. He was too dazed to speak, his head resting against Joss' shoulder as he saw a second gun pointed straight at him.

'Armed *police*. On the *floor*. *Now*.'

Joss took a step forward and sideways, Michael tight in

front of him.

'Let the boy go.'

'Not a chance.'

Michael swallowed. Joss had nothing to lose and he didn't really want to die, not like this, despite what he'd said earlier. He could've talked his way out of this, he *knew* he could, before the heavies arrived and forced the issue. Lee's life was more important.

He could smell burning, but didn't dare turn his head to see. 'Joss, please—'

'I *will* kill him. Dead victim – think of the paperwork. You have twenty seconds to back off.'

Michael's arm was going numb. So was his brain. He didn't doubt the man meant it.

The armed police barely looked human, they had that much body armour. 'Let the boy go and put down your weapon,' one of them said tonelessly. 'Last warning.'

Joss didn't reply this time, but side-stepped towards the door, keeping Michael between him and the police. He took his hand from Michael's wrist to grasp the doorknob, but Michael saw his chance and kicked the door fully closed.

'Stupid, Mikey. Very stupid. Ten seconds and you're dead.' Joss wrenched his arm up higher and Michael howled as broken bones crunched.

In response, Lee rolled over, fell off the sofa and coughed up a spurt of bright red blood.

Michael was off-balance already and he couldn't stand up any longer. As everyone's attention was on the body on the floor, his legs gave way beneath him and he crumpled in a heap at Joss' feet, vomiting over the carpet. Barely conscious, he managed to register two things that would remain in his memory as long as he lived – the sound of a single gunshot and a body falling on top of him, making him scream even louder in white-hot agony.

Dimly, he felt someone picking him up; he kicked out and yelled at them to leave him alone. There were voices calling his name but he couldn't hear them properly; there was a smell of smoke – and puke – and when he tried to open his eyes, the room was far away and tiny. At his feet a hole opened up – the blackness got bigger and bigger, until he fell in and the world switched itself off.

They patched him up again at the hospital, encased his entire arm in plaster this time and told him he'd have to come back in a couple of weeks and have it reset properly – reconstructed with pins – once the swelling had gone down. By now, he was front page news again and there were reporters at the casualty doors, but at least he didn't have to answer endless inane questions about the track marks up his arms. They gave him a shot of morphine this time, and he floated away for an hour watching the striplights, and hearing the sound of a gunshot over and over again.

Then Derek came into the cubicle and told him Lee was dead.

'You did your best, Michael,' he said, perched on the end of the hospital trolley. 'There wasn't any more you could have done.'

'I could have got him out of there quicker. If the police hadn't turned up—'

'Lee ran out of time as soon as he shot up,' Derek interrupted. 'Whatever he took was too much.'

Michael tried to rub his eyes. He wasn't going to cry. They'd stuck another fucking needle in his good hand, had attached a saline drip and were keeping him in at least overnight and probably longer. There was a uniformed officer standing in the corridor outside. 'Me and Lee – we were—'

'We all need friends, Michael.' Derek passed him the tissue box.

'No, you don't understand. We—'

'You looked out for each other. That's all you need to remember.'

The morphine was blocking the pain. Did he know? *Does it matter?* Michael wasn't sure. Joss was dead; Michael had felt him die. Eddie knew too but that wasn't important any more, and if Eddie told, well who was going to believe him? Lee had been different.

But Lee was dead too and their secrets with him, and all he had to face now was the trial.

The reporters had gone for the night. Kate and Derek stood outside by his car.

'Is it over?' He unlocked the door but didn't get inside.

Kate didn't know what to say. 'Do you want it to be? Lee's dead.'

'Which is important to Michael.'

'I know.' She thought she really did too. Maybe she'd get that photograph off Derek sometime and give it to Michael. 'We'll be all right. I think.'

'We?'

Kate leaned forward and kissed him quickly on the lips.

Derek said nothing, but he smiled, shaking his head as he got into the car.

THE END

Look out for the sequel to *Hamelin's Child*, which will be called *Paying the Piper*. You can find out details of this and other books at www.debbiebennett.co.uk

Made in the USA
Charleston, SC
07 March 2014